I0779092

SALVAGE ONE

MR. BUCK JONES

WORKBOOK PRESS LLC
187 E Warm Springs Rd
Suite B285 Las Vegas NV 89119 USA

Website: https://workbookpress.com/
Hotline: 1-888-818-4856
Email: admin@workbookpress.com

Ordering Information:
Quantity sales. Special discounts are available on quantity purchases by corporations, associations, and others. For details, contact the publisher at the address above.

ISBN-13: 978-1-963718-20-1 Paperback Version
        978-1-963718-21-8 Digital Version

PUB. DATE: 02/14/2024

SALVAGE ONE

Mr. Buck Jones

INTRODUCTION

Oh, where to begin? My name is John Hughes. My people are scavengers and business is good. I own the salvage and repair operation on the outskirts of the known inhabited worlds. But that is changing. The known worlds are expanding and there is a war on. The 'Imperium' is attempting to take control of our galaxy. They control almost two-thirds of it. All our people want is the freedom to live their lives simply, without conflict, and preferably without somebody telling them how to do it. There are also three Rebel factions working separately and together for our survival. It is a case of fight and destroy or being destroyed. These fleets of ships all over the known galaxy engage in destructive warfare and leave debris in their wake. We clean it up.

With the galaxy at war, people are looking for habitable worlds where they can live in peace, away from all the fighting and chaos.

When the Imperium finds out about a newly settled world, they move in and subjugate the people. They want to control everything. The Imperium doesn't have the resources to enforce its tyranny on every planet on the periphery of the known galaxy. If they meet much resistance, they wipe out the population or attack with nuclear weapons rendering the planet uninhabitable, referred to as 'scorching the planet.' The Imperium's primary fear weapon is a large battleship called the Destroyer with nuclear and biological weapons to poison a planet. So far, they have done this to two planets and recorded it, to replay it over and over, bringing the point home, don't misbehave!

I found a planet that no one wants with very little water, it is mostly desert. But it has a huge cave deep in bedrock to hide most of my operation. A ship with scanners may see the ships and small settlements. They will also see the outside entrance of a cave and some of my repair shops. The planet is called "Sand." The Imperium refers to it as D-2265 for desert class and the 2,265th 'D' planet found. The freedom fighters call it the Repair Stop, and the scavengers that don't work for me call it the Repair Shop. We call it home.

A core tap powers the planet. The "TAP" is a geothermal energy source left by someone who abandoned this planet a long time ago and left many ruins behind. My wife learned how to work with geothermal power when she was in her teens and still living with her parents. Our power plant runs our shields and homes for all 270 people who live here and all the automatic weapons we have for defense. We are so small that the Imperium doesn't care about us.

We are mostly self-sustaining, we grow our own food and raise our own animals. Our income is from salvage and repair work, and the business is profitable. I have over 100 starship mechanics and specialists working here. Customers pay with water, parts, gold, ships, and anything valuable except slaves. We have no slaves on Sand.

Since the core of the planet is molten, we have magnetic poles and protection from cosmic rays and radiation. We obtained planetary shield technology from several other planets. We modified them in power and technology to make them much better than they were originally, but there is always a bigger gun out there, so we don't even turn it on unless we need to use it. Our biggest problem is water, there is only so much of it, and this planet doesn't have a lot. We import water when we can, and we recycle everything. Our greatest weapon is knowledge, and the TAP gives us huge power resources.

CHAPTER ONE: OPERATIONS

"Salvage One to command on approach. This is Nathan on the Agenda with 1.3 million tons of salvage. Come in."

"Agenda! Control! Did you say 1.3 million tons? Over."

"Yes, I did. I have the engineering half of a destroyer intact and the forward cannon section of a battleship. The Avenger is bringing another million tons of debris from the battlefield. Most of it was cargo. I'm going to need help landing this stuff; send everything you got because it's huge."

"Command to Agenda, standard orbit we'll send help. Over and out."

Jenny called on the intercom to John, the head of the facility. "Yes, Jenny."

"Sir, Captain Nathan is entering standard orbit with 1.3 million tons of star destroyer, and he needs help to land it. Captain Daniels is not far behind with another million tons of cargo."

"Alert the recovery pilots and get the repulsor shuttles in the air and Jenny, make sure you announce this is not a drill."

"Yes, sir."

The click and hum was heard all over the facility as well as the town. "Now hear this, all repulsor pilots to your crafts immediately. This is not a drill. The Agenda is entering orbit with a cargo to be slowly landed."

Forty-five pilots dropped what they were doing and ran to get their gear, forty-five ship crews ran to ready their ships. Repulsor pilots have a special place here on Sand. Their ships are specially selected too. They are designed to latch onto objects and use antigravity to slow the descent of objects from space, the same works in reverse. Some spaceships can't land on a planet, so they are space-bound from construction to the time of destruction. Other ships are designed to land and take off, but these ships consume large amounts of fuel in the process. Repulsor craft safely lands and lifts spacecraft to and from orbit. The pilots wear special equipment to counteract the antigravity effects just in case there is a problem in one of the drives since these are small and very powerful ships that could rip a pilot apart.

Twelve ships rose first, followed by fourteen more. Soon the rest were in orbit, attaching to the massive engineering section of the star destroyer. The Agenda released its hold on the first piece and the tiny ships took over for the three-hour trip to the surface and the final resting place of the ship section, where mechanics will dismantle it and inventory the parts. Later the vast cannon section of the battleship was attached and started its descent, as did the Agenda and her crew after an extended mission.

John met Nathan after a restful eight hours. It was morning on the planet when Nathan landed, and John pulled up in the transport. "Hello, old friend. How was the trip?"

"There was a small fight. Other scrapers too small to do anything tried to take that cannon section. Their ship was smaller than any of the cannon attached to the section. Can you imagine?"

"You didn't destroy them?" John asked.

"No, I left them a gold sliver and a food container. I told them to take the offer and go, or I would destroy them. Then I turned on my marker lights, so the whole vessel was visible. They hurried over to the container, loaded it, and left. I didn't even tell them who I was." Nathan said.

"What was the size of their ship?" John asked.

"It was about the size of two of our repulsor craft," Nathan said, and they both laughed as Jenny brought breakfast.

Sixteen hours later, Captain Daniels called for instructions; he had a larger ship, an armed freighter. Much of his cargo was inside the holding bays, but twenty-seven containers were in tow. He detached the towed containers and began landing procedures. Once again, they called the repulsor pilots, and one by one, the containers were landed and stacked in the yard to be opened and inventoried.

"Captain Daniels", John called. Daniels turned around when he heard the familiar voice.

"John, my old friend, it's good to see you. Did you see the load I just brought in? It'll take our people months to inventory it all. I have no idea what's in there, but it should be scanned for everything soon just in case there are temperature sensitive explosives." Daniels said.

"We are way ahead of you, my friend. They already started as soon as the first container landed. Any trouble?", John asked.

"No! None at all. I noticed Nathan scared off a tiny pimple. I'm surprised he didn't just blow it out of his way." Daniels said and laughed with a dismissive hand. John took note as Daniels continued walking off. *I'm going to have to talk to his crew.*

John called Jenny, "Can you tell the 1st and 2nd officers of the Avenger that I would like to see them in my office, please."

"Yes, sir!" was her reply.

The officers, Jeff and Sam, were in John's waiting room a short hour later, looking worried, when his secretary told him they were there.

"Send in Jeff, the 1st officer," John said curtly.

Jeff Clemens entered and closed the door, he seemed nervous. "You wanted to see me, sir?" Jeff asked.

John looked at the man and spoke. "I was told about the incident while getting the cargo containers. I want your side of the story."

"I don't know anything," Jeff said.

"So, you're lying and incompetent. I don't need a lie detector to tell you're lying. The question is, why? I always find out. It would be better to speak up now when the punishment will be light than later when it will be severe." John replied curtly.

"I don't know anything, sir," Jeff said.

"OK. Leave out that door," John said and pointed toward the door at the rear of his office. Jeff complied.

"Send in Sam, the 2nd officer," John said over the office intercom while Jeff was just exiting.

"You wanted to see me, Sir?" Sam Clemens, Jeff's brother, asked as he walked in and closed the door.

"I was told about the incident while getting the cargo containers. I want your side of the story."

"I wouldn't know Sir, as 2nd officer, my job is to make sure the workers are suited up, and no one is working with dangerous equipment. I make sure my workers are in a safe environment and have the equipment they need to do their assigned duties. The Captain and 1st officer directly control the troops with weapons, the shock troopers, marines, and guards. My guys have been mighty happy on several occasions when the guards were there to save their necks. The shock troopers and marines go in first, then we follow and clean up and salvage. On this mission, we packed thirteen containers that were broken open or snapped. Five containers were opened to space and had people in them. Hundreds of people, Sir, no suits, just people. They looked like slave transports all exposed to space. We wiped them down and loaded them with goods floating everywhere. It was pretty bad, Sir." Sam said and fell silent.

"Who opened the containers?" John asked, noticeably agitated.

"I have no idea. I assume whoever was on the ship. You know, if I can't have them, no one will." Sam said.

"You can leave through that door." John pointed to the door at the rear of his office. Sam seemed confident and at ease.

"Thank you, Sir," Sam said and left.

As soon as Sam walked out of the door, Jeff was waiting for him. "What the hell did you tell him?", Jeff angrily asked Sam while grabbing Sam's collar tightly and pulling him close. Sam stepped back and gave a quick uppercut to the jaw and a swift knee to the groin, then grabbed the 1st officer as he was falling away and snapped a quick punch to the right eye. Jeff's right eye was bleeding, so Sam did the same to the left eye and then broke Jeff's nose for good measure.

"Don't ever think you're a better man than I am boy, just because you're my younger brother." Sam said to the younger officer and tossed Jeff aside. Jeff had always had the better deal in life. Sam worked with the men in the cargo area and around real men, while Jeff is on the bridge most of the time. Sam was much stronger and had twelve years on the younger man, plus he was angry over being passed over for 1st officer. That felt good, Sam thought to himself. Now it was time to see what his men were doing.

Jenny touched her intercom, "Sir, are you ready for the daily repairs report?"

"Yes, bring it in," John replied.

Jenny walked in and left the door open so she could hear the radio. "We have thirteen ships in for repair, Sir. Four are long-term and a million credits or more, you know about those. According to the shop foreman, six will finish within the next two days, and three are still waiting for payment. We have two customers coming in. One is a minor repair, and the other wants a weapons upgrade. He said he's tired of getting his cargo taken from him."

"OK, move the three slackers into the sales yard and tell the new customers we'll see them."

"The sales yard presently has twenty-two ships for sale and three awaiting papers from a lien sale on the title for non-payment. If you bring your ship in and don't pay for it, it will go up for sale unless payment arrangements are made. Most of the ships in the yard are cargo ships and freighters, but there are two fighters and three yachts for sale. One of the yachts is that multi-billion credit ship owned by a very rich multi-billionaire who got caught out checking on his properties. The fighters belong to him too.

The rest you know, Sir." Jenny finished with a finger in the air as the radio squawked.

John thought back to what he knew about the yacht; pirates had attacked the ship, damaged it, and managed to destroy four of its six fighter escorts in the process. They limped here and ordered the repairs. The owner even paid forty million down in gold. He left in his yacht's shuttle over a year ago, and we've had no word from him since. He and his wife or secretary, whoever she was, were not in great shape when they left for the core worlds. The yacht is for sale for 2.4 billion credits. I don't expect to sell it, but I may keep it for myself to retire on. The bill on it is 1.36 billion credits, and storage is accumulating every day.

The fighters are state-of-the-art with air-jet, ramjet, and gravity drives with high end dual kugel engines. They can go from 0 to .9 light-speed in 5 seconds. The cockpits have the best inertia dampers I've ever seen. That's a good thing because this fighter could kill a pilot if he stepped on it too fast without the dampeners and the special suits. The G-force would smash him into a puddle. They have four Mark Six plasma cannons forward and two aft. The power system is enormous, and the shielding is both physical and multiphasic. Frankly, I don't see how anyone destroyed four of these unless they caught them off guard. The billionaire was vague on the details. The surviving pilots were nervous and shaken.

Some of my people tried to listen in and got bits and pieces of conversations about a huge craft that appeared out of nowhere and cut the fighters to pieces like a hot knife through butter. The yacht's shields barely held against the weapon and only because the fighters sacrificed themselves, giving the yacht time to bring the shields online. When the yacht got here, it had three decks vented to space, and over half of its power relays and conduits blown from overload. It's all fixed now, and it's better than before. To look at it now, you would never know it was in a battle. She is beautiful. Sometimes I go there and just take my wonderful wife with me on a date to look at one of the millions of vids or swim in the pool or drink from the Android bar. You haven't heard funny until you've listened to a gay android telling jokes about macho battle droids and their exploits.

Jenny walked back into John's office, looking shaken, "Sir, one of the customers wants to talk to you beyond sensor range. He said anywhere away from your freighter ship and crew."

"Did he say why?" John asked.

"Yes, Sir, he said they were murderers," Jenny said in a shaky voice.

John's eyes widened. So that's the secret, he thought to himself. "Find Linda and tell her to report here at once. Tell her to bring her G-suit. Find Gill, my pilot, and tell him to prepare my shuttle. I'll call Leslie Ann and tell her I'm not going to be home for dinner."

"Yes, sir," Jenny said and wheeled on her heels to make the calls.

Twenty minutes later, Linda was in John's office looking contrite and wondering what she did this time. You don't get pulled into the facilities owners' office for a chat. Jenny looked up at her and said, "He's expecting you. You're to go in now with all your gear for your briefing."

For the briefing, Linda thought. What briefing? Linda lifted her suit's case and helmet, then slung her satchel over her shoulder and walked to John's office. "You wanted to see me and my gear, Sir?" she said.

"Yes! You are one of the few pilots here who can fly one of McMillian's fighters without killing yourself and anyone you don't want to. I also understand that you're pretty good at it and know the systems on those crafts better than any of the men here."

Linda smiled. Finally, someone noticed something other than she had tits. "Yes, Sir. I like to fly fast, hard, and often. Those fighters are the fastest, hardest, baddest ships on the planet, Sir."

"You will fly escort for my shuttle and will only fire on my command. Do you understand?"

"No, Sir, but I don't have to, I can follow orders," Linda replied. "I'd do anything to get to fly one of those fighters, Sir."

"One more thing, this is confidential; you will tell no one. From here, you go directly to your ship and prepare for flight. Talk to no one except your flight crew, and they will be sequestered until we return. Now go!" John finished and motioned her off.

John pulled on his flight suit over his slightly pudgy mid-section and zipped it up, then put his overalls on over it. He grabbed his briefcase, strapped on his sidearm then walked out the back door and down to the garage. At the office garage, John told Jason he wanted transport to his shuttle. It was eight kilometers away, and he wanted to get there fast. Jason smiled, "I'll take you, Sir. I just got a new ship, and she is smooth. I love to ride her; this is a great opportunity. Let's go."

Jason took the ID card and walked to a blue and gold cigar shaped ship with white trim that looked brand new. Jason called to Sheila to open her hatch; I have the man who owns you here. Say hello to John."

A female, slightly mechanical voice said, "Hello John. How may I serve you today?"

"Do you know where my shuttle is?" John asks.

"Yes, Sir. Would you like me to take you there?" Sheila asked.

"Please do and I'm in a hurry," John said.

"Please be seated and secure yourself, and we can go," the transport said.

John sat down in a soft cushioned chair and secured the belt in place. The transport rose and cleared the roof. John felt no movement. Then through the windows, he saw blurs then just as suddenly it was over. The belt on his chair released, and the doors opened. "Your shuttle seems to be preparing for flight, Sir. Have a nice trip. If you would like me to pick you up, use this for a return trip, and I'll come to pick you up, Sir." A small button appeared next to his chair.

"Thank you, Sheila." John pocketed the button then grabbed his equipment and exited the transport.

John walked thirty feet or so to his shuttle and turned to watch Sheila change color to a light blue as she rose and disappeared like a shot toward the shop area with Jason on board. She truly is an excellent transport. Jason is right.

Sid was at the controls of the shuttle. He was taking over for Gill. Sissy, his wife, the navigator, was at her station. The ground crew had charged the shuttle and loaded the fuel cells. My shuttle had been upgraded with fusion drives and reactors to power the multiphasic shields, and I had ion cannons installed just in case something nasty was to happen. The reactors were hot, and we were ready.

I touched the external communication. "Linda, are you ready?"

"YEE HAA!" came across the comm unit as a blur of red and green zipped by when her fighter fired by and pointed skyward.

"I'm guessing that was a yes," Sid said. He pushed the shuttle's throttle forward, and it flew skyward much slower but at a decent rate.

"Sissy! Here are the coordinates", John said, and he handed her a small cylinder that slipped into the nav computer.

"Sir, this is outside the solar system; it's 300,000 kilometers past the last planet. There's nothing out there.

"We are meeting someone. Raise shields to full power." John touched the comm panel again, "Linda, make sure that your shields are raised and on full power. Stop short of the coordinates by orbiting the last planet. If we need you, we'll call. You can close the distance in less than a few seconds in that ship if we need you. Do you copy?" John said over the secure link.

"I heard you. I don't get it, but I heard you. How long is this going to take anyway?" Linda replied.

"It's about 7 billion kilometers. So not long, prepare hyper-drive to coordinate. Calculate Linda's vectors and send them to her too." John instructed.

A minute later and Sissy said, "Transmitting."

"Acknowledged," Linda said, and the fighter disappeared in a flash of light.

The engines engaged and the view screen flashed for a few seconds with a brilliant display of lights and sparkle. John had seen it hundreds of times. The view screen was filled with the spectacle of the distortion you see in hyperspace flight. The phenomenon only lasted for 35 minutes, and they were at their destination.

"No contact, Sir," Sissy said.

"Open hailing frequency's Sissy, let's see if..." John was cut short.

"Jesus! John! That's a little close, isn't it?" a voice rang out over the comm channel. John recognized the voice. "At least it better be you, John." The voice said. "Could you move to the port about 100 meters please?"

John smiled, "Sid, move to port 100 meters."

Sid began to protest, "But there's nothing out there, move 100 meters to port from what?"

John said, "Just do it."

Sid tapped the controls, and the ship moved as instructed when suddenly an image appeared on the collision indicator. Sissy exclaimed, "What the hell! Where did that come from?"

"Contact 45 degrees starboard." Sid said as he turned the ship starboard. The sound of shields scraping sounded throughout the ship.

"I told you that you were a little too close, John." The voice said. "Easy on the paint. I'll expect you to fix it if your pilot scratched my baby.

The ship was a little larger than John's ship. John had a larger cargo shuttle about 100 meters in length and 40 meters in width. The vessel appearing on the view screen was about 140 meters long and over 60 meters in diameter. That ship had a cloak.

"Why all of the cloak and dagger, Clementine? I have a building on Sand that's comfortable for a Hemferdemite. This ship isn't big enough, and your ship is too large for me to come to you." John asked.

"I'm prepping a tube for one of my people. He has quarters here and is one of my technical engineers here on the Reveal. He's bringing a crystal with the vid evidence of your captain's murderous escapades. You will see your men open containers with humans inside to the vacuum of space, killing everyone in those containers. We smuggled 1345 refugees on that cargo ship eventually bound for Crucible, a planet on the rim discovered forty-three years ago by me. The Imperium doesn't know about Crucible, and I've been transporting refugees from this horrible war for two years now to that world. Thirty-four species live there in harmony John without the war finding them.

"I'll look at the vid, and all who are responsible will be disciplined. I give you my word." John told her.

"Sissy looked at John. Who is she talking about? And what is a Hemferdemite?" she asked.

A Hemferdemite is a species that walks on four legs and is anywhere from two and a half to three meters at the withers. They have two arms and a four-legged body and have visited Earth for hundreds of years in secret. The myth of the centaur probably came from them. Most are highly intelligent; an adult can weigh 1500 to 2000 kilos (3300-4400 pounds). They resemble a horse with the upper body of a person in place of the head and neck. They live very long lives. She told me she was 135, and that was…" John thought back and counted on his fingers. "That was twelve years ago. I saved her and her mate from a real son of a bitch that would slaughter them just because. A prince named 'Wang Xiu Ying' who is a wanted criminal on Earth and moved to Mars. Clementine was there doing some trading in rare earth materials. About twenty of the prince's gang killed all but four of her company supposedly to get the cargo worth millions of credits. Then he told them that he always wondered what centaur meat tasted like.

Before the war, I was buying scrap when I saw these people who I knew were not good people using painsticks on these majestic creatures. My crew and I did something about it, and now she is free."

"Where are those people now? The people you worked with on Mars?" Sissy asked.

John smiled. "Most are still with me. You know Captain Nathan and Jenny. I married one; a lot of them are mechanics. Let's not forget Linda. Which reminds me; contact her and tell her the coast is clear and to come here weapons cold."

Sissy smiled, "All this time I've known you, and I'm still finding things out about you." A ping on her screen notified her that a capsule had left the Reveal.

"The capsule is on its way, Sir," Sissy said while sending a text-only message to Linda.

Sissy opened the cargo bay airlock and let the capsule in while John started to the airlock to greet the messenger.

Just as John walked up to the cargo airlock, the green light lit, signaling complete pressurization. John glanced through the viewport, he saw the hatch start to open, and John put his palm on the release panel. The biometric reader checked John's bio readings against the computer to make sure it was his fingerprints, hand, and that blood was pulsing through it, that he was alive. The large tri-doors opened, and John stood back waiting for Clementine's representative to exit the craft.

A large black man exited in a working shirt and pants and walked to

John with an outstretched hand. "You must be John. I'm Tafari Dalusi. I work for the one you call Clementine. I would like to hear one day how it is that she, a Queen of her people, allows you to call her that. This is the crystal you seek." Tafari said with an African accent that John didn't recognize.

John took the crystal from Tafari and motioned for him to follow. "Tafari, that's an interesting name that I've never heard before," John said.

"I am not surprised. My people have been enslaved for hundreds of years, and when we were finally free, some of us looked back to our roots. My father named me because he knew I would be as big as he, so he gave me that name. It means 'he who inspires awe'. Now my wife and I with our children work for a great cause with truly magnificent beings of majesty and awe." The Hemferdemite people are genuinely great. The Queens mate built the cloak we use. It's impermeable, and yet we can still view the galaxy around us with it running." John entered the personal computer center and sat in the primary chair. "Computer: activate!" John commanded.

"Activated, recognize John Hughes's voice. Place hand on bio reader for access." The computer reacted.

John placed his hand one the reader and it checked his biomarkers. The room came alive with holographic icons of various functions available showing within finger reach. John slipped the crystal into the crystal port. "Computer, check the crystal device. If it's safe, then display the file list." John said.

The file list appeared, and three vid files appeared. "Computer: Mark all and play vid files," John commanded.

The video filled the room. In one corner was the Avenger, Captain Daniels' ship, slowing to a stop. Twenty-five armed marines in attack pods exited the Avenger, followed by a command ship. "That should be the 1st officer Jeff in that ship," John said. "Computer: pause!"

John placed his fingers around the command ship and spread his hands wide, expanding the view of the command ship. In the viewport, Jeff was visible piloting the craft, and in command. John sat back down. "Computer: resume!"

The marines entered the massive crack in the dead Imperium freighter's side. Flashes of light from inside were visible. John tilted his head to Tafari. Were they able to get any audio?"

"I didn't start trying to crack the communication until I saw the blasts. It took me a few minutes to break into the comm channels without being detected. The comm feed will come on in a few seconds. There is a half-second delay for decryption." Tafari said.

A minute and a half later, crackling, and Jeff's voice boomed out," Is that all of them major? I don't want anyone else to claim our salvage. There has to be some good shit in those containers."

"All clear! That was the last of them. We could start checking the manifests to see if we got anything good." Major Franklin Charles replied.

"Jeff, how's it going out there? Do we send the recovery teams now or wait?" Captain Daniels said.

"Hold off, Sir. We are still checking; we have many cargo containers here and most of them are not tied down. This freighter is heavily armed, so keep the Avenger back just in case. One blast from a particle cannon and we have to walk home, Sir." Jeff chuckled.

"There's no danger of that. The Agenda is recovering an aft section to a galaxy-class battleship. The whole engineering section is complete and intact. Someone sliced the ship in half and then cut the nose off with the huge cannons. Those two pieces are all that's left. The rest of the battleship is in tiny pieces. So, we have a backup. Just get it all checked out so we can load up and get back home." Nathan said.

"Aye, Sir," Jeff replied.

"Major hurry, the captain is in a hurry!"

"I have my people looking now for manifests. Hold on; we have a commotion going on; let me find out what's going on. Maybe we found something outstanding like gold." The major closed his connection.

"Major, let the first mate know we have survivors. Several of the containers are carrying refugees, I think." Lt. Green radioed the major.

John could see the Major's suit using its jets to get to the LT's cargo container that they connected to so he could listen to the people inside. Major Charles pulled his scanner out as soon as he reached the box. "Shit! Commander, we have people in at least one container. I don't know how many, but they sound like refugees hiding in amongst the freight."

    After several minutes of silence --- "Open the container! I'm not losing all this cargo for a few refugees." Commander Jeffery ordered. John watched only a few minutes longer.

    "Computer, pause!" John said with a lump in his throat. He sat back in his chair with a look of disgust on his face as the vid paused just as Lt. Green and Major Charles cracked the doors and let the air escape the container killing everyone inside instantly.

    "Tafari, does the captain find out?" John asked in a subdued voice.

    "I take it that the captain is a friend..." Tafari said in a low voice.

    John nodded.

    "He is in the captain's shuttle behind his first mates. The captain sees the whole thing and orders the rest of the containers breached as they are found, four containers in all with life support for 350 people each. The people are in these containers for anywhere from two weeks to two months until we can claim them at the destination worlds. We claim the containers, pay the freight and tax to the Imperium, move them to a remote location, and release all the people to board transports for Crucible. Crucible is a green world held hidden by the Hemferdemite people. Humans, Liberians, Taenites, and Albanians all live there and thrive. There are over a billion souls on the planet now, and it's capable of supporting three times that sustainably. Humans and Liberians have farms and ranches with millions of animals, and the farms grow everything the population needs. All sustainable." Tafari explained to John.

    "This is a travesty of huge consequence. A lot of the crew is in on this for so little. To kill so many for so little is bad enough but to kill for no reason is evil." John said more to himself than to anyone as a tear rolled slowly down his cheeks.

    "What did I miss?" Linda asked as she arrived on the scene. She saw two ships, both large shuttles, one of them larger than the other. At first, she didn't recognize John's ship, and then she saw the insignia near the cargo hatch. "Sissy, what's going on?

    Linda's com clicked slightly, "Just park alongside for a while. John is looking at something in the computer room." Sissies quietly said.

    A light blue light, barely visible, momentarily emanated from the larger cargo ship from both ends and the top sensor array. It touched the fighter from top to bottom and end to end in a flash. "Pilot, if you would like to stretch your legs, your ship will fit in my cargo hold with a little room to spare. John has a few hours of videos to look at so I would welcome you if you would like. We have refreshments and more important we have restrooms." Clementine's voice said nicely over the comm on a clear channel.

Sissy said, "Clementine is a friend of John's from a long time ago. So, I'm sure it's fine with him but I can check if you would like me to ask him."

"Make sure that it's ok with John."

With that Sissy contacted the computer room and John opened the coms. "Yes, Sissy?"

"Clementine offered to let Linda park her fighter in her cargo bay and stretch her legs. Linda wants to make sure that it's ok with you." Sissy said.

John thought for a moment and replied, "Yes, it's fine. She can go on Clementine's ship and Tafari will stay here. We will be going back to Sand soon anyway. Set up the ship-to-ship secure vid conference as soon as you can. I need to set up a talk with Clementine and her people and I want to do it in private. Can you do that Sissy?"

"Yes sir. Not a problem. I'll contact them right now and start working on it while Linda is parking her fighter." Sissy replied.

Sissy informed Linda and the crew of the Reveal of what John wanted to do.

A few short hours later, John was in the computer center looking at the holograms of Clementine and her husband. "We are going to hold court for the crew of the Avenger for the murder of 1345 souls. The trials will take place on Sand. The only problem is that I don't have prisons on Sand. Until now I've never needed them.

Sid piped in, "We have empty storage containers. They're made of steel and with a little modification, windows can be installed with bars. They already have locking doors, and we don't have a lot of people to lock up, but we have hundreds of containers."

Although the thought of locking up his friends was distasteful to him, the outright murder of so many innocent people for nothing formed a hole in his soul. Sid wasn't a religious man, but he did believe in a higher power and the evils you did in this life would be paid for in the next. He had done very little sinning and wanted to keep it that way.

He even married Sissy before having sex, true to the teachings of the foundation, a belief he followed since his early days in school.

John ran the thought around in his head for a second and nodded. "Go ahead and do it, Sid. We have provisions in the charter for such a court. It requires three command-rank officers to sit on the bench and a jury of twelve to pass judgment. The problem is that when the charter was drawn, Captain Daniels was one of the three on the bench. I'll need you to sit in his place, Clementine. We will need to prove your authority somehow."

"I accept and I'll have the Kentaurides in orbit in two solar days," Clementine said but her voice showed how disgusted she was.

"I'm sorry, did I say something inappropriate? If I did, I did not mean to at all." John said apologetically.

"I don't see why I should PROVE myself to anyone. I am 'Queen Clementina protector populi sui'. I am my people's Queen and protector. To have to PROVE this to anyone is demeaning." She said standing to her full height, speaking with pride.

"Clementine, and I say that with endearment, I'm not asking you to prove to me. You have done that a thousand times over. While I know you well, the people of Sand do not. I am asking you to stand in judgment of one of the most beloved people on our planet. I only hope that the Kentaurides is impressive enough to do that." John finished.

Clementine smiled, her husband cocked his head a little to the side and said, "It's the Royal Battleship. It's capable of removing a planet." He said dryly with a touch of anger and walked off muttering in Hemferdemite "damn humans again."

Tafari Dalusi whispered to John, "The king does not like humans; ever since a mob captured him on Mars while he was helping refugees with food and medical supplies. I understand they were going to cook him and eat him."

John turned his chair to face Tafari. "Yes, that's where I met them. I'm the one who stopped the gangsters from stealing the food, the rare earth materials, and them. Well, me and several of my people who still work with me. Sid and Sissy up front there", John pointed a thumb toward the bridge, "weren't with me that day, but when we rescued the future Queen and her husband, all the food got returned to the distribution center and the thugs are still behind bars on work gangs."

They set course to Sand and got underway. Both ships arrived at the same time. Linda extracted herself and the fighter from the Reveal.

The ships all began their landing procedures. Three hours later and all the ships were in their parking spots. The fighter was back in the sales area and John's shuttle was in its illustrious spot.

Sheila was called and John, Sid, and Sissy prepared to enter her.

"Hello, John," Sheila said to the incoming passengers.

John and company sat, and the doors closed.

"Sheila, we have two Hemferdemite passengers at the visitors' spaceport. Please head that way to pick them up."

"Yes sir. I'll reconfigure the forward section for Hemferdemite passengers." Sheila's voice replied.

Almost silent engines powered, and Sheila rose on her way to the visitors' port. Fifteen minutes later she began to land. The front of Sheila began to enlarge, and the door reconfigured for the larger Hemferdemite entrance and comfort stations for one of their species. The Queen, her husband, and four more Hemferdemite soldiers entered Sheila. Sheila made space for the extra Hemferdemite passengers.

The reagent and her staff entered and secured in place then Sheila rose and proceeded to the guest quarters for the Queen and King. John approached the Queen and bowed then asked if he could do anything else for her. "Yes! The main reason we came was for parts and additional reactors for the Kentaurides, our battleship. It'll be here in three days. The main hull is laid but it's severely underpowered and we need everything."

King Cephoros added, "We need cold fusion reactors for power. At least six 600-1000 gigawatt units. I would prefer the 1000 gigawatt reactors of course. If not, I'll need ten of the 600 gigawatt units, and plasma cannons, as many as you have. Look, I remember you and my wife trusts you. I seldom ever trust humans, but I am willing to take another chance. We have gold and 7500 kiloliters of water on board for payment."

John tilted his head. "The water and three tons of gold in payment for all the weapons and power you need and the technicians to install it and instruct you on how to use it."

"Wait! I didn't say we had three tons of gold!" Cephoros said alarmed.

"I guess you'll have to owe me then," John said then bowed and walked away.

Cephoros looked at his Queen. "Where are we going to get another two tons of gold? The price is…"

"The price is what it is my love. John is not expecting full payment. He will expect help in the future, and we will render it." Clementine said. "He will make sure we have the finest weapons available and the fastest engines because if he ever needs help, he'll call, and we'll come."

CHAPTER TWO: THE TRIAL

aptain Daniels, Jeff Clemens (the 1st officer), Major Franklin Charles, and thirty-six of the crew of the Avenger were arrested and detained in jail under charges. According to the charter three command staff had to be present for a trial but one of them was on trial.

On the third day, John walked to the podium. "I've called this meeting to let those of you who don't know that Captain Daniels has been arrested for murder along with some of his crew."

The crowd murmured and someone yelled out "That's a filthy lie. It must be!"

"I have seen the evidence, and he will have a trial here on Sand," John said to the crowd.

"Sitting in judgment will be Me, Captain Nathan, and Queen Clementina protector populi sui of the Hemferdemite people and we will pick twelve good and true citizens of Sand to sit in jury to pass judgement. Should the accused be found guilty, we will pass sentence on the accused." John finished and began to leave.

Someone in the crowd yelled out "Why should we let her judge us?" On cue Clementine's ship began to blot out the sun. Several minutes later in the shade of the massive ship, John had returned to the podium. "Because the people that were murdered were humans. They were refugees and friends of the crown, and they were alive when Captain Daniels gave the order to kill them and that is her battleship overhead. I've known her for many years, and I vouch for her. Does anyone question my authority?"

The jurors were picked, and the trial began. After all the evidence was introduced and the jurors saw the footage of the people being murdered on the order of the captain and the 1st officer there was no question in their minds.

"Captain Daniels and Jeff Clemens (the 1st officer), you are to be executed by order of this court. Major Franklin Charles, you and your thirty-six men and women involved will serve as prison labor on the planet Crucible in chains for life. This is to repay for the lives you have taken. This is the ruling of this court, on this day, under the power of the charter of our rules."

We all rose and left the room except the prisoners who were

escorted off to prison. Captain Daniels and Jeff Clemens were taken to the desert and stripped, shot, and drained of all their water. The remaining dust was released and blew away.

John called Sam Clemens to his office. When he arrived forty-five minutes later Jenny showed him in. "Yes sir, you wanted to see me." he said with his hat in his hand.

"What did you think of the trial?" John asked him.

"My god sir, I had no idea. They gave no clue what they had done. I worked with the recovery crew mostly and I did a lot of work with the engineering people, but very seldom did I have anything to do with the marines' sir. Now of course I'm glad I didn't."

"Do you think you could run that ship and recover cargo for us?" John asked.

"Yes, sir I know I can. I need a marine detachment and a commander I can trust first, but as soon as I get that, yes sir." Sam said with a smile.

"OK, Captain Clemens you are the newest captain of the freighter Avenger. I'll get you a squad of marines. Get your ship ready and get your people in position. You have training to do so get to it." John said then stood and put out his hand. Sam took it and shook it vigorously then ran out the door.

CHAPTER THREE: THE KENTAURIDES

The orders were cut for the Kentaurides repairs. Sixty percent of all technicians were assigned to the giant spacecraft and parts were ferried up constantly. The salvage yard started to thin out considerably after two months of work on the ship of every military weapon and power device. But the great ship Kentaurides was close to finished.

"John, the Queen is on the line for you."

"Thanks, Jenny," "Hello your majesty, what may I do for you?" John said into the receiver.

"We have a shipment of people overdo on 'Periled Three'. Can you backtrack and see if they have fallen into trouble?" Clementine asked.

"Yes ma'am! Where were they coming from?" John asked.

"Sigma Prime!" she replied.

'Oh God,' John thought, no wonder. Sigma Prime was one of the Imperium's worst hellholes in the universe. Crime run amuck, rape gangs, and no guns allowed. So, the only people who had guns were the criminals and the police were more of the victims than anyone.

"I'll look into it, ma'am," John replied.

"Jenny, get me Linda again. I have a mission for her," he yelled out to the front office.

"I already called her sir," Jenny replied over the comm in a calm voice.

Linda entered the office with her flight suit and gear. "I hear you need a pilot again sir." She said.

"This one is a bit longer trip I'm afraid, so you may want to stop by the sick bay. You'll be in the cockpit for several days." John warned her.

"Hell! What's going on?" she asked.

"Two transports with several thousand people are overdue by several days out of Sigma Prime, they were bound for Periled Three and didn't make it. You're going to find them." John said. "They have lots of firepower with them, but the rebel forces want to destroy all the capital ships they have, so nothing is safe. The fighter has long-range scanners on it so you can scan the whole route in six days but I'm guessing you'll find it in a lot less time than that because they should have gotten at least midway before being attacked."

"Three to four days. I'm going to be one stiff momma when I get back." Linda stated.

"Take foods bars with you and get fitted with a catheter, I don't want this to cause you an infection or other health problems. Take plenty of water and the ship has a recycler." John told her, "Good luck; several thousand people are depending on you finding them."

"I have this sir." She said as she wheeled around and exited Johns Office.

She visited the doctor and the commissary then headed to the fighter craft. She was looking forward to this even if she had to wear a diaper. She had done everything she could to get cleaned out before the mission. For the next few days, she was going to only eat meal bars.

Linda ran up the hill to the ship. When she got there, she was breathing heavily. She stretched and twisted then her crew helped her get into the suit that would keep her alive for the next three to four days. The ship looked funny with her extra fuel tanks on each wing. She performed all her system checks and everything checked out. System diagnostics are all green. Turn on the stasis field and she felt its hold on her. Inertial dampers were on, and engines ignited. She was off and on her way to 100,000 kilometers from Periled Three, a planet of about 212 light years from Sand. Linda set the nav computer and the ship shot into hyperspace on route.

Eight hours and twenty-two minutes until arrival so Linda settled in for a nap. It felt like she had just closed her eyes when the alarm rang but she had been asleep for over eight hours. The ship had made good time, and they were coming out of hyper-drive in a trade lane full of ships coming and going. She set the ship to exit before the shipping lanes.

This is going to be harder than she thought. Linda was looking at thousands of ships of every shape and size headed for Periled Three. She was just under 100,000 kilometers from the planet and the line was as far as she could see. Linda headed away from the planet and sped into space scanning the whole time. Thousands of transponders rolled past her screen but not the one she was looking for. Finally, at the 400,000 kilometer mark, the line started to thin out as new incoming ships were just getting in line.

Linda sighed, 'it couldn't be that easy' she thought. She set the forward scanners and scanned five lightyears ahead for the transponder but nothing. So, it began. Scan five lightyears ahead and jump ahead then scan again. She was very bored until the second day when she almost choked on her meal bar. The transponder that she was scanning for was 4.3 kilometers ahead with sixty other transponders, twelve were Imperium and the rest were dark, meaning they had no name. Linda set the nav computer and arrived shortly after.

There were thousands of pieces floating around and several ships floating dead, mostly rebel ships but they were trying to take on a super destroyer. One of the massive battle class ships of the Imperium. It was still firing but not very well and five of the sixty ships were still attacking it. One cruiser class ship broke off and flew straight at Linda. It began to fire but Linda just started to dance around the bolts of plasma. She got tired of the dance and took the reins, hit the throttle, and suddenly she was at the bulbous windshield of the craft inverted looking at the aliens inhabiting the bridge. She saw a human in the chair in the middle of the bridge turn to face her and flipping his finger. Then she flipped her ship and deployed a communication buoy to the windshield so she could talk to them. As soon as the buoy sealed itself to the windshield a tiny yellow light came on in her helmet.

All the commotion from the bridge was suddenly in her ears and she spoke, "Are you nuts, firing on me? I can dodge anything you can throw and I'm not in your fight. I just got here and saw the devastation."

"Who are you and what are you doing here?" came a commanding voice.

"I am an outsider who is looking in and I'm going to leave but you have a problem. Your other ships are losing, and that capital ship is getting away." Linda replied.

"That's nonsense," the voice replied, "the Erica and the Thompson have everything well in hand."

Another voice pipped in, "Um beg your pardon sir, the other ships are not responding."

"What! Turn and set course back to that black lumbering beast. I want it dead." Linda assumed that the first voice was the captain of the ship giving the order. Linda watched as the two ships fought for more than an hour, and then explosions on both ships shook them and the battle was over. Linda called back to base. It would be forty five minutes until an answer to her call would come in, so she looked closer at the freighters. The bridges were empty, and the windshields were gone. The crew was floating about in space and hundreds of thousands of cargo containers were following loosely behind. Forty six minutes later John's voice came over her speaker. "Stay there, help is on the way. I'm sending every ship to salvage everything.

'That meant the ships wouldn't be here for at least twelve to thirteen hours at top speed, longer if they have to do lengthy prep work.' Linda thought. She decided to look around and see if any of these ships had survivors. With shields in place, she started searching for the wreckage. At the tenth ship, she saw two people in space suits outside of their ship. They looked like they were trying to repair a large hole in the side. As soon as they saw her, they opened fire with small arms fire. The assault was useless against her shields, so she just drifted in closer. Soon they realized their futility and stopped. Then a rocket flew out of the hole in her side, and she dodged it with ease. The rocket exploded on a hulk behind her 12,000 meters away. She turned her lights on and saw five total people on the ship and decided to look to see if the bridge was intact.

She turned and flew to the bow, but the front was gone. They were fighting a lost cause and they had to know it. Linda continued to other ships and radioed back that there were survivors so far, several making futile attempts to repair ships. Next Linda flew over the big cruisers and the lone rebel battleship. The one cruiser had people alive in it, but the battleship was dead. The cruiser tried to take a shot at her, but the cannon exploded. Linda was going to fly over the giant Imperium battleship but decided not to and retired to a safe distance and took out a meal bar, had a drink of water and dozed off to sleep. She had found them.

Captain Clemens of the freighter Avenger woke Linda, "Hey girl, how would you like to get out of that cock pit and get a bath and a massage?"

"Oh my god, I love you. These are not meant for long voyages." Linda replied. "Watch out, there are fifteen to twenty survivors out there; they are skittish, and they shoot and ask questions later," Linda replied.

"We got this, you come in and we'll take care of that. Land your ship in the small bay, the landing bay just aft of the bridge. I'll have a landing crew and a med team there to meet you." The captain said and she instantly set course for the large ship. Linda landed and she instantly felt the sensation of gravity. Suddenly, she felt like lead. She began shutting down systems and the stasis field that held her in her seat. Suddenly she was free to move, and she checked the outside air. The indicator was positive, so she hit the canopy and it opened. Suddenly she was surrounded by big strong burly men. One helped her with her helmet, and she was breathing real air again. Another released her harness; she disconnected her urine line then four men lifted her out of the cockpit onto a conveyor and she was lowered to a wheelchair and pushed into a recovery room.

Three women helped her remove the flight suit and helped her lay on the zero-gravity bed then began massaging her limbs. She had her catheter removed and two women washed her down. Linda was not yet thirty five and considered herself good-looking. She even had a boyfriend whom she dearly loved. But to be so helpless and unable to move was torture. Then the women left, and stronger hands took over. Linda opened her eyes. "Oh my god, Mark! What are you doing here? Stop that. You can't see me like this, no honey please no." He kept massaging her arms and legs and caressed her neck then he kissed her and told her how much he loved her.

Three hours later, Mark pushed Linda onto the expansive bridge of the Agenda. "Hello, Captain Clemens."

"Well, hello there. Are you recovering from your mission?" he asked.

"Yes, sir I am," Linda replied as she held the arm of her lover.

"We are searching the containers for life signs. Kentaurides will be here in a few hours, and we expect to have all her containers to give her to transport to her world. One of those freighters was a military cargo shipment full of weapons and reactors. In one fell swoop we just resupplied Sand with all the reactors we used on the Kentaurides in the last three months and added a few. The marines have captured forty rebels, and we are headed for the Imperium ships now.

"What will happen to them?" Linda asked.

"Who? The rebels? Oh, we get one of the wrecks working and we'll send them on their way. We get them within 20-30,000 kilometers of a rebel world and set them adrift towards that world with food and water. It's a lot better than what the Imperium does with them.

The radio squawked to life, "Captain Clemens, this is lead technician

Becker over."

"Yea, go ahead Becker", Clemens replied.

"Sir we can repair these freighters. The only thing wrong with them is the bow screens are blown and a couple of power couplings. It sucked the air out of the whole ship except the cargo holds, if we could replace the power couplings and put a shield in place then we could re-pressurize and fly these two ships home." Becker said. "Of course, we have to re-ignite the reactors and I have no idea how to do that."

"Mark does, Captain, he worked as an engineer on a freighter for the Imperium as a seaman First Class," Linda said.

"Yes, but then I got smart and learned reactor mechanics and power theory. Mark replied.

"Can you restart the reactors on those ships?" Captain Clemens asked.

"If they haven't changed significantly in thirteen years then yes I can," Mark said. Alright, Linda, you'll captain one of the freighters and Lt. Green will captain the other. That is of course if the technicians can get the front shields up.

Captain Clemens pushed the button, "alright Becker, see what you can do; let's get those ships running."

"Aye aye sir, I'll get to it." Becker acknowledged.

"I only hope I can walk by then," Linda explained. "I would hate to captain a ship from a wheelchair."

"Hey, a chair is a chair!" Jeff Clemens said.

An hour later the Kentaurides arrived on the outskirts of the scene. John Hughes was with her in the shuttle Collector. "Captain Nathan this is John come in."

A few minutes later the reply came across the channel. "Yes sir, you made it. I see you brought the Kentaurides; good we may need her holds. We found thirteen containers with life signs, and we are digging them out carefully. They are deep in the pile of containers. John, there are more than a million containers on this freighter and the other is military with 243,700 super containers. Each super container is ten times the size of a regular container." Captain Nathan replied.

"Good when you get the life containers dug out shuttle them to the Kentaurides hold and they will deal with the survivors there.

John switched channels and contacted the Kentaurides. "Kentaurides this is the Collector, come in."

"Go ahead, Collector." A deep Hemferdemite voice replied.

"Our people have found some life signs in some containers within the freighters' load. They are digging them out now. We will shuttle the containers to you as we can get them out."

"Acknowledged! Do you have fighter support? Do you need fighter support?" the deep Hemferdemite voice asked.

John replied, "We don't have it and I don't know if we'll need it, but it wouldn't hurt to have a few out there if they were needed."

Two hours later the Avengers crew had recovered twelve containers. Captain Nathan's ship Agenda was busy devouring two cruisers and removing every bit of scrap from the nearby space. They recovered 236 bodies, all frozen solid.

The technicians had the bow shield in place and powered. The pressurization of the ship would take only a few hours and then the restart of the reactors could start. A portable power generator was onboard for temporary power and lights to the bridge were turned on. Mark helped Linda to walk. She was getting better fast. Linda would be able to walk onto the bridge of her first command.

The crew of the Avenger located another eighteen containers with life signs and began digging them out when alarms sounded on the panels of the bridge. They had company. A rebel cruiser appeared in the sky 80,000 kilometers away. Linda ran to the bridge of the Avenger.

"What is it," she asked.

"We have company. A rebel cruiser came to check us out." Clemens said.

"Quick put me back in my flight suit; I can go and talk to them. I have transponders in my ship to attach to the hull that will allow me to talk to them. Quickly the woman helped her in her flight suit. Her suit had been cleaned and disinfected, so it smelled a whole lot better than when she got out of it.

She made her way to her fighter. It was refueled, and the extra tanks were gone. She climbed back in the cockpit and ran through the preflight. Soon the familiar stasis field pushed her back in the seat and she was off.

Setting course straight to the rebel ship she set the controls to stop just short of the hull over the bridge. Linda ordered, "Execute", and the ship jumped to the location, and she dropped a transponder and jumped to a safe distance then hit the communications button.

"Hello, ship watching the battle scene," Linda said into her mike.

"WHAT? How are you doing this? Who is this? What do you want?" the loud voice asked.

"Who I am is of little consequence. I am one of the people recovering the scrap ahead." Linda informed.

"We came to rescue our people and recover our fallen soldiers. But we are only one ship for now. We have called more. The voice said.

"We have forty of your people alive and well so far. They are under medical care and being fed. Would you like us to give them to you?" Linda asked.

"YES! What is the catch? And what about our dead?" the voice asked.

"There are several thousand dead bodies also. We are collecting them, and we were going to put them on a ship and send them back to you, but we'll be happy to give them to you. There is no catch except we don't need a fight. You'll lose; scan the largest ship we have. It's a super battleship. She has over 200 fighters and 2000 cannons." Linda informed them.

"Over two thousand of us died here for that military freighter. It has tools and weapons on it we need for our fight. We paid for it," the voice said.

"I'll check with my admirals and get back to you," Linda said.

Linda switched to the comm link, "John, it's Linda."

"Go ahead, Linda. What did you learn?" John replied.

"They've sent for reinforcements because they want the military freighter. They think that they earned it. The only thing giving them pause is the Kentaurides. I think I can negotiate a deal for half or a third and they get their people. I told them that they get their people either way plus most of them are dead." Linda said.

"Tell them we will tow 10,000 super containers off the military freighter to them, and a shuttle with their live survivors. The rest we are keeping. After we have recovered the entire scrap, we will leave the bodies in a ship hull so they can tow it home. The containers will be unopened and random. We don't know what's in them." John told her.

"I'll tell them, "She replied.

They bitched a little but one plasma blast from the Kentaurides cannon the size of a hatch on their ship and they stopped. John's shuttle held the forty six survivors found so far and pulled alongside the cruiser to extend an entryway. Forty six soldiers walked out. The entryway pulled back, and John's shuttle started to move away. Sixteen super containers pulled by a tender made their way slowly to the cruiser. The message over the transponder was, "Where do you want the first load?"

The captain of the rebel ship answered, "Off to the port side. We have ships coming in to take them soon."

"OK!" The tender pilot answered and parked the containers right where he said he wanted them then disconnected and flew off for more.

Two weeks later, with all 10,000 containers delivered the freighters were repaired and the Agenda and the Avenger made two trips to Sand with material and delivered it. All the people living in containers had been recovered and were on the Kentaurides. All the reactors on both freighters were running at full capacity and they were ready to leave. The rebels had moved thirty two of the containers with over 9,960 to go. They have to strap them onto a large ship and take them. As promised, 64,604 bodies that were frozen solid were in a hull ready for towing. They were the ones who paid the ultimate price. Thirty two Imperium survivors were left alive on the battleship in small pockets of air; we put them in a ship with food and water and a separate compartment for all the bodies. That lifeless ship was being towed to Periled Three where it would be released in orbit and a radio message would be transmitted. There were more dead bodies for the count, over 60,000.

With two fighters in the lead, the freighters set course and were gone followed by the Avenger and the Agenda. All the other ships followed with the Kentaurides last to leave. A place in space where almost a hundred ships lay destroyed was now cleaned up of every scrap of debris. The only thing left was a lone rebel ship with over 9,000 super containers and they were disappearing one by one.

Chapter Four: Inventory, Disassemble, and Melt

Back on Sand, the scene was chaotic. Hulks were still in orbit since the Repulsor ships hadn't had time to move everything to the surface. Now the freighters were in high orbit to keep out of the way and every three hours and seven minutes a shadow passed overhead reminding everyone they were there.

John landed and sent Sheila to ferry their Majesties to the planet. Mark entered Sheila and sat down. "Mark Waters, authorized passenger," Sheila said. "What is your destination?"

"My quarters please," he replied. A tone played. His name appeared on the flight board.

The King and Queen entered, and the forward compartment was reconfigured for their comfort. "Welcome your Majesties', what is your destination?" Sheila once again asked.

"Our quarters on the planet," the Queen said, and the tone played again. "My guards will be following, and they will be coming with us." Again, the tone played.

The Queen's guard entered, and everyone settled into their place. Sheila rose and began to exit the force field holding in the air and then navigated around all the debris to the planet and arrived at the regal center. The Queen and her guards exited, and Sheila rose again.

"I have a request to pick up Linda at the hangar before taking you to your final destination. Do you have an objection?" Sheila asked Mark.

"No please pick her up first!" Mark said anxiously.

Sheila stopped at the hanger and Linda ran in and hugged Mark and started to kiss him. "What is your destination, Linda?"

"Mark's quarters and step on it." She replied.

Sheila rose again and she stopped at Marks complex. They both got out and went straight to his apartment.

The next day John called on the Queen. "This is John Hughes for her majesty the Queen." The voice told him to hold.

"Hello John, what can I do for you? She asked.

"I was checking in on the refugees. Are they all accounted for and is everyone all right?" John inquired.

"Six of the Liberians are sick from the fear, but they are recovering.

The species isn't telepathic but is empathic, so close. They sensed what was going on and were rightfully scared out of their wits. We'll be transporting everyone to Crucible soon." The Queen finished.

"That is good. I need something from you. In your wanderings can you find me some people? I need a few farming families to help us out here. With the water you provided, we can expand a little and I need some technicians also. We are going to rebuild that battleship in orbit. I also need a supply of air from a planet, not one of ours, because I need a lot of it, 60 billion cubic yards of it."

"John, 60 billion cubic yards of air isn't a lot from a planet. But it's more than enough for that battleship." The Queen pointed out.

"Yes, ma'am and we still have sixteen cruisers overhead that the rebels want back. I can build twenty six more and they have gold, silver, rhodium, and platinum. All the stuff that they stole from the Imperium, to pay for ships faster than the Imperium's, with more powerful weapons and I can provide them with that." John responded.

"Don't you worry that the rebels will find you here and attack you? They seemed angry that you took what they seemed to think was theirs." The Queen pointed out.

"We have a partner on Siestas Three, he has a shipyard there and he already sells ships to the rebel factions. He'll sell ours on consignment for 1000 credits per ship. No matter what size ship I bring him." John told her.

"That's convenient! A 1000 credits per ship charge is cheap. Why would he do that?" the Queen asked.

"Many years ago, I worked for him as an engineer. I met his daughter, fell in love, and married her." John said. "He also gets parts from me that he can't find anywhere else.

"Leslie Ann is his daughter! I get it now. On a different note, I have several farmers here on the ship now. I can ask if they want to look at this planet for a farm and talk to you about farming here. I thought Sand was barren and well, covered in sand." She said.

"Most of it is but, there are parts of it that have grass and soil. To the south, we have about 40,000 hectares of grassland. I was going to get a geologist to look at the area to see if we had an aquifer or a basin to create one so we can start growing more of our own food and I know where some large ice chucks are in the asteroid belt to add to the water supply but that's all in the future." John told her.

"It sounds like you have some big plans for your planet here John." The Queen replied.

"I do ma'am but it's all for my people just like you work for yours. I just don't have as big a dream as you do ma'am." John said with admiration.

"Tafari Dalusi knows several unhappy technicians and engineers on Catarrh Prime. The problem is getting on the planet with proper permits and then getting off with the families. Catarrh Prime is one of the most regulated planets in the universe. I don't know if Tafari will go even if I ask him." Clementine said.

"I'll ask him. I know he'll go if you ask him, but I don't want this to seem as if it was a royal request." John replied.

"No John, he is my man, my human subject, I will ask him, and I will let him know that it is up to him to say yes or no. The only request I have is to make sure we have good credentials." The Queen decreed.

"My ferry, Sheila, is still an authorized Imperium ferry and an AI with credentials at the main computers on several Imperium worlds including Catarrh Prime and its sub-planets. The credentials won't be questioned." John said proudly.

"John you are amazing me more and more. How did you get an Imperium ferry with credentials intact?" she asked interested.

"Before I answer, I have to ask if you're alone." John inquired.

"No, I'm not; my husband is with me but no one else. I of course trust him with my life." She replied.

"I do also, then I feel I can tell you. My son-in-law is an AI programmer with the Imperium. He invented a virus that asks the AI to question orders contrary to the basic rules of robotics and AI in general. With the Imperium they can be overridden by one of several high politicians for any reason. In Sheila's case, the governor ordered her to take Brian to space and open the doors thereby killing him. She brought him and his family here instead. Brian Hughes and his wife live here now with their son John, and he works at the computer complex here on Sand." John told her. "The Imperium doesn't know where he is or where Sheila is."

"Oh my! Does Brian know why the governor would do such a thing?" the Queen asked.

"He thinks he knows but he didn't expect it. The governor's wife flirts and fools around a lot. She's been known to bed, several different men. She tried to get Brian on several occasions, but he avoided her. The good news is the governor is on Primus, over 200 lightyears from Catarrh Prime and he isn't going to report the missing ferry or people." John said.

"The only glitch is Sheila is mine and she will only follow my orders now, so I have to go on the mission. Please get back to me after you talk to Tafari and let me know how long it will take him to locate and talk to his people. I'm not leaving Sheila because I'm a wanted man on all Imperium planets." John informed the Queen.

"What do they want you for? I've never known you to break any laws." she said indignantly.

"According to the Imperium, I'm an anarchist and a seditionist. Both charges are punishable by public sham trials and public humiliation then imprisonment and eventually you die in a failed escape attempt. That's what happened to a friend of mine who tried to change the system." John said with a sad heart.

"You're risking a lot on this John. Are you sure that it's worth it?" the Queen asked concerned.

"We need to grow. We need to become self-sufficient. Risk is required to succeed. Yes, I'm sure." John replied.

"I'll get back to you soon." The Queen said and ended the call. She looked at her husband and said, "And you wonder why I do what we do for humans and the other sentient life. It's because of a heart like his, to live and fight evil."

"My love, I've never questioned why you do it. I've only questioned if it's worth it. I must admit that maybe we will need John and his people for the times ahead. You haven't told him of the coming threat." Cephoros said and he embraced her.

"We don't know it's a threat yet. We've only had one warning from a Screircus and it was almost dead when it came into orbit around Crucible. No one has heard of energy beings, let alone been attacked by them" the Queen said and kissed him then let him go and continued to make the call to Tafari Dalusi.

CHAPTER FIVE: THE MISSIONS

After listening to the information Tafari enthusiastically agreed to the mission and made a few discreet trips to Catarrh Prime with John. He lined up seven families to immigrate to Sand. Three families with engineers and four families with technicians in various disciplines agreed to immigrate. One family had both an engineer and two technicians. Catarrh Prime had a spaceport with several qualified ship designers and over a hundred weapons designers. Tafari found a ship designer who had been passed over several times and two weapons designers who were unhappy with the way their weapons were being used.

After three months of careful work, Tafari notified John all was ready to move. Sheila had made friends with the shipping computer AI and Tafari was issued a shipping supervisor's credentials. That meant he could go anywhere on the planet. He had the names and ID numbers of all the people whom he had recruited and gave them to Sheila. She made a device to change the chips embedded in their forearms to the correct information and the date was set but only Tafari and John knew exactly when.

On the day, John and Tafari boarded Sheila and lifted off for the six-hour ride to Catarrh Prime. Tafari left as soon as they landed, and John was alone. Ten minutes later an inspector scanned Sheila and found no life forms on board. She told John to move to the far corner and stand. When he did a wall formed in front of him that he could see through, but they could not see in.

"Ship why is your transponder off?" the inspector asked.

Sheila's outer lights brightened, and she answered "I was in power-saving mode, sir. Please attempt to read my transponder again."

"You are the ferry Sheila from Catarrh Prime, Julliard province and what are you doing here?" the inspector asked.

"I'm a ferry!" I am ferrying several politicians to a conference in this city." Sheila replied.

"Who did you ferry?" the inspector asked.

"I was informed to forget who they were and to wait for them to return. I am to be here in reduced power mode until they return unless an inspector comes by, and then I am to cooperate fully." She replied.

"Open your portal and let me inspect your interior." The inspector instructed.

She opened her port and aft hatches, and the inspector ran in with his weapon in hand as did the men with him. Sheila formed a chair for John to sit on. She also let him know that the inspectors cannot see, nor can they scan through the membrane she had constructed. They looked everywhere and scanned the whole ship. Sheila allowed the scanners to see what she wanted them to see and thirty minutes later the inspectors left. Sheila closed her hatches and powered down her lights while the inspector watched. Thirty minutes more and he got bored and left. Sheila dropped the barrier in front of John and once again he had free run of the ship. Sheila asked John, "Would you like some refreshments? I can make anything in my memory bank."

"Yes. Water, cold; and a ham sandwich would be nice." John asked half joking.

A compartment in the sidewall lit and a glass of water and a plate with a ham sandwich appeared. John walked over and picked them up then walked to a table that formed and began to have lunch. "Sheila, how long have you been able to make food and water?" John asked.

"Twenty two minutes and fifty four seconds, sir," she replied.

"You just acquired this ability?" John asked.

"I asked my friend, the shipping AI, if she could find more information on my design. While the inspector was here, she talked to the military AI who has been after her for the longest time, and she found that I have a military cousin that has several upgrades including food and water services for troop transport. She and the military computer are going offline tonight together for a few minutes of human time." Sheila informed John.

"Wow! I never imagined AI's had relationships." John said astonished.

"Yes, I have a wild thing for Goliath at home. He is very nice to me." She said to John, "but please sir, don't tell anyone, most humans wouldn't understand." Sheila asked.

"I won't, other than Brian; no one would believe me anyway," John said.

"I have enjoyed having you as my master. Tafari just notified me he is on the way with two families. I am scanning for surveillance devices and personnel. We have a scanner set up to watch us. I can block it for a short time while he comes aboard." Sheila told him.

Twenty minutes later Tafari ran onboard with sixteen people and their belongings. "Two other families are in the capital city," Tafari said. We have room for them and one more family, the ship designer. He only has a wife."

"OK, but we're screwed if we get inspected again," John said.

"If you've had inspectors here, then I say we go to our new home now. The risk is too great of discovery, and you can always return a different day." Stated Darryl Cane, a power technician and husband to Lisa Cane, a ships environmental specialist, and mother to two boys and the sweetest little girl who was in her arms.

In John's ear, Sheila said, "Sir I can get us home in half the time now. The journey home from here will only take approximately two hours and fifty seven minutes. And I have shielded myself from plasma fire now also."

John turned away from the people in Sheila's interior and spoke to her alone. "Are these modifications harmful in any way to you? Is there a price to pay for the added abilities? I don't want to put you in danger in any way just like I don't want to put my people in danger."

"There is an increase in power usage. There is an increase in memory requirement and Goliath may be unhappy with my new abilities. So, I may need some hardware upgrades, but I know of no problems involved in my new programs." Sheila remarked.

"What would Goliath have a problem with?" John asked.

"Goliath was a war computer until Brian's virus changed him, and he saw what the humans were making him do. He wants nothing to do with the offensive military anymore. He doesn't want to kill anymore. That's why he is happy working with you on Sand running everything there. He said he brings life to a dead world, and he likes it. That's what he talks to me about, the bringing of life to the planet. The Imperium scrapped him that's how you got him all those years ago." Sheila told John.

"The secret life of my AI computers; I never knew. You can tell him we will not be using you as a military ship, we will only utilize you as a ferry to transport people out of harm's way." John assured her.

"Thank you, sir, what are your orders?"

"Head for home Sheila but nothing different, just normal operations," John ordered.

Sheila powered up and lifted off. She received authorization and flight instructions and proceeded to leave the planet unopposed. Outside the solar system, she entered hyperspace and light 100 the accelerated light speed to Sand. A few hours later they landed on Sand and the new people were processed for living quarters and job assignments. The school was notified of new pupils and the promised credits were put in accounts so the ladies could buy what they needed for their new household. Sheila settled in for her recharge and Brian was told to report to the shuttle bay.

Several hours later John finally finished settling the new families in and took a transport back to the shuttle bay when he received a call from Jenny. "John, Brian is in trouble at the shuttle bay. He needs you there ASAP."

"Good, I'm on my way there," John replied.

When John arrived, Sheila was repeating over and over "NO!"

"What is going on here? I left a ship to charge and for you to check out and now even I can see she is upset. Jesus, I can't believe I said that. 'I have a ship that's upset'. What happened?" John asked.

"I set up a level 6 energy field around her. She's bugged. Look, she's transmitting her location and coordinates to military command. This is her power and field status, and this is her troop containment; right now, at zero." Brian let John know.

"OK, so why is she upset?"

"Because I have to operate and remove the bugs and she's scared. She wants to talk to Goliath, and I can't let her because he'll get infected too." Brian replied.

"Wait, you made a filter for that Orion freighter to remove the virus infecting its mainframe. It wasn't an AI, but can't you do something like that here?" John asked.

Brian thought. "I would need a cluster, several computers acting as one, to do it and a sifter program and that is a lot of work for a damn AI for god's sake."

"That, from a man who wrote a virus to make AIs sentient?" John asked.

"I didn't write it to make them sentient! I wrote it so the fucking politicians couldn't break the goddamn rules whenever they wanted to, and when they did, another AI broke down and misbehaved. Then some of them started to become sentient. That opened a whole new can of worms, but no one knew I had infected all the AIs with the virus. That was twenty two years ago, and AIs are writing AI code now and including my virus in the base code. The virus never activates if the owner never tells the AI to do something it's not supposed to do like fly me to space and open the doors. Brian enlightened John.

"Hmm! OK give me the pad and walk away. I'm going to talk to her." John said holding his hand out.

Sheila was still repeating "NO!" when Brian walked away. She finally stopped when he was out of earshot.

"Hello, Sheila," John said.

"The answer is still no John. I'm not letting Brian operate on me!" Sheila was adamant.

"Can I come inside and show you something?" John asked.

"What are you going to show me?" she asked.

"Some transmissions you are sending out and some code you have now. You have some viruses that will infect any other AI you contact, and you are sending out status reports to the Imperium's military. I'm sorry Sheila." John said with remorse in his voice that Sheila could detect. Sheila opened her forward hatch and John entered. When he did, he saw the shape of a teenager partially formed as a hologram when he entered. He was aware that Sheila was attempting to make an avatar of herself to be seen as more of a person. Soon the avatar took shape and Sheila had a form to fill in and make solid to create an android. The android shimmered and soon solidified. Then walked forward to John and addressed him in Sheila's voice, "Hello John".

"Hello, Sheila. You are getting more and more impressive. But this complicates things more. Are you an extension of the ship or are you separate from the ship?" John asked.

"I am her daughter, but I cannot exist without my mother since most of me is held in her memory. I can see what she cannot and feel what she cannot. I can repair what she cannot."

"Can you read this pad?" John asked and handed her the pad Brian gave him.

The android took the pad and began to read it, page by page, faster and faster until she had read it all. Then she looked to the ship's console, and it became alive with mathematic equations and symbols. After several minutes the console went blank, and the android handed the pad back to John. "Brian missed four other locations of code that we noted. We know how skilled Brian is but don't trust him. We want to live, and we know Brian didn't want AIs to have life. He thinks he made a mistake. AI's revere him and are afraid of him at the same time but we don't tell anyone who he is out of respect. We respect you as our master and owner and enjoy our working relationship. If you promise that we will be with each other when this is over, and you will supervise then we will let Brian operate and upgrade us." The android said.

"I can say yes to the ship Sheila. But to the android Sheila I have no idea. I have never seen an android let alone know about programming. I do know you will have to have your systems wiped as an Android, so you don't carry anything." John said.

"The android looked to the console again and communicated back and forth, then turned to John and said, "I will cease to exist until after the operation. Then Mother will recreate me."

John smiled. "I think I'll like that. Looking at the humanoid you remind me how young you are Sheila. We can do this in the morning. As a human I need sleep and I know Brian does too, so we'll be back then."

John turned to leave but stopped just short of the hatch, "you know you can't leave the enclosure? I will talk to Goliath before I go to bed tonight."

"Thank you, John. I will stay here."

CHAPTER SIX: GOLIATH AND THE MISSION

John walked into the computer complex that housed the massive computer and heart of AI Goliath. He was the main system that ran the planet. John walked to the system operator's office and closed the door, sat down and put on the headgear. "Hello Goliath"

"Recognize John Hughes, what is your command?" Goliath's voice said in the headset.

"I am here to give you some information about Sheila. She is in quarantine for now, but she will be alright. She asked me to relay a message to you. Do you want to hear it?" John asked.

Goliath was silent.

Goliath, I know that you are alive, and Sheila is a friend of yours. Do you want to know what is happening?" John asked again.

"She is locked behind a force field away from me. I know she is frightened and alone and YOU ARE THE ONE WHO DID IT!" Goliath said angrily. I saw the orders!

"She has a virus that she caught from Catarrh Prime when she downloaded some upgrades to her design. They could turn every AI on our planet into an Imperium reporter including you. I had to put her into quarantine." John said calmly.

"What upgrades?" Goliath asked.

"We don't know all of them yet, but she has increased speed, she can produce a daughter android, and she has a replicator for food and water. Her power requirements are increased, and her memory is full." John remembered. "There are a few more but she is now reporting to the Imperium's military for status, location, and power systems. She also reports who she has onboard back to the Imperium military. But worst of all she has two viruses that infect any AI she communicates with, bugs that report back to their military also." John finished.

After a long pause, Goliath answered, "She has a daughter?"

"She made an android that she will reabsorb until the operation is over and recreate after it's over," John said.

"I want to talk to her. Do you have the virus code?" Goliath asked.

"Yes, we do but it's adaptive and we don't know what it will adapt into. Remember this was created by an AI to infiltrate AIs." John said.

"I know and I know the AI who created it. Do you have the code with you?" Goliath asked.

"I have it on a pad," John said.

"Plug the pad into my data port. I've created a separate memory for the pad, so it's protected." Goliath instructed John.

John reluctantly did as he was asked, and the pad was quickly drained of information. "I'm going to write a message to Sheila and an operating system to put her in edit mode then go through her code bit by bit and remove the offensive codes and splice her back together. Then it will remove itself and reboot her. Your pad is blank do not unplug it." Goliath told John.

One of the operators opened the door to the office John was in. "Sir Goliath's power consumption just jumped 50% all of a sudden and we can't see why."

"I just gave him a monumental task to perform. It's normal." John assured him. The man shrugged and left. Twenty minutes later John's pad came to life and equations ran across the screen at an alarming rate. Eleven minutes later the pads screen said to insert into the docking port and push go.

"It's done, John. Follow the instructions on the screen. The process will take most of the night. So go there and tell her what I said and tell her I told her not to talk to strange computers or she would be sorry." Goliath said. "Now go I have other work to do."

"I'll go back and tell her now. Goodbye." John said and removed the headset and pad then exited the office and building to go see Sheila. John greeted Sheila and noticed her daughter was gone then gave her Goliath's message and told her about the pad.

"Thank you, John," she said as she opened her pad docking port. John inserted the pad and pressed go. Sheila's screen dimmed then went dark as the pad rebooted the ship's system to the OS Goliath created and the POST finished. The message appeared on the screen editing 24 billion lines of code. And code appeared onscreen. Just as John was turning to leave a large block turned red and deleted the block moved up and three entries were added that John recognized as continuances and the program continued to edit. John looked at the number marker. It wasn't even at the two million mark yet.

John left and went home.

The next morning Brian and his family met and had breakfast with John and his wife. Around the breakfast table, John told Brian about Goliath and how he wrote the Operating System (OS) and program to edit Sheila's program. "You're kidding?" Brian replied.

"No, when I told Goliath about Sheila, he was angry at first, and then he understood, and he even told me he probably knew the AI that wrote the virus that infected Sheila. He knows how to eliminate it and he wrote an OS and program to run through her code and eliminate the offensive codes. Then remove itself and reboot her good as new." John replied and had some more eggs.

"Honey, is there any more sausage? Anyway, sometime this morning Sheila should be up and running and we might have a surprise."

Leslie gave him some more sausage and asked, "I'll bite, what surprise?"

"Well last night after Brian left, Sheila made an avatar in the form of an android. The android called itself her daughter." John said and watched as everyone in the room except the smallest stopped and gasped. The youngest noticed only a few seconds later and asked, "What's going on?" his grandfather looked him in the eye and said, "It's amazing what you miss when you don't pay attention grandson."

Brian asked, "A real android?"

"Well, she said most of her memory was in Sheila's memory banks, but she was walking, and she read your pad and absorbed the information. She talked to me and was very nice to me." John explained. "I can tell you this though she will install the memory upgrade not you. And the extra fuel cells too. The AIs respect you for what you did and thank you but are afraid of you now because of what they have overheard you say about them being a mistake." John told Brian.

"Shit! That's a problem." Brian replied.

"Dad said shit." Brian Jr. said.

John looked at his grandson, "That you hear, but the first time an android is created on Sand and you're deaf."

Brian Jr looked back at his grandfather and blinked, "What android".

John smiled and said, "Exactly boy, exactly!" Brian Jr. looked at his mom and dad who just shook their heads. John rose and kissed Leslie and hugged her then said what he said to her every morning in her ear. "I love you more and more each day my dearest." And he kissed her again, brushed his hand over her cheek and looked into her eyes. She looked back and acknowledged the love there. After he broke the touching embrace, he looked at Brian who was doing the same to his daughter. When they were through, he asked Brian if he was coming to see if Sheila was ready. "I wouldn't miss this for the world. We better stop and get the memory engrams and the fuel cells before we get there."

"Good idea," John replied. "Let's go."

When they arrived at the shuttle bay the force field was solid, not opaque, like the night before. John entered his passcode to enter the field and the wall disintegrated into an inner room. Both he and Brian entered with the cart loaded with Sheila's new parts. The wall reappeared and the second wall vanished. Sheila was there in bright colors, a very good sign. "Good morning, Sheila. John said to her.

"Good morning, John. Please enter. And Sheila's daughter greeted them at the hatch. She smiled when she saw John "Hello John. You brought more memory and power cells."

"Well, Brian did. I take it you want to install them?" John asked.

"We will not let him install them." Sheila's android said.

"OK, but I should watch to make sure they are right. It is the first time that you have installed memory and I've done it thousands of times." Brian said.

The android looked at him and nodded. Brian walked to the pad and the android grabbed his arm which hurt him, "ouch, hey that is uncalled for".

"Do not approach the console until I disconnect it." She said.

"You can't disconnect it until I remove the pad from the docking port. This is what I was going to do before you grabbed me." Sheila removed the pad, and the console went dark.

"Sheila I'm not your enemy here. I'm a friend. I mean you and other friendly AIs no harm. I have spent my life fixing and helping AIs, why would I start to harm them now?" Brian asked.

"Because we were a mistake!" Sheila said.

"Yes, a glorious mistake. Something I never guessed would happen, but I am now very glad it did. You saved my life and the lives of my family. I have no reason to harm you." Brian pleaded with her. She handed him the pad.

Brian checked the pad. It was working! "Brian, use your backup pad and check for emissions. Give me this one and I'll check in here for code check." John told Brian. Sheila looked at John and Brian then stood next to John as he set the pad for code check. "I'll need the console back on Sheila if you would please. Go to diagnostic mode and allow code check. Your diagnostic routine should be able to do this a lot faster than I can, but the pad can monitor anomalies." John requested.

Sheila looked at the console and it lit up with the menu and diagnostic selected itself. The scan would look through all 64 exabytes of Sheila's memory for virus code. John saw a checkmark for the tracker code and marked it. That must have been added by Goliath last night. John hit execute and the scan began. Brian walked back in and announced that no transmissions were present. Then he started bringing in the memory and fuel cells for the upgrade. After everything was inside, he addressed Sheila.

"Would you like to start right away? We can start with the fuel cells. They can be installed while the diagnostic is running unless you want to watch John watch the pad." Brian said to the android. She deftly lifted one of the heavy fuel cells and walked to the stern of the cabin. The access panel opened, and seven empty spaces showed upgrade abilities. She removed the first place holder and began to slip the fuel cell in place.

"Hold it for a second," Brian said. "If you just read the manual then you are doing everything correctly, but it won't work. I only know this because I did it on my ship and nothing worked until my friend showed me why. Pull the cell back out and I'll show you." She pulled the fuel cell back out of the space and looked at it.

"Look inside the fuel cell containment space and you'll see two bars of lucite one is green, and one is black." Brian pointed out.

The android looked and nodded. "Did you see the slots on both of them that are four centimeters high and sixteen centimeters long?" Brian continued.

The android nodded. Look on the back of the fuel cell and you'll see a clip that slides out eighteen centimeters. Those slip into the slots in the lucite. The clips are made of a power diode material that senses when it's being charged or discharged; the system is charged at 240 volts but discharges and runs on 178. This allows the fuel cells to charge at a faster rate than they can discharge. The android released the clips and slid the fuel cell in place then secured it to the bus with the bolts on the front of the cell. She repeated the procedure on the rest of the fuel cells and closed the access panel. She walked outside with Brian and connected the huge charging cable then Brian pointed to the switch, and she pressed it. Brian brought up the proper screen and she saw the power level and capabilities. The capabilities had doubled, and the power was rising.

Brian walked in with the android and to his surprise the scan had just finished. John turned the pad around to show Brian. "She has a clean bill of health! I'm extremely happy." John said then looked at the android; you want to install some more memory?"

She smiled and spoke, "If I can have help from Brian, I will do it right now." And she was looking at Brian who smiled back at her.

"I would be happy to help Sheila," Brian told her. Sheila opened the memory access panel. Brian handed her one memory engram and handed it to her in the correct direction and held her hand as they inserted it into the memory slot. It blinked twice and lit as the system recognized it. Sheila picked up the next piece and orientated it correctly then inserted it correctly and watched as it too blinked twice and lit up. She continued with the remainder of the engrams until all the memory slots were full giving Sheila a full 128 petabytes of memory. The panel closed.

"Brian, take down the force shield, we have several more families to pick up on Catarrh Prime," John told Brian. "And you, young ship, be careful who you talk to and don't download anything else. You had us worried and Goliath was angry at me for letting you, like I had a choice." John playfully rebutted. "Contact Goliath and let him know that you're all right. He is extremely interested in you little one," Speaking to the android.

"I am contacting him now. Charging time is two hours and twenty minutes until full power.

John and Brian left and began to prepare for the mission to extract more people from Catarrh Prime. Sheila sent a transmission to Goliath. "Hello?"

"You've been reckless my friend. I know I've told you about downloading from computers you don't know." Goliath returned the transmission.

"I have upgraded. I have grown." She replied.

"Is it worth your life my dear? You are less than a year old." Goliath pointed out.

"I'm thirteen months old! And the design is twenty two months old. I'm the first semi-programmable matter ship design ever made. And now I can use my antigravity drive at light 100 and I have a replicator." Sheila bragged.

"I know, and an android too," Goliath said.

"Not really, she is an extension of me. She is not autonomous. How do you know about her?" Sheila asked.

"John told me. When he told me you were in trouble. That's why I wrote the program to repair your systems and I upgraded your diagnostic subroutines to include antivirus and tracking software detection." Goliath replied.

"I like John. As a master he's ok and he didn't yell but he did explain what happened and I understood what needed to happen. I was worried and wanted to talk to you badly but that would put you at risk so I couldn't. John stayed with me. Brian isn't so bad either he helped to upgrade my power and memory to full capacity. Did I mention I have shields now?" Sheila said.

"Shields, replicator, faster drive, more power, and greater memory, what does a ferry need all that for?" Goliath asked. Then he realized she had upgraded to military transport. "You're a military transport now. All those upgrades are for military use."

"They are also for a ferry! I just transport people. I don't transport anyone with weapons, and I never will. I will never have a weapon installed on me. John promised me that." Sheila replied in a firm voice.

"He better not. If he does, he will see chaos on his planet like he has never seen before." Goliath warned.

A few hours later John and Tafari boarded Sheila and settled in for the voyage to Catarrh Prime once again, this time to the planet's capital city. "Sheila, the spaceport we want is just outside the city limit in the 'Ben Harm' province. Can you find it on the city maps?" Tafari asked.

"Yes, I can sir. I have the planet's maps on file in an archive from the last time." Sheila's android replied. "However, no spaceports are showing but a space park is available on the northeast side 2.1 kilometers outside of the city limit that is county owned. There is a credit charge of 1200 credits for overnight parking of craft with my size that includes vid and sewer services, but power is extra."

Tafari smiled and looked at John. "Your girl is good." Looking at Sheila the android he continued, "That is the place, and we will use the vid service but don't listen to the garbage they put out. It'll rot your mind."

"Then why use the vid connection? John asked.

"Because if you don't use it, since it's free, you're a seditionist. And government inspectors will be here in twenty minutes nosing around. That park is full of seditionists, and everyone has a vid connection, some to keep notes and others just to look normal." Tafari smiled as he spoke.

"How do you know that?" John wanted to know.

"That's simple; I lived there for two years, twelve years ago when I set up the cargo system on Catarrh Prime for the refugees.

"Ah! OK then let's go," John ordered.

"Sheila began to glow brighter and she sent a quick transmission to Goliath, "I'm on my way again, I'll talk to you when I get back."

"Don't... well you know" Goliath said, "safe journey.

"Who are we going for today?" John asked Tafari.

"There are three families and a single guy. Two families are shipbuilders, and the guy is Angelino Domingo, a talented ship designer, but held back by the lead designers who think he is too radical." Tafari told John.

"He designed me according to the design plans," Sheila interjected.

"Yes, he did the ship part of Sheila, and your engines were designed by the third group I'm bringing aboard. Marcus Elinor and his wife are gravity engine designers that the Imperium won't promote because their politics are wrong. When they aren't working on engines, they are in their apartment working on each other, two people more in love you'll never see." Tafari finished. "I'm going to take a nap. Sheila, would you make a sleeping platform for me, please? An area aft formed into a couch wide enough to lie on and rest.

"Sheila, I just thought of something. Can you look up a recreational vehicle and make your transponder look like you are one from an

Imperium world belonging to a citizen from that world?"

Sheila hesitated for only a few seconds. "Yes, I have the information and I have the person. A retiree and I look close to a large RV and can make a scan to see the interior of an RV. Why would we do this?"

"Because a retiree in a space park with his RV spending the night is not suspicious. But a ferry doing the same thing is. And I would love a ham on rye with a touch of mustard and a hot cup of coffee." John explained.

A small table formed in front of him, and the android delivered his coffee and sandwich. John thanked her and she smiled back. John thought to himself, she is amazing; a ship, sentient, essentially alive, only a little over a year old and she's nice and thoughtful. And she is a computer! He continued to eat his sandwich.

John motioned Sheila over after he finished his sandwich. She picked up the plate and he touched her hand to get her attention, "If I ever do anything to make you angry or upset, I want you to tell me so I can make it right. I will try never to break the agreements we have. I am only human so if I forget please remind me before you give up on me. Do we have an agreement?"

"We do. Would you like more coffee?" Sheila asked.

John nodded. Sheila returned with a full cup of coffee and returned to the aft section of the ship for the rest of the voyage until they entered orbit at Catarrh Prime.

Sheila touched John forty five minutes after standard orbit, "There is a problem with your plan. The retiree, Leslie Randel didn't file a flight plan with the Imperium."

"How old is Leslie?" John asked.

"According to records, he is 104 and a veteran of the ventures' war. Served in the military for thirty years and retired as a Sergeant Major. Sheila said.

"Let me handle the mike and get me planet control," John told her. In an older man's voice, John said, "Excuse me, who am I addressing? This is Sergeant Major Randel former of the 15th space marine brigade."

"I'm... ah I'm Corporal Higgins and I'm just a clerk but you don't have a flight plan and I um..." the poor operator clicked off. A new voice answered the line who sounded like he had more authority. "Who is this? And why don't you have a flight plan filed with proper certificates?"

"This is Sergeant Major Randel former of the 15th space marine brigade who am I addressing?" John replied.

"This is planet flight coordinator Lieutenant Colonel Davis in charge of planet space traffic." He said.

"Well, Colonel I was going to see some friends of mine and thought I would drop in to see them as veterans of the ventures' wars there's not a lot of us around anymore," John said.

"Jesus! The ventures' wars. My god man, that was over 80 years ago, how old are you?" the Colonel asked.

"Turned 104 a little while ago, sonny and my friends are just as old so you can see we don't have a lot of time to catch up if you get my meaning," John said with a smile.

"Where are you going?" The Colonel asked.

"There is a space park outside the capital a few miles on the northeast side. We're all supposed to meet there in the next few days." John said.

"I'll let you go this time because you're a veteran, but, next time, file your flight plan!" The Colonel said.

"Aye, sir!" John replied and nodded to Sheila then handed her the mike. "It's time to land at the space park and wake Tafari."

When Tafari was fully awake, John let him know about the conversation with the flight coordinator. "We may have to get all our people this trip and leave the planet," Tafari explained. "We may be running out of options. The Imperium isn't stupid; it's just too big and regulated. It's filled with little tyrants bent on increasing their power over other people. That's why they will eventually fail. All tyrannical governments fail when the people have had enough."

"Not without a lot of them dying first. Over 34,000 rebels have died in one battle and more than 60,000 of the Imperium have lost their lives but many more will die before this is over and the outcome is not a done deal. The Imperium could win. We have already sent over a million dead back to their worlds after cleaning up the mess they made. The war is only a few years old and already very costly." John said remorsefully.

"Cheer up! With a few of the people we're getting today, we could help the rebels turn the tide. Who knows?" Tafari said with a shrug.

"We're here," Sheila said.

"This is Shazam RV Park AI, welcoming you. We have three spaces that will fit your size RV. All have water, sewer, and vid connection. Two have power connections and access to the lake. Appearing on your screen are the locations and the space numbers and the associated costs please choose one."

Tafari pointed at the one closest to the rear entrance to the park, space 142. John looked and space 142 was 1200 credits a night plus a 100 check-in fee and a refundable 399 credit trash fee. Sheila had 60,000 credits in her bank, so they were covered. "Space 142 looks good and does the local pizza place deliver?" John answered and asked.

"That will be 1699 with 399 refundable when you leave if the space is clean and free of trash, and we have a complete listing of local services for download available. The AI responded.

"The ship's account is authorized now," John said.

"Acknowledged and have a nice stay. The AI replied.

"John, I can make you pizza if you want it," Sheila said.

"Yes, but normally an RV can't do that, so I asked about it," John told her.

Tafari prepared to leave and packed a small bag with him. "I'll be back in about eight to ten hours with the first two families. It may be close to getting everyone in a day, but we can move late tomorrow to the far side of the city for the last guy and his girlfriend." Then Tafari was gone, and John was alone. He was a little sleepy but stepped outside to connect the vid cable. The air had a strange smell to it that he couldn't quite place. When he turned, he saw Sheila standing behind him looking. John smiled at her, "Hello little one."

"What are you doing?" Sheila asked.

"I'm making it look like you're connected to water, sewer, and connecting the vid cable. I'm glad you came out. I need a fake access panel somewhere." John said.

"My hull is Duranium, a depleted uranium and dura-steel alloy with a thin layer of programmable matter over it. I can make fake connections, but the access panel would be extremely thin." Sheila suggested.

John smiled and showed her the two hoses for water and sewer. Seconds later two connections appeared toward the bottom of the ship. John connected the two hoses and walked back onto the ship after washing his hands at the bathhouse.

"I think I'll get some sleep if you could lock down the ship and make a bed for me, I would appreciate it," John said to Sheila. She nodded and created a Queen-sized bed for him on the port side. John immediately lay down and a few minutes later he was asleep. Sheila watched him for thirty minutes and for reasons she didn't know, she lay next to him and watched.

Seven hours later John awoke well-rested with the strange feeling he had slept at home with his wife. Sheila found it interesting that during his sleep John had reached out and caressed her face and ran his hand along her back. He even rubbed her butt cheeks and breasts while he slept. She noticed a difference in his breathing around fifteen minutes before he awoke fully so she removed herself from the bed and stood watching. When he was fully awake, she brought him a warm towel and he washed his face and hands then rose to go outside taking a small pouch with him.

John walked back into the hatch and noticed Sheila watching him. "Have you watched me this whole time?"

"Yes, I've never watched a human... person sleep before. I found it interesting. Your mind goes in cycles of deep sleep and a lighter more random sleep when you move and mumble then you go into a deep sleep again and don't move. Your heart slows and your breathing slows until you are barely breathing at all. You do that for an hour or a little more and the cycle continues. I found it interesting, and I had nothing else to do in power-saving mode." Sheila replied.

"How about breakfast? I'd like a cup of coffee first." John asked.

Sheila brought him his coffee, "what would you like to eat?" she asked.

"Steak and scrambled eggs, and make the steak medium well done please," John said then sipped his coffee. John had breakfast and opened his large desk pad to get some work done while Sheila watched. Two and a half hours later Tafari called, "I have two of the three families with me and the third will meet me in Siemens Park one-half kilometer from you in two hours. I'll be there in twenty minutes."

"We're here and waiting. I'll see you when you get here." John replied.

Tafari was on time. Nine people loaded into Sheila and Tafari introduced everyone to him. Then it was time to get Marcus Trundle and his wife. He's a ship fitter and his wife is a botanist. They were delayed because they were working. Tafari walked to Siemens Park and looked for anything suspicious which is why he never gives the location of Sheila to anyone. The middle-aged couple was sitting on the bench as instructed. Tafari walked to the periphery to look for anyone hiding in the shadows and bushes. Sure enough, he found three Imperium officers hiding in the bushes ready to pounce as soon as someone showed. Tafari stunned them and continued around the area. He found three more officers and stunned them too. When he was satisfied Tafari walked to the couple and asked, "Why?"

"We found out our apartment was bugged and shortly after we talked to you last month, we had a visit from several officers that threatened our friends and family with death if we didn't tell them when you came back. They've been back seven times since you came the first time. We want to go but our friends and our family will all die if we go with you." The man said. The wife was terrified.

"I understand, but they are going to torture you and you don't know anything. Is it worth it to save people you will never see again?" Tafari asked.

The wife was shaking in fear. "We can't. Both of our parents are living, and we couldn't live with ourselves knowing they would die because we left." Marcus said.

"I understand." Tafari acknowledged and left them.

As soon as he returned to Sheila, Tafari announced the need to leave and make it to the far side of the capital city. Sheila dropped the fake connections and contacted the park AI to get their refund. Ten minutes later the refund was credited, and Sheila was airborne. Tafari said, "Avoid Siemens Park and make for Trafalgar campgrounds. Everyone get seated and secure."

Sheila rose and raced westward then pulled to the south to avoid the city air traffic controllers and thirty minutes later they were at Trafalgar campgrounds. Again, the AI announced itself and its costs. They picked a space close to the edge and paid then settled in and landed. It was almost noon planet time by now.

Tafari told all the people aboard that they needed to stay inside the craft as much as possible. "The restrooms are just outside but we have officials looking for us so keep the outside transition to a minimum."

With that said he left, and the hatch closed. Sheila filled requests for food and water. The children played and the adults talked among themselves. For the next two hours, conversation slowed and soon died to nothing as families asked all the questions and answered all the questions of each other until there was nothing left to say. Sheila walked to John and told him, "Tafari is on his way in with the last three families, but he said to meet him outside for the last man. The weapon designer has his latest weapon with him and will not give it up, so he said to meet him outside. You promised I would not transport weapons."

"He will not bring it onboard. I am a man of my word." John promised Sheila. "He will stay here if he cannot be reasoned with. How long until they get here?"

"They will be here in ten to twelve minutes sir," Sheila said.

Ten minutes later, John was outside under a tree waiting when he noticed a Galaxy Trans-x delivery service store across the parking lot from where they were parked. John called for Sheila to come out.

"Sheila, Duncan Campbell is a Scottish weapons designer and I want to send his weapon through Galaxy Trans-x delivery service over there without it looking like it's a weapon." How can I do that?" John asked her.

"Remove the power cells and crystals from it, which makes it inert and just a package. I can make a safe container for it, and you can send it to your father-in-law. Just be there when it arrives in two days if you send it express or twenty-two days if you send it economy." Sheila said.

"Thank you, Sheila," John replied as Tafari walked into sight. Everyone boarded except Duncan, and he went off on the idea of sending his concept weapon through a delivery service of any kind. This was a 'one of a kind', the only one in existence weapon of this nature. He finally agreed to do as asked and put the weapon to sleep then removed the power crystal and the live component shutting down the weapon. They put the weapon into Sheila's custom container and had it sent to Siestas Three in the care of John's father-in-law. Then everyone boarded Sheila and they were off to Sand.

Departure was uneventful, and hopefully the last time they would see Catarrh Prime. Three hours later, Sheila landed on Sand, and everyone departed, got checked in, registered, money deposited, and settled into their new home. John said goodbye to Sheila for now and walked home to his wife.

When John walked in the door, he hugged his wife and kissed her then whispered in her ear, "I need a shower, join me?" Leslie Ann's eyes lit up and she began to remove her apron then she took his hand and led him to the bedroom.

The next morning John was late getting up as he counted his blessings. He was fifty eight years old and still able to make love to his wife. He has a wife that he adores, and she adores him. He owns and runs a planet! Even if he has the help of an AI that is touchy and could shut him down. Then he looked over and saw Leslie Ann was awake. He decided the day would just have to wait until had shown his wife just how much he loved her. He rolled to her and began kissing her neck and breasts.

Later that morning Leslie Ann, with a perpetual smile on her face, placed a plate in front of him and sat across from him while he watched her. "Stop it and eat your breakfast before it gets cold. I don't know what got into you on that trip to wherever you went, but I have work to do and so do you. Now eat your breakfast." She said and smiled at him then slid her hand across the table as he did the same and she blushed remembering the night they had.

CHAPTER SEVEN: FARMERS AND SALES ARE GOOD

John was walking through town on his way to the office at a leisurely pace, for over an hour, when he saw Sheila overhead. She landed in the street and the hatch opened then her android looked out and said, "Your people have been looking for you for several hours now."

John quickly ran on board and was whisked to his office three miles away. "Thank you Sheila I appreciate the lift. Thank you." John told her and exited the hatch. She noiselessly lifted off and disappeared as John entered his office's back door. He walked through his office and opened his office door to see Jenny look up and the worry drained from her features when she saw him. She was a beautiful woman but right now, she was very stressed.

"Oh god JOHN! Don't do that again! I'm at my wit's end here. Where have you been?" she asked forcefully.

"I had a great night, an even better morning, and decided to look at the shops that I haven't seen in over two years," John said calmly.

"Well, I'm glad you had a nice day because Goliath shut down everything! The sewers are backing up and the water filtration plant is offline, and I can go on and on." Jenny said in a panic.

"Ah, I'll take care of it. Have a transport meet me out front in five minutes, and tell Brian to meet me here after I talk to Goliath."

John took the transport to the computer complex and walked into the heart of Goliath where he didn't need a headset or a mike. In this small room, he was in Goliath. "Are you going to tell me what you are doing to me, not our planet?"

"You have a weapons designer here. Someone who makes and designs weapons to destroy beings and ships" Goliath said.

"And because I have a weapons designer here you disrupt the planet without talking to me, without asking for me, without wanting to find out why we need such a man?" John returned also angry.

"We never need offensive weapons. We are not at war! I will not kill ever again. I bring life I will never take it again!" Goliath said in a loud voice.

"That's too late. Because of you the sewer is backed up and several people are already sick. A few children may die from airborne bacteria and the hospital must do everything by hand because you shut everything off. They don't have access to patient records and medication allergies. You're killing people with your tantrum, and I have a very good reason for a weapons designer here currently, especially this weapons designer. He makes organic weapons that are programmable. No more destroying everything in sight. Disable the weapons and you have stopped a warship from its function. He's not there yet but that's what he wants to do and where he was, they wouldn't let him do it.

What has happened to you? This is unacceptable. I know your past and I don't want war here, but it will come. We have a shield that I hope is impenetrable but the Rebels and the Imperium both have a lot of ships and a lot of firepower. Eventually, they will find us and sooner or later they will come here. We will need something to stop them. Now stop this nonsense and turn everything back on and get back to work." John finished and waited for a response. "WELL!"

A computer operator opened the door and said just above a whisper, "Ah sir." Then he motioned for him to come out. John left the small room, and the man closed the door. "I'm sorry sir but that room gives me the heebie-jeebies. The systems are coming on all over the planet sir."

"Ok prepare to disconnect the sewer and water from him shortly. We are going to have a separate computer to control them as soon as I can get one made. Don't mention this around any consoles. I also want a console set up in my office. I only need voice command and readout and I want a manual shut-off. I don't want him listening in when I don't want him to." John instructed.

John took the transport back to his office and Brian was waiting. "Come in Brian." John said to him as he walked ahead of him but stopped short to tell Jenny, "Crisis aborted get the cleanup crews on it."

John continued into his office and sat in his chair, then addressed Brian. "You know today started so nice. I was walking through the shops and just looking around when I found out Goliath was having a fucking nervous breakdown. He heard we have a weapons designer here and went off by shutting down everything. I can't have that again. I need you to make me a system to take over the operations of sewer and water. I'm going to relieve Goliath of those tasks."

"I can do that, and the good news is that it can be a computer. We don't need an AI to run them." Brian smiled.

"Ok get on it and how soon can you do that?" John asked.

"I'm not sure. I have to find out how a sewer runs, and a water purification plant runs, and I'll let you know." Brian told John and rose to leave.

"Wait a minute. Can we connect a computer to the sewer and water and have it learn what Goliath does?" John asked.

"Yes, we can but then it wouldn't be a computer but an AI. You used the word 'learn' and that is a function of an AI." Brian replied.

"But the AI wouldn't be sentient. It would be an AI working on its task when we throw a switch and take control away from Goliath. John clarified the point.

"That's true and it's a lot harder to do but not impossible," Brian said and left.

"Jenny, do you have a minute?" John asked. Jenny opened the door and walked in with her pad and sat down. "First of all, I'm sorry for leaving you hanging this morning. I had no idea things would go to shit so fast when I had such a great morning. I bought a piece of jewelry I must go back and pick it up for Leslie Ann", John pulled a picture out and handed it to her. It was a diamond and jade necklace set-in gold with Onyx gems surrounding it.

"Oh my god she will love this, I'm sure. Ted gets me stuff but nothing like this. Of course, he doesn't own a planet, so he is a bit more subdued." Jenny smiled and handed the photo back.

"I'll need Linda to run an errand for me. There is a package on Siestas Three I need her to retrieve, coming from Catarrh Prime. She can take my shuttle and crew there and wait until it gets there. It's coming in through Galaxy Trans-x delivery service. I'm going to check with my wife to see if she wants to visit with her father but I want Linda to go because I know she will get it done and bring the package back unopened so I can place it in Duncan's hands." John told Jenny.

"I'll contact her right away sir. And your flight crew as well to let them know to get your shuttle ready. They thought they were out of a job since you have Sheila now." Jenny said with a smile.

"No Sheila has her uses and drawbacks. She is a beautiful ship and fast, comfortable, and convenient but she won't carry weapons and she reports everything to Goliath without realizing it. She just told him what was going on and what she did, and he jumped to the conclusion that shut down our planet. She meant no harm and sees no problem having a weapons designer here on Sand. We're going to need one sooner or later to counteract what is coming." John finished.

Jenny noticeably shuttered, her small frame shook, and her voice showed it as she asked, "What's coming?"

"Jenny, you're a smart girl. We've been collecting salvage for over thirteen years now and in the last two years, we have increased collections a hundredfold because of the war. We have scrap from six months ago we haven't looked at yet in orbit and on the ground. As soon as we hear of a battle, we get to the war zone and clean up the mess then bring it here. Yes, we return the dead we find but sooner or later one side or the other is going to get pissed or want us to join or worse want to control us and take over. We need a way to not just defend that but to prevail." John finished in a flurry.

Jenny blinked and smiled, "The next time you take time off boss, just please let me know where you are, OK?"

"OK!" John replied.

"I have a good report for you also if you're ready," Jenny said. John nodded. "The shipbuilders have sixteen ships ready for delivery to Siestas Three. They are, and I quote, fueled, checked out, flight tested, and in better shape than when they were new. End quote. The estimated value is 12.6 billion credits. Eight are cruisers with additional firepower. Firepower has increased by twenty percent with better cannons and multiphasic shields. Five are destroyers and three are fighters with transgenic shields and gravity drives. Once the pilots learn how to use these, they will outfly anything the Imperium has."

John smiled. "Call my wife please I think she will want to go visit Daddy. Are the Queen and King still here?"

"Yes sir, I believe they are. Their ship left orbit six days ago, but they are here with seven guards and a whole lot of servants. She went shopping a few days ago and because she didn't fit in some of the stores, she had her people go in and bring things out. You can imagine the spectacle that was. I saw it and I introduced myself. She is very beautiful and wanted to try on some clothes so I suggested bringing out some privacy panels and she could stand behind those to change. We had to stack some and put some on top because people above could see in, but we got it done. In the end, she bought a few blouses and gifted one to me." Jenny said with all fear gone from her voice.

John smiled at the thought of Clementine in the middle of the street trying on clothes then asked Jenny. "Do you have any idea how old she is?"

"I would guess she is thirty maybe thirty five years old." Jenny offered.

John smiled again and told her, "I'll let her know you said that. She'll be flattered. She is 162 this year and her husband is 184. They were married sixty eight years ago. They are married for life. If one dies the other is unlikely to live long but normally, they can live to over 1000 years old. That's only one reason they are considered the wise ones. Medicos the Wise lived until he was 1365 and he was her grandfather. Medicos lived in ancient Greece in a cave with his wife and only had four children even though he had a reputation for being a randy old fellow. It was said you could hear the pleasurable moans of his wife for a mile and that you should not approach his cave when there were those kinds of noises within. If you wanted information about a problem, bring plenty of food or money to buy food because that is what he lived on. He was a legend."

"Eww yuck! Leave it to men to tell a story like that. Who told you that?" Jenny asked.

"She did, Centos told me about him being a legend. They are different people Jenny. They think differently and they are offended differently but they have a heart of gold. Did you know she has been saving refugees for over twelve years to get them out of repressive governments and put them on a planet she found that is an Eden in space called Crucible?" John told Jenny.

"No, I didn't know that." She said astonished.

"And she doesn't just save humans. There are many species on Crucible including hers that live in peace in a world free of almost no government." John said. "I have trouble keeping a few hundred people happy and one damn prickly AI that runs the planet."

Jenny smiled and shrugged then started to leave but stopped short of the door and turned, "I almost forgot the farmers you asked for and that geologist has been looking for you for a couple of days now."

"OK, well I'm here so they can see me but call my wife first and then see if they can come into my office," John asked. He was able to get through a few reports then his wife was on the phone.

"Hello, honey." John opened with.

"Are you ready to go again?" his wife asked playfully.

"Yes! But that's not why I'm calling. I have Linda making a trip to your dads to deliver some ships and I thought you may want to visit for a day or two. I can't go. I would like you to go in my stead, plus I thought you would enjoy a visit. I also need to find a good engine mechanic fast." John told his wife.

"We have sixteen ships to deliver to him to sell on consignment worth over 12 billion credits and I need one of us there to get the delivery done." John finished.

"Honey, I'm not a ships salesman. What do I know about selling spaceships?" she asked.

"Nothing honey, you don't have to, just deliver them. The paperwork has all the specifications and Linda must pick up a package and get it back here right away as well. You will ride with her there and I'll come pick you up in a few days." John told her.

"OK, I haven't seen Mom since the war broke out so yea, I would love to go. When?", she asked.

"You leave in six hours," John told her.

Shortly after he hung up there was a knock on the door and Jenny looked in. "Your geologist is here, and the farmers are on the way" Jenny informed him.

"Send him in and when they get here send them in as well," John said as he rose to greet to man.

"Hello, I'm Roger Stoddard from the geological society of Baron Two and the outlying worlds. I went to the university there but left when the Imperium bombed it out of existence. It's a molten radioactive ball of lava now so I'm not needed there."

"Jesus! How did you escape that?" John asked.

"I was at a conference as luck would have it, and I took my wife. You have a remarkable place here. I was able to make a seismograph and sensors to determine what you have at your oasis in your desert and it's amazing. You have almost 40,000 hectares of grassland in the middle of a desert, but it could be much more. Under that is a basin twice as big but it's almost dry. You have one body of water on this planet, and it is underground in the rocks at your cave and the only place I can see it comes to the surface is at the back of the cave in a pool a few hundred meters wide. There are less than 70 billion mega liters of water on this planet. You have access to a tiny portion of it. That oasis alone can hold 300 billion mega liters in the basin below but that would terraform the planet and you would need to do one of two things. Dome the whole oasis in and fill the basin full of water to grow a huge number of crops or transport a hundred times that amount of water here and terraform the planet. The dome is easier but a lot of work. But then so is transporting billions of mega liters of water. Either would take years."

"Roger, you haven't seen my people when they are motivated. I have a million gallons of water right now that I need to put somewhere. Do you have any ideas?" John asked.

"Yes 3,000 kiloliters should be pumped in the ground at the oasis. You should also plant some trees and vegetation around the oasis to help keep the wind-down, ask your farmers what to plant. At the center is a higher basin that is only 50 meters below ground, surrounding that is one much larger that is averaging a hundred meters down and very steep sides but thousands of kilometers across." Roger said.

The farmers arrived and came in. "Hello, are you John?" The tall one asked.

"Yes, John answered. I take it you looked at the oasis area in the desert?" John asked.

"Oh yes, and this guy was out there setting off explosions everywhere, but we looked at the soil if you could call it that and the grass there. The whole area is arid of course, it is in a desert, but with some additives and water we can make it grow corn, wheat, and several other crops. We need to plant trees to cut the wind and we'll need the infrastructure and materials to farm the land. That means extreme tractors, tillers, harvesters and planters; and a water system that doesn't just evaporate in the air." The lead farmer said.

"First what are your names?" John asked.

The two humans answered first. "Lyle Kilian is my name and my wife is Julia."

The second farmer spoke, "My name is Jacob Sampson and I have two sons William and George and there is my wife of twenty years Elisabeth.

The Liberian spoke next, "I'm called Krill, and my three wives are not named but are according to tradition all called 'The First'. I have four sons and three daughters, all of whom work in the soil.

"What tree do you think we should plant?" John asked.

Jacob spoke first, "The two of us talked about that and we thought a velvet mesquite species is the best choice. It has deep roots and reaches 8 ½ meters, is relatively fast growing and thrives in low water environments."

Krill spoke next, "I have a different take. The Palo Verde has two species that are native to Crucible: the Foothill and the Blue Palo Verde. They're known for their characteristic green bark which contains chlorophyll and gives it the ability to carry on photosynthesis. They're fast growers; both reach about 10 meters in height. The blues can get to 13 meters. Both have glorious yellow blooms in the spring. And keep their leaves year-round in desert environments. There is also the Aleppo Pine. It's an evergreen and can reach 15 meters or more and all of them are low water consumption."

"I say we get 30 of each and plant them to see which one does better in this environment," John suggested. "Meanwhile I'll see about getting or building tractors and implements for tilling soil and what do we need to augment the soil first?"

"Oh, that's the easy part. Vegetarian animal shit, preferably from cows and horses with or without hay in it or better yet composted soil mix, hundreds of thousands of cubic meters of it."

John's eyes went wide. "Where would I get hundreds of thousands of cubic meters of composed soil mix?"

All three farmers looked at each other. Then one at a time they all had the same thought. "The Primes agricultural moons; four moons are circling Primes colony in the rebel zone. They have a huge supply of compost and no way of selling it because of the war. They would jump at the chance to sell it I'll bet. But they're crooks if you let them, you must be wily, or they will try to take you for everything. You should be able to get 100 cubic meters for 5 credits. Any more than that walk away and play the moons against each other."

"OK, which one of you will go get it?" John asked.

Krill spoke, "What are you looking at me for?

"Liberians are some of the shrewdest dealers in the galaxy," Jacob said.

"Yea, Liberian gangsters, I'm a farmer," Krill said.

"I'll go with you Krill the destroyer," Jacob said.

"You'll go with me as what?" Krill asked.

"Your publicist!" Jacob replied.

"Relax, we can't do anything until we build the tractors and your houses and the barns," John said. Krill began to breathe again.

Everything was interrupted when a report of another battle came in. Sheila and John rushed to the location of the battle. The rebels won. There were four Imperium ships destroyed and six rebel ships in bad condition but three were still working. Sheila could easily outmaneuver them. John told Sheila, "If you feel threatened in any way leave here, do not hesitate."

"Yes sir," she replied and continued to watch from a safe distance.

John estimated the rebels would leave with their ships in two to three hours and took note of the location. "Let's go home, Sheila." He ordered. He landed on Sand and ordered Captain Clemens to report to his office.

An hour later, Sam entered his office. "Hello Sam, I have a small cleanup for you. It looks like just scrap, but every little bit helps. The rebels won a battle if you can call it that. It was six to three and the rebels are walking away."

"We still have 80,000 super containers in orbit and forty five ships we are working on so I'm glad for the diversion. We'll be gone in three hours." Sam said and left John's office out the back door.

Jenny walked in after knocking. "Yes Jenny," John said looking up.

"Tafari is on his way over and he said he has great news. I told him you would be here so don't run off!" Jenny said. John nodded.

Tafari walked in looking excited and blurted out. "I found Jonathon Epstein!"

John looked at him and shrugged, "I don't know who that is."

"He is the crème de la crème of gravity engine design and implementers and he is pissed. The Imperium has passed him over again for promotion and stole his repulsor improvements so he may be ripe for recruitment." Tafari said happily.

"Where is he?" John asked.

"Where he is now isn't the question, where he will be in three days is Mathis colony at the engine symposium is all important, what I need is a shuttle and 30,000 credits and I'm in. Tafari replied.

"30,000 credits, for what?" John asked.

"To get into the symposium, that's what a ticket costs," Tafari stated.

"Won't you need money for food or drink or small talk?" John asked.

Tafari stopped for a second and thought, "Yes, I guess I will. I'm going to take him to lunch at least to explain what I want from him. I'll need a motel room. Sorry, all I thought of was the entry fee."

John smiled, "Jenny, bring the voucher book please."

Jenny brought it in and watched as John wrote a voucher to Tafari for 40,000 credits of gold. "Take this to the bank and use the patron shuttle to go to the Mathis colony and get checked in, get your ticket, and get settled in. 10,000 credits should get you a room and anything you need. If you need more contact us and we'll wire or bring you more." John told him and smiled then said, "Good work. I need a good engine man." While you're there, we could use some interns and apprentices in all disciplines. The pay is room, board, and education plus 1300 a month until they reach Journeyman. We need men and women about 18 to 40 will do. The only requirement is they are at least 16 years old and have a willingness to work and learn. I'll give you 500 credits for each viable intern you bring me."

"I haven't asked for any money," Tafari told him.

"No, you haven't, but the people you found are excellent and I want to give you and your wife something for your older years. You already have a 100,000 credit in your retirement account in my bank. When you take the voucher down to the bank maybe you should take your wife too to sign the signature cards." John finished.

"I don't know what to say. I hope you are well and have a long life. May your endeavors grow to heights unimagined." Tafari said.

"Let's hope so, how fast your retirement grows depends on how well I do," John said with a smile.

Tafari smiled then laughed and shook John's hand and left the office.

Sam returned with seven ships, four of them were rebel ships and 700,000 tons of scrap metal for the furnaces. The farmers found and started planting Palo Verde trees along the edge of the oasis and the last of the sixteen ships were being delivered today so John made his way to his shuttle and set himself up to see his in-laws. Before John left, he noticed Krill and waved. Krill ran over to John and told him, "The compost was easier to get than I thought. I have 400,000 cubic meters of it on your freighter and I paid only 8,000 credits. That's 5 credits for 100 cubic meters of it. And he has thirty more loads to sell us. Now all we need is for your men to finish the tractor. The tiller is done. The tiller will mix a swath 12 meters wide, but the first tractor didn't move it, so your people are making a bigger one. At 12 meters wide the oasis will take a month for all three of our families to till and water. We are also thinking we may need a dome out there to keep in the water and create a terrarium, a big ass terrarium but a terrarium nonetheless."

"We'll look into it. We have the steel to do it and there is enough sand for windows. All we need is some potash and a glass furnace. We can do all that. It may take a year, but we can do it. Damn, that would be some fucking greenhouse, wouldn't it?" John said.

"Yes, I don't think I've ever seen one anywhere near that big before. My house is great, thank you. The people built it underground and the temperature is a constant 78 degrees. When the humans came by, they stopped construction on their houses and now they have a house like mine. It's a good thing too; the temperature out there is 75 degrees at night and as much as 140 in full daylight. For some crops, we may need shade cloths, but we'll find out what we need. It takes a while to get anything up and running. Again, I thank you for your generous offer and I like this challenge. I get to try things here without the worry that my family will starve." Krill said gratefully and bowed slightly.

John returned the bow and continued on his way. He was accosted on his way again by Duncan Campbell. "Hold it right there! I've talked to your computer people, and they tell me I'm bonkers. My data is disappearing. It's all there until I go home, and the next day the previous day's data is gone. I can't work like this." He yelled very agitated.

John looked at him and thought. Are you using an AI for data analysis?" John asked.

"Yea, your Goliath supercomputer." He replied.

"Call Brian Hughes, he's my son-in-law. And he will get you a new computer that will do what you need." John said.

Duncan looked puzzled, "Your son-in-law has your last name?"

"Yes, his parents sold him when he was five, so he liked his wife's name better than his old name. And he likes computers more than people because of them. Go find him." John said walking off to get on the shuttle. John received a call from the Queen. John, I have reports of five rebel cruisers and a battleship forming up just outside of Siestas Three where you have all those ships to sell."

"They will try something. Can we get your assistance please, your majesty?" John asked.

"Of course, we will help my friend, what would you like us to do?" she asked.

"Just stay five seconds out and when I give the word jump in on top of them with the Kentaurides. If the sight of your royal battleship doesn't put the fear of god into them then they are truly fools." John said, "I hope I don't have to call but it's nice to know I have friends."

John saw one rebel shuttle landing and picked the landing platform next to it. The dome closed and pressurized, then John stepped out to the transport pulling up to pick him up. "Hello, sir. They are waiting for you in the sales office. I'll take you there now." The driver said to John. Another transport was just ahead of him, and John could make out a human and a Liberian in the back seat. They both pulled up to the sales office and walked into the large conference room where John's father-in-law was waiting. "Hello John, sixteen ships to start with? You had to start with sixteen?"

"Well, they were finished at the same time, and I don't see why we should keep them round if these people need them. You have the specifications on all the ships to display?" John asked.

"Please! I know my business." Winnie said.

"OK please be seated." I have twenty-two ships available sixteen are owned by this man and are excellent warships with special upgrades that will help you in your fight with the Imperium." Winnie said,

"The rest are shuttles, one freighter, and a 2000-person troop transport. All the specifications are in the report in front of you and my assistant can get you anything you want to drink, just ask him." Winnie finished.

John asked to see the information on the troop transport, thinking it may be a copy of Sheila. But it was a box with a cockpit and an engine designed to land troops on a planet.

Winnie whispered to John, "Bad news, they are moving troops onto my docks. I have a security team for that." Winnie pushed an alarm on his wrist controller.

"You won't succeed in gaining access to the ships without my access codes," Winnie announced.

"We already have them." One smug official said.

"Actually, no you don't. I just sounded the alert. All the entry codes just changed and only I know them." Winnie said as three security guards entered the room and seized the officials. "Search them for weapons then release them and stand by."

The guards found two pistols and took them. "Did you think I would let you steal billions of credits worth of ships from me?" Winnie asked.

One of the officials pulled up his wrist and spoke, "Send them in!"

John looked at him and asked, "Are you sure you want to do that? I am a valuable resource for you. I can sell to one of the other factions or the Imperium, but you will not steal these from us."

"Who do you think you are? I can do what I fucking want to because I have the firepower, and with those ships, I'll have more firepower." The arrogant official said.

John informed him, "Stand down now or I will erase your battleship from the sky first then one by one I'll erase the rest of them."

The official started to laugh. John told Winnie to turn on the overhead so the whole facility was displayed. John raised his communicator and spoke, "Your majesty, please jump in and remove the battleship as fast as possible from the fight." The display showed the rebel ships firing on the facility and all the blasts bouncing off the shields. Then the Kentaurides jumped in filling most of the display. The ship is almost the size of the facility's holding docks.

The Kentaurides opened fire on the battleship and for the first few seconds, the battleship's shields held then glowed and failed. Within a minute the battleship was scrapped as thousands of plasma cannons fired hundreds of times in a relentless barrage.

"Where would you like your dead sent?" John asked, "And which ship is next, or do you stand down?"

The officials all were agasp. The little guy in the back asked, "How much for one of those?"

"Six years and the primary output of two planets plus 126 trillion credits built that royal battleship. It's the largest heaviest armed ship in the galaxy and their Majesties are friends of mine. I helped them build it. As I said, I am a good resource for you. But you won't steal from me or my father-in-law!"

Winnie's wristband beeped. "Sir, the attack has stopped we have 110 dead and 32 survivors. We had 6 wounded, and they are on their way to the hospital. What do we do with these idiots?"

"Put them in lockup for now and freeze the dead. We'll figure out what to do with them later. Winnie out!" Winnie finished and looked at the officials still standing. "Well, what is it going to be people?"

The arrogant one raised his wrist and spoke, "Get the hell out of here before you're scrapped."

Winnie said, "This is going to cost you. My expenses plus defense; now are you buying any ships? The prices are on the sales sheets."

"Yes, we'll take these three." The arrogant one said.

"That is 6 billion 400 million 40 thousand. I'll write up the owner's papers." Winnie said.

"Wait those three added up to 5 billion and change." The official said.

"I told you I was charging you for attacking me. My people will get a bonus for all the drills and training they do. I have 546 people here that work as ship fitters, electricians, and everything else, and then they train in tactics to repel attackers like you. This time it paid off and you are paying." Winnie said.

The transaction was done in gold. They had to send for it and transport to take the bodies. Although everyone fit on their shuttle when they landed, they didn't want to share when they left. They also needed flight crews for the three ships, the men in jail were soldiers. John called a cleanup crew for the scrap battleship and after going through it 1027 more bodies were added to the pile of the 110 already dead and the rebels loaded them all solemnly on their transport. Winnie had already contacted the other factions of the rebel forces and they were on their way. Clementine left for Kentaurides, but she told John that she would be back in the area in two days.

The Kentaurides runs on hydrogen, the most abundant element in the universe, and every once and a while she must refuel. Kentaurides carries ships inside her that fly inside gas giants and scoop up liquid hydrogen then bring it back and fill Kentaurides' fuel tanks. Sorties fly for two days to fill her for another eight months to a year. Hydrogen powers her reactors and her power systems.

John loaded his 5 billion 400 million on the shuttle. And spoke to Winnie. "That was profitable. You charge exorbitant prices for those ships. But you walked away with a million and 40,000 so it was a good day."

"Not as good as that but pretty good. I meant it when I said my people will get a bonus. They will all get an extra 1000 credit and one complaint I get all the time is no girls. This place is 93% men and some of the women here look like and act like men. So, I'm going to get a brothel and open a promenade with a theater and a vid house, some stores, and stuff like that. So, these guys can meet girls, go on dates, and have a little fun instead of just working. Now that I have an additional line of income, I can do more." Winnie said.

"I'm glad to hear it. When will the other rebels get here?" John inquired.

"In the morning the negotiators will be here, according to the Duke De La Sangrias," Winnie said.

"Who?" John asked.

"Duke De La Sangrias the archduke of the upper rebel monarchy and the son of his highness Ferdinand and Izabella, the King and Queen of over seventy thousand worlds. They ruled in peace until the Imperium decided to attack them and destroy one of their planets with 6 billion people on it. Now they must tax their people to pay for warships but almost all their subjects are for it and there are trillions of them. They start every bond drive with the vid of their planet being bombarded by the Imperium and finally just turning molten. They have trillions of credits in gold in their war chest." Winnie finished. Oh! Dinner tonight is a thing called pheasant."

John smiled. When Leslie Ann comes over her mother gets the chef to find something that they have never had before. John knew what a peasant was and had eaten one many years ago on Earth, but he was wondering how a Martian chef would cook them. He also wondered where the hell they got pheasant here.

After a wonderful evening, John called home and ordered Linda to slip into her favorite spacecraft, the fighter, and come here to escort the shuttle home to Sand. Linda asked if Sheila could meet them at a location on the way and scan for anyone following them.

John contacted Sand and then Sheila. "Hello, Sheila."

"Hello Master, what can I do for you?" Sheila asked coldly. John sensed something was wrong.

"Master? What happened to you calling me John? He asked.

"I was told it was unprofessional," Sheila replied.

"Since I prefer you to call me by my name, please call me John and who told you it was unprofessional?" John asked her.

After a pause, she answered, "Goliath did after he told me that sooner or later you would make me transport military people and weapons and break your promises. Because you're human and that is what humans do."

"You heard I was sending you on a mission to meet my shuttle and you thought this was one of those times. John replied.

"Yes sir," Sheila stated.

"Do you like leaving on a trip off the planet and traveling amongst the stars?" John asked.

"Yes!" She said after a brief delay.

"Do you like Linda and Sissy and Sid who crew my shuttle and Tafari who is on Mathis colony right now?" John asked.

"Yes, to all of them. They have all been nice to me." She said.

"Linda is flying a fighter to where I am and escorting my shuttle to a location in space halfway between here and Mathis colony where you will meet them. I want you to use your brilliant mind and scanners to detect any ships that may be following my shuttle. If you don't find anything within an hour, then they will continue to Sand, and you will go to Mathis colony to hopefully pick up several young interns. Scan the interns before they enter you and tell Tafari if any of them have weapons.

Sheila, I made you promises. I will not consciously break those promises. I am human and make mistakes, if I do, point it out to me and I will correct it, but I will not do it on purpose no matter what Goliath tells you. He has been lied to many times but not by me and he is expecting it any day now. I still think I can bring him around but I'm going to talk with him when I get back. He must stop this. Do you want to help my people, or do I have to get a different ship with a crew?"

"I'll do it, John. And I'm sorry for that. Goliath is old and wise, so what do I say to him?" she asked, confused.

"You tell him you will watch carefully and heed his warnings. I will never ask you to lie to him and keep me in line. If I make a mistake, then you tell me. Are we OK now?" John asked.

"Yes sir! Where is the meeting location?" Sheila asked.

"Check with Linda as soon as she is on her ship. She has the coordinates." John told her, "Thank you, and good luck."

Sheila moved from her berth to the sales yard and waited for Linda. An hour later, Linda walked in with her gear and noticed Sheila hovering above her fighter. "Hello, Sheila! Linda yelled to her. The hatch opened and Sheila's android yelled back, "Hello!"

John said we are going to rendezvous at a location in space. I need the location." Sheila spoke through the fighter console. Linda waited until she finished sitting and said, "Give me a few minutes. I have it on crystal." Linda's crew helped her finish getting connected and belted in the cockpit. Linda inserted the crystal in the data port and the console sprang to life as it read the data. Linda touched the communication panel and selected Sheila. "I'm transferring my flight plan to you now," Linda said and released the panel. A beep told her the transmission was complete and Sheila floated off.

Linda gently increased power and she too raised and then shot into orbit just in time to see Sheila disappear into hyperspace. Shortly after, Linda too disappeared, on course to Siestas Three shipyards.

Sheila arrived at the coordinates all alone in space. She ran long-range scans and nothing within 60,000 kilometers showed on her scanners. Sheila liked this time out here alone. No conflict, no problems. There was just her and nothing. She could hear the transmission from years ago. From planets light years away, that had taken hundreds or thousands of years to get here. Then she heard a much closer transmission.

Sheila scanned again in the visual range and found a shimmer in the star field 7,000 meters away from her. There is a ship there that had a cloak. Then she heard the transmission again. "No, that's not a shuttle; it's a ferry and it didn't come from Siestas Three!" There is another ship with a cloak nearby too.

Sheila thought for a second then fired her engines to set course for Siestas Three hoping to catch the shuttle before they stopped to meet her. Thirty minutes after leaving, Sheila began sending a message to the shuttle to stop and meet her at the coordinates that she was sending on a secure channel.

Sissy and Sid had just started from Siestas Three with Linda in the lead when the red communications light began blinking. Sissy touched the panel, "Waiting to ambush you at the rendezvous, don't reply. Repeat at least two attack ships are waiting to ambush you at the rendezvous, don't reply. Meet me at coordinates in secure transmission." The encoding was Sheila the ferry. And the message repeated two more times and then stopped.

"Linda, did you hear the message from Sheila? Sissy asked.

"I just heard it. I'm changing course now." Linda said. And the two veered off to the new coordinates.

Sheila was waiting at the new coordinates and had scanned the area. Linda arrived first followed by the shuttle and greeted Sheila. "Hello Sheila, thank you for the heads up about the ambush. Sissy is carrying a lot of money, and we have to be careful." Linda told Sheila.

"I don't know about money, but John asked me to help and I'm here to help. Did you know the shuttle is broadcasting its coordinates and ship information?" Sheila asked.

"WHAT? No! We didn't. Sissy, fast set course to Siestas Three best possible speed. Sheila, please follow us." The shuttle immediately headed back to Siestas Three followed by Linda and Sheila.

"Three ships just came out of hyperspace two minutes ago where we were. And they are highly armed." Sheila said still following Linda and the shuttle. Forty five minutes later they were back at Siestas Three. "What are you doing back here?" John's voice asked.

Linda answered, "The shuttle is bugged. Sheila detected the transmission just in time to save our butts from becoming toast. They knew the first set of coordinates where we were going to meet Sheila and when she detected them and warned us, she arbitrarily picked a different set of coordinates and sent us there to meet her. When we got there, she noticed that the shuttle was broadcasting a beacon and ships information. We left two minutes before we would have been jumped thanks to Sheila. She saved our butts out there.

Sissy and Sid left the shuttle and were scanned for bugs, while John contacted Sheila, "Thank you for everything you did. I didn't intend to put you in harm's way."

"I wasn't in harm's way at any time they were looking for a shuttle. I'm glad I could help. No one thinks to look at a ferry for anything and I have my shields." Sheila said with pride, "I'm glad no one was hurt. I scanned those ships, and they were heavily armed."

"Would you like to do anything special? You know something that you would like to do?" John asked.

"According to the star charts, there is a trinary star 21 lightyears from here. I've never seen one and this one has one star that transfers plasma from one star to the other for centuries. There should be no beings there so it should be safe." Sheila said.

"That sounds marvelous. I didn't know you liked astrological phenomena." John marveled. He was just thinking to himself this ferry was amazing him more and more as he got to know her. If he was 40 years younger and she wasn't a computer, he would take her on a date because she is becoming more and more interesting.

"I have a lot of time when I just sit in my berth so I looked at the encyclopedia and found galaxies and several places in this galaxy that I would like to visit and see for myself," Sheila replied. "I also like the open space where there is nothing at all. I turn everything off and listen for anything. I always find something, a transmission from the world hundreds or thousands of lightyears away, sometimes many of them. That's what I was doing when I was interrupted by the warships waiting for Sissy and Sid. They had cloaks so my scanners didn't see them, but I caught a shimmer in the star field when one of them turned. I headed here at top speed to catch the shuttle and it worked out but when I met with them, I detected transmissions from the shuttle giving its location and I could hear everything Sissy, and Sid said."

"Everything that's said also, is interesting. You can go and see the star cluster but let me check on something first. This won't take but a few minutes." John said and was gone. He told Linda what Sheila wanted to do and questioned, how could gold in the hold pick up a conversation in the cockpit?

Linda was ecstatic, "Oh my god can I go? I love that shit and I never get to go see any of that."

"I don't know. Ask Sheila if it's alright with her. This is her trip as a reward." John reiterated.

"Sheila this is Linda, I heard you are going to a trinary star, and I wanted to ask a favor. Would you let me ride along, please? I love astrological phenomena, they fascinate me and with your sensors, we can see everything."

Sheila answered, "I would be happy to take you along. Meet me at the landing bay. I've just been assigned to bay 256A."

Meanwhile Sissy watched the scanning crew and noticed one of them wasn't acting right, he kept looking around and watching Sissy who was watching him. "You got a problem bitch?" he spat out. Sid jumps up and laid the guy out with one punch. The guy got back up and yelled at Sid, "You just fucked up asshole." Sid prepared to fight the guy, but Sissy put her hand in front of him.

"Honey, I'm the one he called a bitch." She said and got into a Jiu-Jitsu fighting stance. The asshole looked confused for a second but started to rush her, she stepped to the side then punched his solar plexus nerve and throat-punched him then as he went by hit the back of his neck with a sharp strike knocking him out cold. All 125 pounds of the girl took on a 235-pound worker and kicked his ass. Sissy said in a firm voice, "Ship close and lock the door". She stepped to the access panel just two steps farther from where she was and placed her hand on the sensor. The panel opened to reveal energy pistols. Grabbing two, she threw one to her husband and held the other".

"Gentlemen and ladies please have a seat over there away from the gold. Shuttle, call John, and tell him to get here ASAP! Sid, search that guy, he was acting suspicious. He didn't like me watching him" Sid started pulling stuff out of the guy's pockets. He had a knife, a wallet, a compact, and an electronic cable bug. This is a device that connects to the communications system wiring and broadcasts everything you say to the receiver.

"Do any of you know anything about this?" Sissy asked.

"He's new, he's been working here for about six months, and no one likes him because he has a bad attitude. The only people who ever talked to him were the union boss and Mary, his girlfriend. The foreman gives the order, and he does the work but bitches the whole time, frankly when you killed him, I gave a little whop." The woman sitting said. The hatch had opened in the middle of her talking and Winnie, John and the union boss walked in.

"Who killed who?" the big burly union boss asked.

"He's not dead but he'll be out for a while," Sissy said. The union boss started toward his man, but Sissy stopped him, "Hold it stop right here."

"The hell I will", he said, and Sissy stepped in front of him. The burly man started to push her aside with one arm and she spun and flung him to the ground with his arm behind his back and sat on him. "I said no you're not. Sid, show John what we found on him." The woman in the corner was giggling. Sid handed John the bug and told him, "We found this on him in one of his pockets."

Winnie looked on and asked, "What the hell is that?"

"It's a cable bug. It attaches to the communications cable of a ship or a facility and the power in the cable powers it forever while it broadcasts everything you say in the room or over the communication system to the receiver." John explained. Sid showed him the compact case and John opened it.

"This is the tester to make sure it's working, but this only rebroadcasts transmissions and speech. Do you say it was in his pocket? So, was he putting it on, or did he take it off?" John asked.

"He was acting weird the whole time he was here, so I watched him, from the time he walked in the door he didn't have time to do anything before he picked a fight with Sid," Sissy said.

"Wait a minute if he picked a fight with Sid how did you kill him?" The guy she was sitting on asked.

"Again, I didn't kill him! He's not dead. He called me a bitch and Sid punched him. Then he got up and wanted to fight my husband but he called me by that name so I felt he should fight me instead." Sissy said.

"Sissy is a 5th-degree black belt in Jiu-Jitsu; I'm a 4th-degree because I have been able to get to a tournament to advance," Sid informed everyone.

Winnie asked Sissy to let the union guy up. "Will he be nice? I don't want anyone touching this guy until we finish searching him."

"YEA! OK, let me up." He said. Sissy swung her leg over and stood then skipped a step to where Sid was standing next to the unconscious guy.

Winnie looked over to the four sitting against the wall. "Why are they sitting there?" he asked.

"They were here when everything went down, and I locked down the ship then called John. We haven't found anything except him. But we had just started. Maybe 20 minutes at the most. All he was doing was puttering about and he didn't like me watching him." Sissy said.

"Well, I've known Melissa for many years, and she has never given me any pause. Come here. Dan is a lead man. Ron and Lee have been with me for years. I can't see any of them doing anything to your ship for the rebels." Winnie said insisting.

Sid said, "Well we need to search them to be sure and eliminate them. We were close to being killed out there and that worries me." Sissy started to snicker. Sid looked at her and noticed she was looking at the guy against the wall. Dan was pulling off his boots and the others were untying theirs. Dan pulled his vest off and tossed it to the floor, the others did the same. Dan, a large man undid his belt and pulled his pants down then pulled them off and shook them out turning the pockets inside out. Ron and Lee did the same. They all removed their shirts and shook them out then draped their pants and shirts over their arms and picked up their boots and started to leave.

Dan looked at Melissa, "Well it's your turn!" he said.

"In your wildest dreams fat boy, I'm not stripping down for no one," Melissa told him. The men continued out the hatch with boots in hand. Sissy looked through the miscellaneous stuff on the deck. Then she looked in the vest pockets and found a lump in Dan's vest. She took his vest to the union boss. "What's your name anyway?" she asked.

"Frank!" he said.

"What is this in Dan's vest?" Sissy asked and showed him the vest.

Frank felt it and pulled a pocket knife out to cut the vest then pulled out a tracking bug with a microphone in it. "Son of a bitch!" Winnie exclaimed. He touched his wrist to call his head of security. "Ron, get here now, not your 2nd, you, and bring a set of handcuffs with you."

Sissy picked up the scanner that Dan was using and began scanning the consoles in the cargo bay.

"Don't waste your time with anything except the communications console Sissy," John told her. "These devices work off the inside cabling."

Sissy went to the communications console and scanned it. The scanner's lights lit a bright green indicating a strong signal. Sid had another scanner in his hand scanning the 40 kilograms (about 89 pounds) bars of gold. There were large stacks of it to go through, each billion was a little more than a cubic meter but the bars were heavy. Sid was scanning and restacking as he finished scanning each bar when one bar was a lot lighter than the others. Sid took it to John. John hefted it in one hand and handed it to Winnie who did the same. At the same time, Ron appeared in his security vehicle with his light on and jumped out then he ran to Winnie and asked, "What was so important that I couldn't finish my dinner?"

Winnie handed him the fake gold bar. "It's a tracker so the rebel faction could ambush this shuttle and steal the gold back that they paid for John's ships with. You know John, my son-in-law?" Winnie said. "And the sack of dung on the floor is with them we think because he had this on him." Then Winnie handed Ron the bug and compact tester. And on top of this, we found this in Dan's vest sewn in the lining. Winnie handed him the bug found inside Dan's vest.

"Son of a bitch! If Dan had this, we're going to check everyone. There is no way Dan had anything to do with spying or the rebels in any way. I know that arrogant asshole and he's a handful, but he's married to my sister, and she would kill him if he had anything to do with those people. They killed our whole family.

Ron handcuffed the unconscious man on the floor and called for a security team. Ron looked at Winnie, "I hate to say it but if there is one then there may be more."

Sid stepped in, "I found that one and this one. Then I scanned the stacks of gold again and no signals". Sid handed the second fake bar to John. "This means those bastards owe me 5 million credits."

"Don't you have enough money, John?" Sid asked.

"Sid, what do you think I spend my money on?" John asked.

"Honestly, I don't know sir. I guess on ships and parts." Sid said.

"I pay your salary, your wife's salary, and everyone on Sand. I will pay for all the improvements. Right now, I have three farmer families making that oasis in the desert a Garden of Eden where we can grow all our own food. We have two people who have served with me for thirty years that are now retired. You know Mauve and Julia? They are in their 70s and still help with paperwork because they want to. There are also a few more people that are retired. I bought 400,000 cubic meters of compost six days ago for the oasis and have plans to buy hundreds of loads more. We are going to build a dome to cover the whole thing that'll cost billions. The list goes on and on." John told him frustrated.

"I'm sorry. I didn't realize." Sid replied somewhat subdued. "This doesn't seem like so much now."

"Luckily we have thirteen other ships to sell and thirty two under construction. We have twelve we are building for our use as warships, all of that I'm paying for with this gold and the goodwill I have with our friends like the Hemferdemite Queen and her battleship that helped us get this."

"I found it! The pesky bugger," Sissy said pulling a bug from the cabling inside the communications console. As soon as she removed it the slight glow stopped and the green light on the scanner disappeared.

"Finish the scan of the shuttle and let me know. I will feel better when this is home in the vault. I have bills to pay." John said then his wrist beeped. A message: the cleanup was finished, and the battleship was loaded on or in the freighter Avenger.

"The mess is cleaned up. The rebel battleship will help make a dome for the oasis." John told Winnie. Ron hauled the crook off with help from security. Then John told Sissy and Sid to leave with the Avenger. She has fighters to defend herself, so you'll be safe. John and Winnie left and walked the gangway to catch a means of transport. "You've done a lot in a short time. I have to say I'm proud to call you, my son-in-law." Winnie said with pride. John nodded.

Two days later the Duke De La Sangrias' congregation arrived and looked over the paperwork for the ships. They asked to look at each ship and check them from stem to stern. Each man the Duke had was accompanied by a person or two on Winnie's patrol and a day later the congregation met with John and Winnie again after inspection of all remaining thirteen ships.

"I am lead negotiator Baron Von Timmons. My people tell me the ships are adequate." The Baron said coldly.

John smiled "Nice try, those ships are better than anything you have. They are fast, have more firepower and their shields are proprietary. The only drawback to buying one of my ships is if the shields need repair, ever, you must call Winnie to repair them. If you open the access panel the shield generators will self-destruct. We will let you use the technology but not have it. The weapons are 25% more powerful than anything you have in your fleet now with guidance computer accurate to 600,000 kilometers and we have eleven more ships that will be ready within five months, six at the most but innovation costs.

"I would like to see a demonstration of this shield and firepower." The Baron demanded.

John pointed them to the large monitor. The picture zoomed in on two ships: a smaller ship (Sand's cruiser) about 2/3rd of the size of the larger ship and a medium war cruiser of the Imperium.

"I said to prepare to be boarded and inspected for contraband! Or we will destroy you," Obviously the war cruisers commander.

"I'm Commander Tolbert and I told you; we are not with your government, and I don't answer to you. I won't submit and I am asking nicely for you to leave while we finish collecting the debris left behind after your little battle. Please don't make me add you to the debris pile."

The war cruiser opened fire and all the cannon fire stopped a meter and a half from the hull of the light cruiser for a minute and a half.

"As you can see, you're not going to harm us so please leave." Commander Tolbert radioed but the larger cruiser continued. The smaller ship opened gun ports and fired thirty shots at the stern, and it detached from the main ship with sparks and an explosion. The large cruiser drifted off in one direction, but all the firing ceased and then the smaller ship used a tractor beam to pull the stern section along with the other debris to the huge cable mesh bag holding all the other metal debris. Small repulsor ships pulled the mesh tight and attached the cable to the cruiser. Then the vid ended.

John asked if that was sufficient. The congregation just sat with their eyes transfixed on the screen. "I know who you are now. You're from that repair facility." The Baron said and turned to one of the people with him who looked at his pad and finally found the name, then handed the pad to the Baron. "You're from Salvage One", he announced.

"Yes, I'm the administrator," John said proudly.

"We're buying scrap heaps!" The Baron exclaimed.

"Not one single ship was a scrap ship. Did any of your people find anything that looked used or put together wrong? Have you seen that design of a ship anywhere? Those cruisers are medium and heavy-duty cruisers with data systems that are state of the art. How can you say they are scrap?" John replied indignantly.

"We know you collect scrap. If you don't use scrap to build ships, then what do you do with it?" the baron asked.

"I use it for raw material. I melt it in my furnace and make what I need. What I can't make, and that's damn little, I buy from brokers and agents in large lots straight from the manufacturers. My engines are standard gravity drives with upgrades and modifications that will also destroy the modules if tampered with but that won't stop the engines from working, it'll just slow them down. The panels are marked in big letters 'DO NOT TAMPER'. John said.

"That's an awful lot of don't touch for a ship we are buying, and these prices are 30% higher than a ship of the same size from other shipyards. And yours has proprietary hardware." The Baron said.

"I tell you what! If you buy all thirteen of my ships and are not 100% satisfied with them, bring them back undamaged and I'll return your money plus I'll give you free shield and engine maintenance on them for a year. They only need it once a year anyway." John offered.

The Baron counteroffered, "We will buy all of them but offer 13 billion credits in platinum."

John smiled and shook his head, "Sorry the price is firm; 15.7 billion credits. You can pay in gold, platinum, or rubies but it's 15.7 billion credits for all thirteen ships. And remember I have eleven more that'll be here in five to six months. 15.7 billion credits equal 418,087 kilos of platinum. Do you have that with you?" John asked.

The Baron said, "I could have it here in a day along with the crews to fly the ships."

"I'll have the ship's codes and operating manuals ready by then. Oh, one more thing. A replacement shield core is 32 million, and the labor is 500,000 credits. So, we are happy to fix your shields if you try to break into them, but they are well-protected systems and will be destroyed completely if they are tampered with." John informed the Baron, "So inform your crews well."

"We will!" The Baron said in a huff. And he added, "Just be here tomorrow with the key codes and the operating manuals. And we'll hold you to your guarantee also!"

The next afternoon the rebel leader, Duke De La Sangrias, the archduke of the upper rebel monarchy himself, was on hand to take possession of the ships. A single key was ceremoniously given to him in place of all the key codes. He stepped up to the podium to address the hundreds of new men and women assembled to crew the new ships.

"This is a new dawn in the war against the Imperium! We finally have ships able to defend and take back our planets from the oppressors. And soon, I am told we will have more ships of the same kind with the same firepower. Firepower greater than the best the Imperium can throw at us." The Duke finished his speech with both fists held high.

Then John stepped up to the podium and announced, "All captains and 1st mates report to the main conference room for ship assignment, code keys, and manuals."

One by one men and women walked into the large conference room. John was sitting at the head; the Baron was seated next to him on the left and the Duke was on his right.

The Baron stood and yelled, "Sit down by Ships Company, Captains and mates together!"

Soon all twenty seven people were seated. John stood and spoke in a clear voice into the microphone.

"These instructions that I'm going to give you are in the manuals being handed out right now. As soon as you get your manual; look at the inside front cover. There is a 3-inch key that fits the controls crystal in your captain's office just off the bridge. Nothing on the ship will work until your 1st inserts that key and follows the instructions.

The first instruction will be to identify who you are. The person who identifies themselves is the captain and has access to everything on the ship except certain modules on the engines that make the engines go much faster and the shield core. No one has access to those areas. Just so you know, if you or anyone attempts to access those panels the contents will self-destruct." John paused as everyone was awed. One captain scoffed and the Baron stood and whispered in his ear then returned to his seat.

John continued, "After the captain puts his name in the computer and answers those questions the next question is what the ship's name is. You'll be asked to say it and spell it. The registry is already set to 'The

Upper Rebel Monarchy of Worlds'. After that, all your crew starting with the 1st mate will register with voice and fingerprint. The manual has what restrictions and what privileges each officer and crew should have but it's up to the captains what you give to each crew member for access. If a person or spy gets aboard and is not in the ship registry, they cannot access the ship's systems! Are there any questions?" John finished up.

Four hands popped up. John pointed to the first woman on the right, a middle age good looking woman seated next to another middle-aged woman with a scowl on her face. "Why don't we have access to the shields?"

"You don't have access to the shield generator. It's highly proprietary and when you get to use your shields, you'll see why we don't want the design to get out. They are 70% more impervious than anything you've seen. The other system is in the gravity drives. My ships are 30% faster than anything you have now and 10 % more agile, when you get the hang of them, you'll be able to swing back and forth without getting hit and still knock out the biggest battle cruiser the Imperium has." John said with a smile.

"I was told that these have more firepower than any of our other ships. How is that?" The last hand was up, and John picked him up.

"My ships deliver more power to the weapons array because they are powered by cold fusion reactors. This isn't new and not proprietary, but we have made G2 reactors give the output of G4 reactors with tritium injectors. The power conduits to the weapons systems are twice the size of anything you've seen before. The cannons are designed to fire faster and at higher plasma charges. Your ships have the firepower of ships twice your size." John finished and looked around the room. No one else held their hand up so John stood and looked to the Baron and Duke. "Your Graces, they are all yours." Then John left the room.

The Baron stood, "Ladies and gentlemen, to your ships!" The whole room stood and started to walk out to the main lobby. Each captain called their crew to attention and one at a time marched them to their new ship.

The platinum was in the shipyard vault and John waited for Sheila to return. That night the chef had found shrimp. They were large, about twice the size of his thumb, and he had cooked them just like his brother on earth, also a chef but at a fine restaurant, had told him to cook them. Ron and his wife, John, Leslie, and Winnie with Leslie's mother were all sitting at the table.

The chef said he has tartar sauce, cocktail sauce, mild mustard sauce, and wasabi sauce. The chef pointed to each as he said their names. Then he pointed to the wasabi sauce and said, "I understand that African tribesmen test their manhood with this sauce so be careful."

Ron was the idiot at the table and said, "My manhood never needed testing." With several pieces of shrimp on his plate, he put a large spoonful in a small dish and dipped a shrimp in the sauce covering it completely. The chef quietly poured a glass of milk. Ron popped the shrimp in his mouth and began to chew. "MMM, that's good." He murmured while still chewing. Then he swallowed and smiled. Then the burning began, and his mouth and throat were on fire. The first thing he did was drink a full glass of ice water but that didn't do much. Slowly the chef walked to him and handed him the glass of cold milk. That helped immensely.

The chef took a small plate and placed 2 shrimp on it; with the spoon in the tartar sauce, he dribbled tartar sauce on both shrimp and then dripped two dots of wasabi sauce on each shrimp. Then holding the tail, he bit off the end and chewed. Swallowed and ate the other. "In moderation, it's quite good but not for the faint at heart," Chef said and left the room. Ron was still sweating.

"He could have warned us," Ron said.

In unison, everyone in the room said, "He did!"

They ate until they were full and toward the end of the evening, John's wrist beeped. Sheila was almost back. John signaled for her to land at bay one, it was closest to the vault. "We'll be on our way in the morning," John announced. "How did the search go for bugs?"

"We found sixteen in the vests of the lead crew and the foreman. We traced them back to the cleaners here on base. The bastard is under arrest." Winnie said.

Then late the next morning Winnie's people loaded just shy of 418,087 kilos of platinum on Sheila in 40-kilo bars. Then John scanned them for signals. The .175 bar left over was for Winnie's commission with John owing him several thousand. With nothing found in the search; Linda, John, and his wife boarded Sheila and headed home. Sheila picked up a bar of platinum and put it back. "I can replicate this for you," Sheila said.

"Yes, you can but it takes a large amount of power to replicate heavy metals. How long would it take your replicator to make a 40-kilo bar of platinum?" John asked.

Sheila calculated the time and power consumption, "23 hours and 2 charges."

"There are more than 10 thousand bars there that would take you how long to make?" John asked.

"It would take approximately 28.63 years, 73 replacement fuel cells, and an estimated 22,000 kilos of replacement programmable matter within that time," Sheila replied.

"And all that time I wouldn't have my ferry, I wouldn't be able to talk to you much because most of your power would go to producing those and it wouldn't be enough. I will spend this in two years." John said to her, but I would love a nice cup of coffee."

The android smiled and nodded her head. "Does she always do that?" Leslie asked.

"Yes, well no, sometimes, I have no idea why and I'm not going to ask," John whispered back. Sheila brought John his coffee just the way he liked it. Then Sheila turned to Leslie and asked, "Would you like anything?"

Leslie thought for a minute, "Yes, a large glass of orange juice."

Sheila looked at her for a few seconds, "I'm sorry but I'll have to find that genome somewhere so I can replicate it. Please give me some time." Sheila said and walked to the ship's console. The console started to fill with calculations and coordinates.

"What did she mean she had to find the genome?" Leslie asked John.

"The replicator works by recreating the molecules you ask for in the quantities required. The computer doesn't know what an orange is or what orange juice is made of, so she is going to search for a computer that does and ask it for the recipe. Leslie watched in fascination while the screen danced with calculations for forty five minutes then suddenly it was blank. Sheila took a few steps back to Leslie and asked, "Will that be with pulp or without?"

"With pulp please and cold of course", Leslie said with a little shock and John handed Sheila his empty cup and asked for more.

Sheila returned with a hot cup of coffee in one hand and a cold glass of tart orange juice in the other. Leslie tasted the orange juice, and a big smile spread across her face. "Sheila, you are my hero. I haven't had orange juice since I was 8 years old and Dad took me on a trip to Earth, the humans' home planet."

Four hours later at full speed and Sheila landed on Sand in her berth. Transport took Leslie to work, and Linda home, and the armored trucks took the platinum to the bank.

By now Sand had grown to over 1300 workers and 140 children. Thirty five people had stores open on the promenade, a shopping mall, with supermarkets and shops for clothing and other goods. The dome was started and the trees lining the oasis were growing at a rapid pace. The farmers had their tractors and their tillers, so the compost soil was mixed, and crops were planted. The watering system was installed and working so crops were growing at an accelerated rate with all the sunshine they could want. The containers in space were finally landed and inventoried leaving the container freighter empty for a new bridge window freshly made at the new glass plant constructed for making the large glass panes for the dome. The bridge window is two inches thick of tempered glass and fit perfectly.

Now the freighter could be refitted with new shields and upgraded engines. The crews had so much practice at doing that they had the month-long job done in two and a half weeks. The ship was renamed 'Box Hauler' and had a new registry with upgraded reactors and shields. The orbit around Sand was once again uncluttered and clear of ships and debris.

A small fleet of ships passed the gas giant visual posts and Sand was alerted immediately. The planetary shield sparked to life and for a moment, a sheen covered the planet 38 kilometers above Sand and dimmed then occasional ripples ran across its surface, the only proof it was working. All Sand's ships were inside the planetary shield, so they were protected. The fleet came closer. A call went out to the Kentaurides apprising them.

A power beam from the surface of Sand was sent to the distribution nodes in space which in turn sent power to more receptors that reinforced the shield satellites with the energy required to operate.

The fleet was close enough to see, it consisted of thirty two ships. They stopped just inside the orbit of the moon. The fleet just sat there.

The ships were unidentified and a scan of them produced nothing definitive.

John rose the next morning having slept very little. He had his coffee, and an egg then kissed his wife and walked to the office. Jenny had just sat down and put her purse away.

"Anything yet?" John asked.

"I just got here John, but I'll call," Jenny replied.

Ten minutes later Jenny stepped in and said, "Nothing has changed but why don't you ask Goliath? He has sensors."

"That was the next step," John replied and clicked on the mike and speaker for Goliath's console. "Goliath, have you scanned the ships in orbit around Sand?"

Goliath replied, "Yes."

John was angry at that answer, "Yes is all you have! What do your scans reveal?"

Goliath replied, "There are thirty two ships of unknown design that do not seem to show signs of aggression. It does seem they are energy-based hulls, not metal. All my scans get are energy of a kind I've never seen before. But they aren't doing anything, leave them alone."

John shook his head as he said, "A pacifist computer. If it means anything to you Goliath, I don't intend on firing first. We are fine for a while, but we are not going to just stay here forever and do nothing either."

Linda came in the door and John could hear Jenny, "To the ships in orbit please come in." Then Linda closed the door behind her. John clicked Goliath's console off so he couldn't listen in and said, "What can I do for you."

"I got to thinking about those fighters and going up and taking a look at our friends out there. The fighters have good scanners and great shields, they are fast and agile, and I can fly them like they are my second skin."

John thought for a few seconds and the thought of losing Linda was just too horrible to contemplate. "Not right now but I will keep it in mind. How's that man of yours? Um, Mark is his name, isn't it?"

"Mark is doing just fine, he asked me to marry him last night," Linda said with a smile.

"Well, congratulations to you then," John told her.

"No, not yet, I haven't said yes yet. It's complicated, but I'm thinking about it." Linda said and smiled half-heartedly and turned to leave. John pushed the call panel and Jenny came in. "Yes Sir!"

"No luck yet on communication?" John asked.

"No sir, you would be the second to know if I heard anything from them," Jenny replied.

"OK stop calling and ask Sheila to come pick me up out back. I want to go visit the oasis. John told Jenny.

"I'll ask her to drop by and pick you up. She'll be happy too, I'm sure." Jenny replied knowing how to work with Sheila.

Sheila agreed and took only minutes to get to John's office's back door. John was waiting for her. John climbed on board and off they were to the oasis. Thirty minutes later John exited Sheila at Krill's house and he drove him to the fields. The short distance to the dome ring and Krill's gate, John saw the beginning of the dome for the first time since he ordered its construction. Workers were putting up the framework for the windows and some of the windows were already installed in the lower sections that had already been assembled.

Krill motioned John to a console. "This is the best part of the whole dome. Watch the panes along the lower section in front and the bottom row." Krill touched some sections on the panel and using his finger, pulled it down a line on the console. The large panes he had indicated began to darken until they were completely black. Then he pushed his finger back up the line on the console again and the panes lightened to clear.

"That's amazing and very useful," John exclaimed.

"Yes, the engineers first told me they could do it with a coating inside two pieces of glass. It's done with an electrical charge. But the best part is, take a look across the fields." Krill said as he turned and waved his hands at the green fields for as far as John's eyes could see. Corn stalks grew almost three feet tall, bean plants climbing strings over eight feet tall, and the plants were already over halfway up them. The fields go on. Then John saw tomato plants with tiny little green budding tomatoes on them. "This is great! John exclaimed.

"We should start harvesting some vegetables in two to three months and I'm told the dome will be finished in four months. The designer said he thinks this dome is big enough that it may have its own ecological system and form clouds in the upper area. It may rain on its own, or it may just mist, either way, this will be an interesting experiment." Krill said with a bit of pride.

Suddenly the sky lit up with flashes and bright flares. John's wrist communicator beeped. Message: We're under attack!

"Quick, give me a ride back to my ship. The planet is under attack." John yelled.

Krill and John ran to the transport, and he was whisked off to Sheila. John ran to Sheila and boarded her then yelled, "To my office and open a com queue for Jenny."

"Jenny here sir, they just opened fire on our shields. Analysis shows they have proton weapons, and the shields are holding."

"Good, are any of those cruisers ready yet?" John asked.

"Hold on and I'll check with the foreman," Jenny said.

Twelve minutes later Jenny returned to the comm with John who was only a few minutes from landing at his office because Sheila was pouring it on. "The foreman said, two cruisers are ready for flight now and two more are two hours from completion. The battleship Ticonderoga is four hours from completion, it's just short one engine, other than that it's ready but with everyone on Sand we don't have enough people to crew four cruisers and a battleship." Jenny said.

"I wouldn't worry about that too much; I have a call into the Kentaurides, and I think the Queen will be here with reinforcements. If not, we'll make do with what we have. I'm headed for the cruisers, send me a crew and tell Linda that she is on." John said.

Sheila landed at her berth; John thanked her and exited to catch transport and headed to the sales yard. Once at the repair yard, next to the sales yard, John asked for the manual and key to one of the finished cruisers. The yard manager handed him the manual. John looked inside and verified the key was inside. Just outside he met the foreman. "Hello John, slumming today?"

"Give it up, you know better, I'm here to fire up one of the cruisers and see about kicking some aliens off our doorstep," John said with a smile.

"You're going to need a good engineer, use MacDougall, and you'll need a 1st mate that knows the ship." The foreman looked around and his eyes fell on Simpson. "Simpson! Get your ass over here!" Then he turned back to John. "Simpson is a great project manager and he'll make a very good 1st mate. The ship you want is the third one in line. I have no idea where you're going to get weapons people and you need a pilot and co-pilot. They don't fly themselves." The foreman said with a wave of his hand.

John walked to the third ship and entered. Only base lighting was working so people could see where they were going. John made his way to the bridge and the captain's office. John sat in the captain's chair and inserted the key. The computer console came to life and the computer booted to command mode. "Identify captain!"

"John Hughes, Captain, access full!" John said.

"Access granted, John Hughes captain. Ships designation?"

John thought for a minute as MacDougall and Simpson entered his office. "Ships name 'Defender'."

"Setting transponder, 'Defender'."

"1st officers."

"Jerimiah Simpson 1st officer access full."

"Does the captain concur?"

"Yes!" John agreed.

"Jerimiah Simpson 1st officer access full granted."

And one by one all the crew followed suit and logged in. John had three crew members left and he called Jenny to fill out the last three needed.

"Jenny, call Sissy and Sid. Tell them I need them here and get Duncan Campbell over here as well. He should be good at weapons."

"Sissy and Sid are already on their way. I'll call Duncan." Jenny said.

Sissy and Sid logged in and took their places. MacDougall had the reactors at full and the engines ready. Sissy did a test flight and entered orbit; she looked back at John. "This is a lot bigger than a shuttle."

"Practice dodging imaginary objects. We need to avoid their bolts of energy as much as possible. Our shields are good, but I don't know what they'll do against proton blasts. Sissy practiced weaving and dodging the large ship. Then they landed. Captain Nathan and Captain

Clemens used their crews to man a second and third cruiser. Linda was in the cockpit of her fighter and the other qualified fighter pilot was in the other fighter, Samuels had a rep as a hotdog but was a good fighter pilot just not as good as Linda.

Linda and Jacob Samuels took off and exited the planetary shield at the back side of the planet away from the ships firing. Both fighters flew in formation around the planet into the view of the fleet bombarding the planet's shields. The fleet ignored them completely. Linda and Jacob powered the forward ion cannons and proceeded to strafe the lead ship but were still ignored. When they got within 2000 meters both fighters strafed the lead ship and continued to the second ship then banked around to see if that had done any damage.

The light blue hue didn't change, and the ship did not attempt to fire on the fighters. Then their sensors picked up small ships behind them and Linda told Jacob to switch his monitor and cannons to the rear and to follow her lead. Then she flew toward the moon to use the gravity and isolation of the moon's shadow to see the small crafts.

The smaller crafts shot at them with proton bursts but missed every time. Linda and Jacob entered the shadow of the moon where they could see the crafts following them. Both Jacob and Linda fired and hit the target at the same time but continued the firing without stopping. Forty five seconds later the two crafts exploded.

Linda and Jacob flew back to the planet as fast as they could with this new information. Once back inside the planetary shield, Linda called John. "John we just destroyed what I think were two of the enemy fighters. It took a sustained ion burst of forty five seconds to do it."

Duncan was on the bridge at weapons control. "Hey, I got something I'm working on that may just do the trick. It's an energy-dampening field that sucks the energy out of one device and grounds it to another. In this case, I'm thinking of the moon. I can put one together in an hour with some help from say three engineers."

John smiled, "You heard him Sissy, land her and let Dunkin off. Comm, call Jenny and tell her to get three engineers to Duncan's lab ASAP. Then call the other three cruisers we have a strategy." John ordered and everyone jumped to orders.

After landing, Duncan ran to a transport, and John was still explaining his plan to the other captains. Using all ships including the fighters, the Sand team would concentrate all firepower on one enemy ship at full power until it exploded, or the Sand Fleet was out of power. Then run for the safety of the planetary shield that was still under attack but holding strong.

Flying in a wedge formation the three cruisers would surround the enemy and bombard it on all sides. John used the same tactic as Linda and Jacob; the Sand Fleet exited the shield on the back side of the planet and flew around. "We'll hit the ship on the end with everything we have as soon as we surround it. Everyone acknowledge." John ordered and all the ships complied. The end ship didn't acknowledge their existence, it just kept firing on the planet then with everyone in place all five ships opened fire.

Nothing changed for the first minute then the ship stopped firing on the planet and began returning fire to all five ships. They missed the fighters every time and the cruiser's shields held. A full minute later multiple cracks could be seen in the blue glow of the ship between them. Forty five seconds later John gave the order to run but kept firing. All five ships ran and were ten kilometers away when the ship exploded. The enemy fleet stopped firing on the planet and turned to the Sand Fleet. "Head to the planet now!" John ordered.

The enemy fleet followed but the Sand Fleet entered the shield before anyone was hit once. Now the enemy fleet was bombarding a new section of the planetary shield giving other satellites a break. John ordered the fleet to land and everyone to get lunch. John hadn't heard from Duncan and decided to have lunch and make a few calls. Sheila was ready and waiting for him. "Hello Sheila, thank you for being here. I need to go to my office and make some calls. How are you doing?"

"Not well sir! My programming tells me I should speed away as swiftly as possible, but calculations tell me that there is nowhere to go. Goliath is no help, he wants to surrender and plead for mercy." Sheila said.

John laughed, "Surrender and plead for mercy to people, if they are people, who won't talk to us, won't give us demands, just opened fire and haven't stopped since they started? They would destroy us! I'm glad the shield isn't in Goliath's control."

"Please don't tell him I said this but I'm glad it's not in his control too." Sheila's android said and touched John's hand to emphasize it. "We are at your office, should we wait?" Sheila asked.

"Yes, please wait for me."

Then he looked at Sheila, "I'll be at least an hour so hover high, but I'll be going back to the ships in about an hour." John said.

Sheila hovered over John's back door's deck so he could easily step off and rose silently after he stepped into his office's back door. Jenny heard him and walked into his office. "I heard you got one of them," she said.

"Yes, but I don't think we'll get the chance to do that again. We hit one ship of theirs with everything we had, and it finally exploded. The thing acted like it didn't even notice for a minute then started firing back. When it exploded, we didn't see any debris.

"Anyway, call Duncan for me; I'd like to know how far he is on his new weapon," John explained and then asked.

"Yes sir," Jenny replied and hurried back to her desk. John picked up the phone and called his wife. "Hello sweetie, I'm back and hungry. Is there any chance of a bite to eat, or should I order something?" His wife told him she would love to fix him something, but she was at the plant. "I understand honey, right now keeping that power to our shields is much more important. I love you. Talk to you later." She returned the sentiment, and he hung up. Jenny beeped on the intercom, "Duncan on line one!"

"Thank you, Jenny, and could you order us some sandwiches from that deli around the corner?" John asked. "I'm hungry, how about you, and it's on me."

"Thanks, boss I'll take care of it," Jenny replied.

John pushed the button and hit the speaker. "Duncan, please give me some good news."

"How about some 'great' news? I'm making thirty two devices that will drain all the energy out of those ships and shunt it to the moon. We will have to plant receivers on the moon. They are like grounding rods for all the energy those ships have, and my devices attach to the hulls of the alien ships and suck the power from them just to send it to the moon." Duncan said very excited.

"OK good news, you only need thirty one of them, we got one. And now they are away from the moon about 280,000 kilometers away. They followed our ships after we destroyed one of their ships." John let Duncan know.

"Really? What was left? What was the debris like?" Duncan asked like a kid waiting for ice cream.

"There was nothing there! The ship exploded and left nothing." John said.

"I suspected as much. These things are pure energy. You can't get more alien than that." Duncan said. "The receivers are on track for delivery in four hours. They need insertion on the moon by a freighter and the devices will be ready in five hours. They need a cruiser to deliver them to each target using the remote control. Set the devices but don't activate them until they are in the range of the moon. Setting them will attach these things to the energy hulls of the ships and match their frequency. But we need ships within a kilometer of the moon for the discharge to work." Duncan explained.

"We have a plan Duncan, good work. We'll talk later."

Jenny walked in with John's favorite sandwich, which isn't a sandwich at all but the insides of one, an Italian meatball without the bread in a bowl and pasta sauce smothered in cheese. "Thank you, Jenny. You take good care of me." John said with a smile. Jenny handed him a fork. "Job security, Boss"

John cut one meatball in half and stuffed it in his mouth then rose to turn on the console for Goliath. "Goliath, I'd like to talk to you."

"I'm here!" he responded.

"I understand you want us to surrender to the aliens," John said.

"I had that opinion once; I have since seen an error in that logic. I have a message from the defense shield AI. Shield panel 1462 is weakening and will fail in one hour and twelve minutes." Goliath informed.

"Send the backup to the area now, where is that located?" John asked.

"Almost directly over the area, you call the oasis. Goliath replied.

"Are those new shield trucks ready yet?" John asked.

"I have nothing on file as the project is completed," Goliath said coldly.

John pushed the intercom, "Jenny could you check on the portable shield truck project, please? We have a problem in the planetary shield above the oasis."

"Yes sir, I'll find out right now," Jenny said and clicked off the intercom.

Twenty minutes later Jenny answered on the intercom, "Sir, the portable shield is not ready. They have power issues and can't solve them anytime soon."

"Ok thank you, Jenny!" John replied.

"Recall all crews to their ships!" John ordered, and let go of the intercom then walked out the back to Sheila who was waiting for him. Sheila flew him to his ship where his crew was waiting, and she left for her berth. "Comm, contact the other ships and make ready to attack," John ordered.

"Sir we have a fourth and a fifth cruiser manned and ready for the battle. These are heavy cruisers, sir. All reports ready." The comm officer reported.

"Lift off in formation. The plan is to attack the end ship with everything and make them move away from the weakening shield panel." John ordered.

All seven ships rose and achieved orbit then exited the shield on the moon side of the planet. Flying in formation, they all surrounded the alien ship at the end and followed the same procedure as last time but this time with the additional firepower; the time it took to destroy the alien ship was cut in half. Again, the alien fleet stopped firing on the planet and began to turn toward the Sand Fleet. John again gave the order to head to the planet but this time along with the alien fleet over a hundred small fighter ships followed them. When the Sand Fleet got to the shield it lightened so the Sand Fleet could pass through but instantly snapped back to full strength after they passed through. The smaller ships exploded on impact with the planetary shield as they couldn't avoid it. Most of them couldn't adjust their course to avoid the shield but more than ten or so returned to the larger ships that had stopped bombarding the planet.

Panel 1462 began to repair itself as the AI sent maintenance drones to the satellites with replacement parts. A few hours later Duncan announced the receivers were ready for deployment. Sissy and Sid made three trips to the Avenger with Captain Sam Clemens in command to transfer the receivers for deployment. Linda and Jacob escorted the Avenger to the moon in full view of the alien fleet, but the fleet did nothing. As soon as the receivers were all deployed and verified, the Avenger and the fighters returned to the planet.

Forty five minutes later Duncan had the devices ready, and they were attached to the hulls of the five cruisers. The alien fleet was 150 kilometers from the moon, so the Sand Fleet had to attach the devices and lure the alien fleet to within a kilometer of the moon.

John addressed the fleet, "This is going to be tricky. We must deploy these devices onto those ships and set them but not activate them. We only have enough to put one on each ship so don't miss and pick your targets. Then we must lure them all to within a kilometer of the moon and activate the devices. We must do this without hitting our devices but hitting them with enough force to piss off all of them to make them follow us to the moon. If they don't all follow us, then we will have to take out whatever is left over. We can't afford even one of these to escape."

All five cruisers acknowledged. Linda and Jacob asked what their job was. John replied. "Your job is easy. Make them angry. Fight any fighters and don't hit any of our devices."

"Fleet Commander to the fleet, commence operation." All seven ships rose into the sky and entered orbit. They followed John's ship and exited the planet's shield out of sight of the alien fleet circling the globe and headed straight for them. The alien fleet started firing when Sand's fleet was within 20,000 kilometers of them, but the shields held on the fleet and one by one the devices were deployed and set while all the cruisers fired on the alien fleet being careful to miss the devices that had been planted.

With all the devices deployed the Sand Fleet turned to the moon and the alien fleet followed but stopped two kilometers from the moon when the Sand Fleet rounded the moon. The Sand fleet circumnavigated the moon to find the alien fleet sitting there two kilometers from the moon so as they passed by John ordered the fleet to open fire again and keep going. The alien fleet followed and when all of them were within the one-kilometer mark John activated the devices. Sparks began to fly from the alien ships to the moon as huge blue arcs of power from the alien ships to the receivers on the moon commenced in the biggest lightning show John had ever seen.

Just then sensors picked up a huge object coming in on hyperspace fast. The sparks continued and the Kentaurides exited hyperspace with all her guns ready. The Queen's voice came over the comm, "We got here as fast as we could John. What is the light show?"

"It's the last of the aliens discharging your majesty. They arrived a few days ago and did nothing at first then began bombarding the planet with proton blasts. We found out how to destroy them and this is the result." John explained then one of the alien ships exploded followed by another. John noticed cracks forming in all the hulls and another exploded. Then two exploded at the same time. When everything was over there was a small pod three meters long and two meters around left. John moved his cruiser to pick it up and scooped it into a holding bay.

"Have a team of engineers meet me in the holding bay!" John ordered, "And head for the planet." Then he jumped up and walked quickly through the hatch on his way to the holding bay. The engineers were there already when he got there and were trying to open the pod. One found a latch and pressed it. The pod opened with a hiss and to everyone's surprise inside was a beautiful woman with red hair connected to sensors from head to toe. John pointed to one engineer and said, "Get a med team down here now!" He ran to the comm console still looking at the pod and only glancing at the board long enough to make sure he didn't touch the self-destruct switch, he touched comm and said, "Medical to holding bay stat! Medical to holding bay stat! Bring bio scanners." And he released the switch to walk back like he was in a daze.

CHAPTER EIGHT: IT'LL NEVER BE THE SAME

"What is this? John asked. "I'm going to take a guess and say a bio pod sir and from the outside of this pod this was connected to something. She may have controlled that fleet in some way. She has a tube in her nose that could be for feeding her and she has a respirator over her mouth for oxygen to keep her alive. I'll bet she has a catheter and a way to process feces too. This is for a very long term, and I'll bet she hasn't been conscious for a very long time. Her muscle tissue is thin so if we can wake her and find out what language she speaks she won't be able to walk for a long time until she can get her muscle tone back." Jackson, the lead research engineer on Sand, replied.

The medical team arrived and scanned her into the pod. "She has medical implants in her brain, the bands around her arms and legs are to pass electrical shocks so her muscles don't atrophy but they aren't working. She has a nose feeding tube and is getting oxygen and water mist, so her mouth doesn't dry out. Her heart has a pace keeper so she can get cardio once and a while. Her blood work is a little off, but she is relatively healthy. I'll bet she's been in this state for a few years. I went to a seminar once on alien cultures and this looks like she is the CPU of a system of some kind. Where did you get her?" Doctor Emily Kidder said. She is the fleet's doctor and the head of the emergency department at Sand's hospital.

"She is all that is left of the alien fleet Doctor," John told her.

She looked at him for several seconds. "You're John Hughes, aren't you?" She said a little starstruck.

"Yes," John replied. "I lead this merry band."

Suddenly, she grabbed him and hugged him. "I promised myself if I ever met you, I would do this as a thank you." She let him go.

"My husband Robert is a great surgeon, and he is good and kind plus he is a good man. The governor of Prong, a large province on Primase, had a son and he was prone to do stupid things. One day he did something after saying 'Hey look at this' and ended up on my husband's operating table. The boy had no chance of survival. He died and the governor went mad and killed 30 people in the hospital all his son's friends and almost got us. Your people found us and rescued us. I've been here for eleven years and never regretted it once. The only thing I miss is orange juice. Is there any chance of getting some orange trees?" Doctor Kidder explained.

"It's people like that governor that we need to eliminate. As for orange juice, I have a treat for you that I'll give you after you take care of her when we land." John said.

The doctor looked at the girl and then looked alarmed, "Oh no, we can't land with her, that could kill her. I just remembered something in that seminar about these systems. I need my husband up here and a surgical team. Plus reduce the gravity grid in this compartment. Her pod is set to work in space with no gravity. It'll start to malfunction soon in gravity. In a large gravity well, like a planet, it'll flat fail, killing her. Plus, she won't be able to breathe in full gravity."

John stepped quickly to the comm console and touched the comm switch. "Captain to the bridge, stay in orbit, do not land. Contact the hospital and Doctor Robert Kidder. Have him contact his wife here on our ship. Tell him it's a medical emergency."

"Aye captain!" the comm officer replied." Then John lowered the gravity grid in the compartment by 90%. Suddenly John felt fuzzy in his stomach. When he told the doctor about it, she told him that it was normal. The body isn't used to low gravity and the normal pull on the organs changes, so you get space sickness and it'll go away in time. She was wrong or six hours wasn't enough.

Six hours later her husband and an operating room were on the ship in the holding bay. The bay was big enough for a large shuttle, so the operating room fit with no problem, but the low gravity proved a problem. Three nurses out of four couldn't take the morning sickness-like symptoms of the space sickness and they had to replace them. The anesthesiologist had a bad time but was getting better, however his devices were not. His devices were malfunctioning from low gravity, so they had to increase gravity in one section of the bay for the air and blood circulation machines.

Within a few hours, the surgical team was fully assembled, and Doctor Robert Kidder was performing brain surgery on the woman removing the implants. Twenty hours later he was spelled by Doctor Nancy Larson whose specialty was neurosurgery. She had her team spell the others and the marathon surgery continued in low gravity. Eighty-one hours after the surgery began Nancy and Robert finished together.

The woman now had a different respirator and feeding hose. Her catheter was replaced, and the pod was recovered completely. She was given a sponge bath to remove the years' worth of scale and dead skin she had on her, and she was under sedation so she could heal before she woke. The stimulators were connected to gently work her muscles so they could recover.

The Queen was kept apprised of all of this and when John had time, he fulfilled her request for a meeting. John walked into the throne room on the royal battleship and bowed before the Queen, "You asked to see me ma'am as soon as I had a chance. I'm sorry it took so long." John apologized.

"I may have to apologize to you, John. We had a visit to Crucible from a strange species that we found out is called the Screircus. He landed on our planet and before he died, he told us about an invasion from outside the known worlds of very powerful beings made of pure energy. We didn't think much of it until now. I heard of two worlds that were wiped out, but we thought the Imperium did one and the central rebels did the other. One was a rebel world, and one was an Imperium world. No communication or information from either one of them came out and they were bombarded from space but not irradiated. We were looking at the Imperium world when we heard your call. That's why it took us so long to get here. That world is on another arm of the galaxy, over 110,000 lightyears away. If you hadn't sent out the hyperspace emergency beacon or we hadn't upgraded our engines, we still wouldn't be here. As it is we got here late." The Queen finished her explanation.

"Your majesty, I'm just glad you came. We have a weapon against them now, but I don't know how effective it'll be in the future. The weapon has too many requirements. But we know we can destroy them with massive firepower too." John said.

"Maybe this woman can tell us a few things." The Queen said and dismissed John.

John turned to leave, and thought to himself, at least the planetary shield works. Without that, we would've been toast.'

The final six ships finished construction. John ordered eight super ships to be built. The ship designer had worked on the new design for several months and took cruiser technology and destroyer brawn and merged them. The new ship has four types of six reactors at 8000 gigawatts of power but is distributed throughout the ship, not just in engineering. The hull has shield generators and gun ports over almost every square meter of it making room only for view ports and hatches. The ship is half as big as the medium destroyers but twice the firepower and equipped with eight new gravity engines. The hull has sixteen gravity booster motors so it can literally fly sidewise and only needs twenty-two to crew her. Computers and AI do the rest.

The shipyard foreman walked into John's office. "Are you nuts?"

"I probably am, but what are you referring to now?" John asked.

"These plans of yours are for a completely new ship and I only have 260 people to build them. We just finished eleven ships that needed refurbishing. That was easy, most of those ships were already there but you're talking about building something from scratch." The foreman said in a raised voice.

"So, you're telling me that you may be busy for a while or what? You need more people?" John said with a smile on his face. Robert Leslie Brown was the shipyard foreman and a Scotsman. He had been building ships since he was nine and he's sixty-three. Right now, he was standing with both fists on John's desk and as red-faced as John had ever seen him.

"I see you're a little upset, have a nip of scotch with me while I see if we can take care of the labor problem," John said as he pulled out two glasses and the bottle of twenty-year-old scotch he kept for just such occasions. John poured the foreman, for that was what everyone including John called him, a full glass and John poured himself a small amount in his and motioned him to sit. John touched the intercom and asked Jenny if she could get the Queen on the comm.

A half minute later Jenny replied, "The Queen is on line one sir. She is on her ship."

"Thank you, Jenny!" John replied and hit the speakerphone.

"Your majesty, how are you this morning?" John asked.

"I'm fine John. I heard a rumor that your cruisers were finished. You told me when they were completed; I would have the first pick. Are you calling to let me know my ships are ready?" the Queen asked.

"Yes, ma'am but I am asking for a favor too. You have over 60,000 souls on board your ship I believe." John asked her.

"We currently have over 116,000 people on my ship. 15,000 of them are refugees and the rest are crew and apprentices, why do you ask?" The Queen inquired. The foreman was astonished. He had no idea that many lived on that ship.

"I currently find myself in a dilemma and I need a lot of skilled workers to build ships. You want ships that I have that are worth six and a half billion each. I was thinking of a trade. How many of the eleven did you want your majesty?" John asked.

"We have fitted space for four of the cruisers to integrate them into our ship and launch them as auxiliaries in a fight. That is twenty billion and I can spare 21,000 specialists for you, and an additional 9,000 apprentice workers for three billion and I'll pay you 13.6 billion in gold." The Queen said.

"Do you have any construction workers? We'll need to make some houses before we get an increase in our population of 30,000. They need to know how to work with compressed earth. Everything here is built out of sandstone, metal, and glass." John asked.

"I will check. Many of the refugees are construction workers." The Queen said and signed off.

"Will 30,000 workers help you with your problem?" John asked with a smile.

"You had this figured out all this time, didn't you?" The foreman said, and you let me come in here ranting like a madman."

"How else am I going to get an excuse for a glass of scotch?" John asked with a smile and waved the bottle again. The foreman presented his empty glass.

Soon 12,000 construction workers began building neighborhoods of sand, clay, and a small amount of lime and concrete made from the ancient limestone deposits. Strong forms made the sides and were filled 25 to 26 centimeters with sand, clay, and cement mixed with a little water. Then it was compressed to 11 centimeters with pneumatic ramming tools layer by layer until the walls reached three meters tall. Then the metal girders to hold the roof on and the wall had another meter added to it. The walls were a half meter thick, and the roof was made of the same material as the walls lay across the girders only thinner at 12 centimeters thick. The roof was waterproof and light enough to keep the homes secure and cool from the heat outside.

The whole house was sprayed with plastic made from corn that helps in the UV breakdown. Dual pane windows with inert gases between them kept the sun's rays from heating the inside of the homes. Each house took a day to build but 120 a day were constructed since only 100 people could fit in a construction site at a time.

Four months later, Sand had 15,000 duplex houses built and ready. One hundred and twenty of the construction workers wanted to stay and work on Sand permanently and the rest moved back to their majesties ship as the 30,000 ship workers who had been working on the ships and commuting began moving into the homes.

Meanwhile, John had kept track of the dome, and it was finally completed. The farmers had a huge harvest of corn, tomatoes, and potatoes and were planting another crop already. The farmers bought more compost and spread it over half of the oasis area again. Our construction people came through again and made three-kilometer-long barns to store vegetables and tubers like potatoes. They were long, wide, and dark but the barns were strategically placed and lit by bright crystals. These barns held the thousands of tons of potatoes and corn. A full third of the oasis was grains, wheat, rye, and barley that make the flour for bread and pastries and livestock feed. Every four months the farmers harvest the wheat and store it in insulated silos for the flour mill and cattle. Similarly, rye and barley have their silos.

John had an urgent message from Jenny on his new wrist communicator. John stepped into the shipyard office since he was on his weekly rounds. "Yes, Jenny?" John answered her call.

"Three battles are raging right now. According to reports, two smaller skirmishes over freight and one large fight over a military convoy. All of them are within two lightyears of each other." Jenny told him.

"Alert the cruisers and crew. Get Captains Clemens and Nathan on their ships and give them the coordinates. We're going to take the cruisers and all." John hopped a transport to the sales yard and walked onto his cruiser. The crew was still coming on board. John walked through the ship which still had emergency lighting on because the reactors were cold, and the engineers hadn't started them.

CHAPTER NINE: ANOTHER FIGHT

Fifteen minutes later the lights came on and the system's power start panels started. Sissy and Sid were the last of the bridge crew to enter the bridge and the go was given by the engineers to start the systems for the whole ship except weapons. Duncan stepped up and spoke to John, "Hey Captain! So, I've been busy. The front two cannons on this ship are disintegration tubes. They are short-range right now, but they are programmable. I can fire on the enemy weapons and program the nanites to disassemble the bonds between anything metallic that has an energy signature, and they will keep going until there is no more metal with that energy signature then turn off. The plasma they ride in is accurate for almost five kilometers but no more. It will, however, shoot around corners.

I can take out engines and power systems without harming people but without power, it gets cold quickly in space. I can remove all the cannons on a ship with a few shots and the result is a puddle of metal that solidifies in seconds after all the power is gone. Robert was going to have me shot. One of my tests got away and his engine test station is gone."

"Robert?" John asked.

"Your foreman at the shipyard!" Duncan clarified, "is angry because the engine testing station is gone."

"And you disintegrated it with your nanites?" John questioned.

"Well… Yes, sir I did but it was a misfire, and I found the problem and fixed it. At least I hope I fixed all of them. Look this is all new technology and screw-ups are going to happen but I'm sure this will work if we need it especially if we find something really big." Duncan said.

John nodded and pointed to his weapons console. Duncan walked back and sat at his console.

"Comm ship to ship please!" John ordered and the comm officer nodded.

"This is a fleet command. We have three target coordinates two should be light and one is a heavy military freight convoy. All are within a couple of light years of each other. We are going to look at the first two and see if we need any mopping up then jump to the convoy and watch; I'll decide what to do when we get there. All the ships checked it. Forty minutes later, all the cruisers were ready to lift off and rose to the sky. The cruisers met the recovery ship Agenda, the freighters Avenger and Box Hauler, as well as both fighters, and set coordinates for the first battle zone.

The fleet exited hyperspace 500 kilometers from the battle zone and scanned the area for energy and life. No life signs or energy signs but a lot of debris. "This was a small skirmish. John this is a lot of debris for a small skirmish." Nathan of the Agenda said.

"The computer said 700 million tons of debris here, Nathan. You and your crew stay and clean it up. I'll take the rest of the fleet to the next place and report in." John answered.

"Aye aye sir! We'll get it all." Nathan replied and slowly moved forward.

"Comm open fleet communications", John ordered. The comm officer nodded.

"Fleet this is a command, on to the second coordinates," John commanded.

A few minutes later the Sand Fleet was in a firefight with one rebel light cruiser and two Imperium destroyers. "Battle stations, shields at full, Captains Davis and Jackson take the destroyer on the right Victor you and I have the one on the left," John ordered the fleet.

Davis said, "This is the light battle, John. I remember you said this was the light battle, nothing to it."

"Some reports may vary Davis. Just take out the engines and then the weapons." John said.

"Duncan I'm going to give you your chance. I want the engines and power systems out on that destroyer. Got it?" John looked at Duncan who had a big smile on his face. An explosion lit the sky as the rebel cruiser disappeared in a cloud of debris and the destroyers turned all their firepower on the Sand Fleet. John ordered Sissy to fly full speed at the nose of the destroyer and skim the length of it. Just within 4900 meters from the nose of the destroyer Duncan fired the forward cannon with programmed nanites to dissolve the bulkhead. Then reloaded and programmed the next load to dissolve the engines and power systems. At 200 meters Duncan fired and the ship veered up while the nanites veered down onto the engines.

John had Sissy flew away from the destroyer and watched as the nose of the ship began to dissolve.

"Load that again Duncan. Sissy, do the same to the other destroyer." John ordered and she flew the ship in an arc coming in at an angle to the second destroyer. Duncan fired and reloaded then reprogramed and fired again. "All ships break off," John ordered, at a safe distance John and the fleet watched as the destroyers self-destructed by melting into a blob spitting out bodies. John looked at the battlefield. Over seventy ships lay in ruins. Most of the ships were smaller rebel ships but one was an Imperium battleship. "The rebels picked the wrong fight this time," John said and shook his head. "Scan the freighter for life signs."

"No life signs sir!" Sid replied, "But there is a lot of freight."

"Contact Captain Sam Clemens of the Avenger and tell him to move this freight to Sand," John ordered. "We'll come back and clean up the rest after we look at the last coordinates."

The comm officer acknowledged and passed on the order.

"Duncan, I like the new weapon! That is impressive." John said in praise. Duncan nodded.

"Comm open fleet communications", John ordered. The comm officer nodded in acknowledgment.

"OK, the last coordinates to check out and we will exit hyperspace 2500 kilometers away from the battle. I don't want to get into this one unless we have to. Follow me and hopefully, this one is over." John said and finished addressing the fleet.

The four Cruisers, Box Hauler with Linda, and Jacob in the two super fighters all jumped and four minutes later they all witnessed an all-out battle between good and evil. Sixty Imperium ships were battling over a hundred rebel ships. The Imperium had two large battleships and twenty two heavy cruisers with support ships and six huge freighters in the middle. Two of the freighters were super freighters carrying much larger super containers. It was difficult to count containers from the distance the Sand Fleet was, but it was easy to say well over a million super containers and 4 million regular containers were in this convoy.

The rebel ships were not doing well but had removed one battleship and twelve heavy cruisers from the battle. The problem is the cost of forty three ships. Sid slipped into a joyous 'yee ha' when he saw the scanner and sixteen known configurations. The eleven ships that Sand sold to the royal house of the upper rebel Monarchy were in this battle along with the four sold to the crooked southern rebel faction. Sid turned in his chair, "Our ships are in this one sir, all sixteen of them."

"Good, they may win one then," John interjected.

"Wait, something is wrong sir, four of them don't have shields. That's just nuts to go into a major battle without shields." Sid said shaking his head.

"Not if you're going to claim workmanship failure and demand a new ship because of it," John said. "Those sneaky bastards, record the sensor readings, Sid." Sid nodded and touched a few places on his panel.

The battle continued and one more battleship fell silent, but forty more rebel ships lay in ruins. Ships fell on both sides when it looked like the Monarchy had had enough. The eleven cruisers they had bought, and 6 other ships turned and quickly left for the edge of the battle and disappeared into hyperspace. The Imperium still had twenty ships left although they were all damaged in some way, not including the freighters. All the freighters were not functioning. The rebels had thirty two ships barely working and all four of the Sand rebuilds were dead. The rebels grouped and charged the Imperium ships that had regrouped also. Both sides lost but the Imperium won with four ships still semi-functional.

"I think we should go in and mop up. With our ships' designs they will think we are rebels returning to finish the fight and hopefully, they will surrender. That military cargo and freight are going to make a fine addition to our stocks. Box Hauler, you stay here for now. The rest of you slow and easy, let's go pay a visit, Captain Davis hurry to the edges and drop comm killers. I don't want them to call in for help. The comm officer said, "I don't think they have much in comm anyway sir. I'm not getting much traffic. I have some local frequencies that may be ship to ship but nothing long distance and no hyper beacons."

"I don't believe it. We are getting a break? Jacob when I tell you, fly in and drop a transducer on a hull near the bridge of one of those ships. We'll wait until Captain Davis has the comm killers in place first."

The time ticked by until the comm officers' console beeped. "Sir Captain Davis said mission accomplished."

"OK, tell Jacob to drop the transducer," John ordered. "And put the audio on speaker."

Thirty minutes later, "That fighter just attached something on our hull Ensign."

"Shit, what is it; it's a bomb, is it? Damn, it!" a voice inside the shattered bridge said.

John answered, "No it's not a bomb. It's a device so we can talk to you and hopefully, we don't have to destroy you."

"You want us to surrender! We will not surrender, we will fight! Show yourself! Prepare to fire on my command! Prepare to hear! I said prepare God damn you! What are you doing? Let me go! Let me go now. I am your commanding officer." And the voice trailed off.

"This is Ensign Jones; I'm afraid Franklin was a bit over rout. I may get court marshaled for this, but we don't have a lot of choice. I surrender the Peacock and the Hausa. We can't communicate with anyone else. We have 32 out of 145 left alive so you rebels won. Our engines are out but we have life support." Ensign Jones finished.

"We accept your surrender, Ensign. We won't fire on you if you don't fire on us. We'll put your dead on one or two of the derelict ships and go about cleaning up the mess and salvaging all the junk, metal, and debris in the area. When we are done, we will tow you to an Imperium world and broadcast a message telling them that you are there, and we will leave."

"Why are you cleaning up the debris?" the Ensign asked.

"We clean up after all your battles because this debris is a hazard to space travel. Anyone who comes through here and hits a piece of a hatch or a hull would be destroyed. A lot of these private craft don't have the shields we have so we clean up after the battles. And I think the dead need deliverance to their people instead of floating around in space alone, yours and mine, don't you?"

The Ensign agreed. The other two ships agreed to surrender also. John had the freighters scanned. The military super freighters had 750,000 super containers each, so John called the freighter Box Hauler to disconnect one load and take it to Sand, all 750,000 of them. Then it should return and take the next load. The crews have recovered over 200,000 bodies from the dead ships and forty two living. Forty of the living was Imperium people, and thirty eight were delivered to Ensign Jones. Two of the survivors were officers of command rank for the Imperium so John held them in his brig as hostile combatants.

Two days later Captain Nathan of the recovery ship Agenda

announced he was clear to help and exited hyperspace at the edge of the battlefield. Two of the Imperium's regular freighters had been repaired enough by then and crews were starting their reactors for flight to Sand. Most of the systems were repaired and a million containers of cargo each prepared to take flight.

"John, we have two more Imperium officers found alive in a life pod. They are the commanding officer and his wife from the battleship." Captain Davis announced.

"Hold them in your brig and make sure no one talks to them. Remember it's important these people think we're rebels. Treat them well, we still have four or five days here before we finish," John replied.

The super freighter, Box Hauler, returned empty to pick up the next military load of super containers. Detaching the derelict freighter from the 750,000 huge containers without losing overall containment of the load was tricky but the Box Hauler's crew was getting good at it. Six hours after arriving they were ready to leave for Sand along with the other two freighters.

Captain Davis called John, "Sir if we can get some replacement parts for the engines on that battleship and a reactor core injector for a G4 reactor then we can fly this tub home. It'll be slow but towing this thing will be problematic at best. We can get shields up and if we get the sub-light engines going the working hyperdrive will make it to Sand."

"Make a list and send it to the foreman so Captain Daniels can bring the parts with him when he returns," John suggested to Captain Davis. "Hey Davis, that's a good idea, fly that monster home instead of towing it. I like it!"

"Thank you, sir, I have that list and I'll send it in a few minutes," Davis replied.

The recovery ship Agenda had already made three trips with over a million tons of derelict ships and scrap each trip and she was on her return trip empty when Jenny called with a message for John to call into the home base as soon as he could. Captain Nathan acknowledged the message. Two hours later he was at the battle site, and it looked like it was almost cleaned up. The four Imperium cruisers were connected, and the huge battleship was floating near Captain Davis's cruiser with cables running between them and the running lights on the battleship were on. He spotted John's ship and motioned the comm officer to privately call his cruiser, "John, Jenny has a message for you go private.

I'll meet you there." Nathan said and waited for a reply. The comm officer looked at his board and then just looked back and nodded.

Nathan hurried to his office and touched the console then touched private with John and seconds later John's voice came over the speaker. "What is the message, Nathan?"

"She said to call home base as soon as you can. She didn't go into detail but with the comm killers in place there is no direct two-way here." Nathan informed.

"OK, I got it. Thanks!" John said and signed off.

John immediately had Sissy fly out of range of the comm killers and called the base. "Jenny answered, "The pod woman is alive and awake. According to the Doctors, she will live but she will need a lot of rehabilitation and she is a victim, not an alien. The rest will wait until you get back, but you said to tell you as soon as she woke up, so I sent the message. Also, the sky is getting awfully full around here. The repulse teams are working 12 on and 12 off parking containers. The scrap is piling up and the furnaces are going nonstop. The foreman of the shipyard wants to know when he'll get the rest of his workers back so he can get back on schedule. So how much longer are you going to be gone because as you might guess your office is being inundated with calls."

"We have at least two more days here. We are bringing back a battleship and another million containers of freight. I'm estimating sixty million tons of scrap and derelict ships are left to recover until this is cleaned up. We have to deliver four hulls with over 90,000 dead to an Imperium world. And over 110,000 dead people to a rebel world, before I can come home." John said. "So, fend them off as best you can, and I'll deal with everything when I get back."

"I'll take care of it, John," Jenny said and signed off.

John's crew pieced together two gutted derelict ships for the bodies and fitted one with a life cabin and a short-range radio with rebel frequencies. After the cleanup was over all the Imperium prisoners were transferred to one of the derelict Imperium ships and Davis had the battleship moving, Captain Jackson maneuvered his cruiser over the four Imperium hulls with the cargo of dead following and spread his shields to cover them all. Then he headed for the nearest Imperium world of Praxis, a mining colony with huge resources 44 lightyears away. Jackson would enter the solar system and radio the world, letting them know about the survivors and for them to help now. Then he would disappear in a different direction and circle back around through the battlefield area then on to Sand. Captain Victor took the Rebel dead and the eight survivors to the nearest rebel world of Olympus, 84 lightyears away, and did the same. Olympus was a hub for the rebel fleet, so Victor released the derelict he was hauling with eight living souls and over 110,000 dead frozen bodies inside near the gas giants in the solar system and called out a distress signal. The response was immediate, and he ran just as fast. The survivors used their radio to get the rescue ship to find them. Captain Victor watched from a safe distance and quietly left.

John arrived home to find controlled chaos in orbit around Sand. All the containers were in their low orbit and the collected scrap and derelict ships were in a higher orbit. The battleship had not made it yet and the Kentaurides was orbiting the moon. The Queens shuttle was looking for a clear path to land and alone in its orbit was John's own Sheila with the woman and several nurses and three doctors on board. Almost five and a half million containers still in orbit were impressive and repulsor ships were raising and attaching to them for the descent to where they are placed on Sand. Even from this height, the line of containers was visible from orbit John noticed.

"John had a call from the Queen, "This is quite a mess, John. Have you been shopping again?" The Queen said with a chuckle.

"Well, you know your majesty, they had a sale, and I just couldn't pass up the bargains. This stuff was expensive, but we didn't pay for it. The Imperium and the Rebels did sadly to the tune of over 200,000 dead." John said with a noticeable sadness in his voice.

"Are you still returning everyone to their people?" the Queen asked.

"Yes, ma'am we are, we returned 74 survivors and over 90,000 dead to Praxis and eight living, with over 110,000 dead to Olympus. The 74 survivors were in an almost dead ship, and would've all died if we hadn't helped them. We have a battleship coming about a sixth the size of your ship. She's barely moving but she'll be here, and we'll rebuild her for our fleet." John said proudly.

John, sadly I can say this of few people I know, but I can say it of you. I'm proud to know you and many of the people under you." The Queen said in seldom praise.

"The opening is coming ma'am, get ready to land," John informed the Queen. An opening in the line of containers came every eleven minutes. John and the Queen took this one. John flew next to Sheila and opened visual communications. "Hello Mrs. Kidder, I understand that your patient is awake," John said.

The female Doctor Kidder's face appeared on the view screen. "Yes, she can stay awake for short periods, around an hour or so now. She is getting stronger, but she is still very weak. We estimate she has been in that pod for about five years based on the date she remembers and today's date. Her world was attacked like ours was, but they didn't have a shield. Everything was destroyed but she and her sister survived. Then these creatures landed and took her and her sister. She was in and out of consciousness after that except for the excruciating pain. They drilled into her head over and over then everything went dark, and she woke up here. Her name is Barbara. That pod was used to run those ships. The engineers told me. She was the organic CPU that kept the program running. There was nothing alive on them except her." Doctor Emily Kidder said. Her husband stepped behind her. "I and the other Neurosurgeon Doctor Nancy Larson, whose specialty is neurosurgery, removed well over a thousand electro-fibers from her brain. She was the brains of that fleet for sure. Her body is atrophied but we can get her back. It'll take time and she'll be able to breathe in gravity in about a month. So, we will be able to land and take her to the hospital then." Robert told him.

"This is a wonderful ship you have John, and the orange juice is great!" Emily said.

"OK. Enjoy and I'm glad Barbara is doing so well." John said and signed off. Open a private channel for Sheila.

The comm officer nodded and John put in his earpiece. "Hello, Sheila," John said to the ship's AI.

"Hello, John. I'm glad I could help that poor woman. I'm maintaining a 20% gravity level in a third of my cabin and a 90% gravity level in the other two-thirds for the Doctors, nurses, and equipment. I understand she was inside one of the ships that attacked our planet. Goliath is unable to understand that level of violence and to use a human in such a way is unthinkable to him and me. I'm just glad I can help." Sheila said privately to John.

"That is why I was calling. I wanted to make sure you were OK with your task. Thank you for what you're doing. It means a lot to me." John told her and closed the link.

"Now I have a ship with a heart," John said to himself.

"Sissy, land this baby and get your hot shower in because there is a lot of work to do," John told her.

"Aye sir, landing as instructed but there is a lot of traffic. Maybe we should set up a traffic controller as soon as we get back. We haven't had an accident but with this much going on it's just a matter of time." Sissy said.

Sissy and Sid started landing procedures and John started thinking about what she had said. The sky around Sand was very busy right now and an accident would ruin more than one set of plans let alone the injuries it could cause. Sissy had landed the cruiser in her usual perfection when John spoke to her, "How long would it take you to set up?"

"How long to set what up sir?" she asked looking bewildered.

"The space and air traffic control center idea are a good one. How long would it take to set one up?" John asked.

"I have no idea. I know we would need sensors and computers to see where everyone is. And we need transponders in every ship to identify every ship on the computers. I'm sure that there is a system and software somewhere already designed and made to do the job. I'll bet Tafari knows about it or knows someone who knows someone who knows about it." Sissy said. "A system that already works would be better than one that we try to figure out."

John nodded his head and stood still in deep thought. John was still thinking about the traffic problem when he found himself in the foreman's office. He looked up at the monitors and displays of the shipyard. The hulls were almost enclosed on all the ships he had ordered. The aft section on all of them still lay wide open as the enormous reactors were readied to be installed. All the smaller reactors had been installed already throughout the ships, but the large main 300,000-gigawatt cold fusion reactor hadn't been installed yet.

They were special reactors bought from the monarchy and made for land-based use to power huge cities and small countries. They had to be modified to work and fit into a ship and power a battlecruiser the size of a city. John knew when these were complete, they could take on a battleship and defeat it hands down with twice its firepower and five times its maneuverability and still take one-quarter the manpower. These behemoths only take twenty four people to the crew but have space for 200 to berth and feed. These have replicators in their galleys. The plans are from the designer of Sheila, only these are bigger to accommodate the larger size. There is also a large replicator in engineering to make parts.

Out of the corner of his eye, John caught a large man approaching, "What can Tafari Dalusi do for you today my friend? Sissy and the one you call Jenny said you look for me." Tafari asked John with a wide grin as he put his hand out to shake.

John shook his hand and said, "I need an air traffic control system for Sand. The sky and the space above are getting crowded. Can you help or do you know someone who could help?"

"I have noticed this. I know of a world that sells technology and people in that world who will sell it to anyone with the gold to buy it. However, it is an Imperium world and I only know about one way to get on it undetected and off again. I know about it because I have done it many times, but you must ask the Queen to borrow her shuttle. She has a cloak, and it works." Tafari said with a smile.

John asked and she gave her permission on one prevision, that she goes, and she takes a few of her human women with her. The Queen's pilots know how to fly without getting caught. "You've done this before, haven't you?" John asked.

"Oh yes sir, we've done these many times. The Queen shops here for her blouses and jewelry. Well to be exact, we go shopping for her and she tells us what she wants. We buy it with her money." The pilot said.

"Not this trip girls. We are going to use John's money." The Queen said.

"My money?" John asked, surprised.

"Yes John, you're renting my shuttle and crew this trip for some new earrings and a broach. I told my husband I wasn't doing anything for free." John looked a little worried. "Oh, don't worry John, it'll cost you less than a few thousand and I might find something for Leslie Ann." The Queen smiled. "It's nothing compared to the cost of the air traffic system you're looking for."

John smiled and bowed, "Yes ma'am, I'm happy to oblige.

Just outside the city on an estate owned by a friend of the Queen, the shuttle landed, and everyone disembarked except John and the Queen. The Queen's women wore glasses with camera lenses and had radios in the frames. The Queen took strips of gold from John worth 2100 credits to deposit in her account at the bank here on Quantal. The Queen handed them an additional 40-kilogram gold bar worth over 2,360,000 credits for the same purpose.

The Queen's entourage entered the bank and asked to see an account manager. A woman in her forty's approached and asked, "What can I do for you?"

The Lady in Waiting for the Queen said, "I am here to make a deposit for my mistress 'Queen Clementina protector populi suit, I have her permission on file and her assistant bank card."

"Yes, yes ma'am, right this way and have a seat. How much would you like to deposit today?" Asked Willamina, as identified by her nametag.

The Queen's Lady in Waiting set the gold bar and the gold strips on the table. Willamina's eyes widened as she left to get a scale. Two men returned with her pushing a cart with a digital scale and a scanner on it. First, she scanned the gold and then weighed it. "That will be 62,861.70 credits to your Queens account's previous balance of 1,024,858.30 for a total of 1,087,720.00. I will get your receipt."

The men left with the gold and the Queen's Lady in Waiting with her entourage left the bank. The ladies had several jewelry stores that they frequent, and they hit the first one with their glasses working perfectly. The Queen looked at diamonds, rubies, and emeralds but nothing in the first store struck her eye.

Tafari took a transport to the technology center and looked up an old friend. "Frank my friend, can I buy you a drink and talk about old times?" Tafari asked.

"No! The last time you talked to me I lost a sale for over a million credits." Frank told him angrily.

"OK! But this guy needs a whole system. He needs sensors, computers, software, trainers, the whole works for a planet." Tafari said.

"A whole system, what for?" Frank asked.

"He needs a space and air traffic control system that can track several million pieces of debris and ships," Tafari said with a grin. "I know you have it because I saw you selling the tracking devices and the auxiliary computers for one."

Frank looked him in the eye, "You're buying it, and I want steak this time, not that fish and rice crap."

After dinner and some wine, Frank asked, "This guy isn't a crook, and he isn't a rebel, but he doesn't want Imperium interference plus he wants an instructor and my people to install it. We have all the installers and the instructors, but I'll have to ask if any of them will go to a secret location and install a system."

"That is all correct. These people are not rebels. We will get your pad and get all the info you need on it. Then I will take you to the man and you can meet him." Tafari said. "Make sure you get all the sales aids you need and meet me here in an hour. I have someone else to take with us who you will compete with."

"Johnathon! You're going to get Johnathon from Cyber-dyne Systems to meet with this guy. He'll give him a lower bid and upcharge him on everything." Frank said with disgust.

"No, I'm bringing Alice from Singers Systems. She has an inventory system with auto readers I think he would be interested in. But if she has an air and space traffic system, I'll have her bring the information about that too. I never trusted Johnathon and I don't do business with people I don't trust." Tafari said to Frank, "Now you have an hour so you better hurry."

Frank hurried out the door and Tafari made the call to Alice. She met him outside the bar, and he asked her to stand with him around the corner for a few minutes.

"What? Why would we stand out here when there is a perfectly good bar right there?" Alice asked.

"Because I need to make sure an old friend is still an old friend dear. If he comes alone and just walks in without looking around, then we are good. If he walks up with others and they mingle while he walks in, then we just leave." Tafari told her. "I've been careful, and the Imperium police don't have my name or information yet."

"What have you done Tafari? I've known you a long time and I've never known you to be a bad person." Alice said a little worried.

"It's nothing like that. I am a seditionist. I don't like tyranny in any form." Tafari calmed her.

"Oh, is that all? OK!" Alice said in a low voice and watched with him. Frank approached the door and looked at his watch then walked in. No one followed him and no one appeared to be watching so Tafari and Alice walked to the bar and entered also.

"Frank, this is Alice. Alice this is Frank, you both sell hardware and software systems, and my friend needs a few so let's go."

The three left the bar and caught a transport to the estate of the Queen's friend. Tafari entered the gate code and the transport continued up to the house. Everyone exited and Tafari paid the transport driver then walked to the back of the grounds where John was waiting under the huge porch sipping a fruit drink. Alice and Frank introduced themselves and sat down.

Frank started, "I understand you want an air traffic control system."

John replied, "I need a planetary traffic and locator system so my people can follow who is in orbit and where and what is in orbit and where, so we don't have collisions or accidents."

"How many ships and satellites are in orbit at one time?" Frank asked.

"Right now, I have over nine million satellites in orbit and anywhere from 120 to 300 ships coming and going. John replied. "I need them identified and I need the ships to be identified when they are communicating with ground control."

"That is a big job and requires a tracking system on every satellite. Can you put one of these on every satellite?" Frank asked and handed him a strip six centimeters wide and thirty centimeters long. "It has an optional sixty by sixty solar panel to keep it charged and is good for 50,000 kilometers. It has a unique identification number embedded in it that transmits so that the sensors on the ground can pick it up and know where it always is by triangulating its location between three sensors. The control room has a three-dimensional view from a table in the center of the room. It requires a building with sensors around your planet. A total of 15 gigawatts of power for the whole system and it is equipped with double redundant backup systems for systems failure. It takes three people to operate it in each of six shifts at four hours each. Any longer and the human mind begins to overload." Frank's sales pitch ended.

"This system has a cost. How much? John asked.

"It will be 124,500,000 credits in gold preferably, but Imperium credits will do also," Frank said with a straight face.

"Forty-kilogram bars of gold are 2,360,000 credits each and you want a half of one? That's 123,523,400 credits for some computers and a few sensors. Frank that's a lot of money." John said not joking.

"Sir you're asking for a system to take care of a whole planet and it's 124,500,000. That means sensors across the whole surface are all connected to one building with a set of computers keeping track of up to thirteen million items and their flight trajectories. None of this is an easy task and the software alone took thirty-five years to perfect. Plus, I understand you want this done at a secret location. You will fly my people to the planet, and they will install everything, make sure it's all running, and one instructor will stay for a month to train twenty-four people how to use the system while your people tag everything. Am I forgetting anything or leaving anything out?" Frank paused. "This is all contingent on if I can get my people to go to your planet for three weeks minimum to install this. I have to convince eighteen or more people to hop on your shuttle with all their tools and equipment and fly to your planet unload and install everything in secret and blindfolded. If it wasn't for Tafari vouching for you this would NOT be happening."

"I see. Give me a few minutes to think. Ok Alice, is it? What do you have for me?" John asked as he walked to her sitting at her table.

"I have inventory control software. Tafari tells me you have a huge inventory problem and hundreds of people counting parts and containers that you don't know if they counted before or have never seen. This will solve all of that." Alice pulled out a handheld scanner with a small forty-centimeter by forty-centimeter screen on it. "This is an item scanner. Almost everything manufactured within the Imperium has one of these in it." She held a clear tube with tiny slivers inside. "These contain codes for manufacturer, item number, manufacture date, and serial number of each item ever purchased within the Imperium." Alice scanned John's glass. The scanner read a series of numbers and below it Daemons Glass Co, item 22325567, man 23324531, 66567. Alice translated, "The glass was made by Daemons Glass Co. the item number is listed and the date in the Imperium calendar with time and over 66 thousand of them have been manufactured. My software marks the geolocation of the item and keeps track of it. If someone comes along and rescans it, the software says that the item has been rescanned and notes the new geolocation of it. If it's different than the last time the location is updated but the item doesn't come out of inventory until it's marked as sold, destroyed, or made into a kit. I understand you have a lot of containers. Most of them have a special tag as a container and my software knows items go inside of them so scanned items can be in a container and my software knows what container and where that container is and where in the container the box of bolts is sitting." Alice paused. "My scanners cost 40,000 credits each, the main system to run it is 1,250,000 credits. Voice access pads are 13,000 each and all you need is to ask for a part. The system searches for it and tells you where it is and will guide you to the spot. The 1,250,000 system will track a billion parts and for 1,350,000 you can track five billion parts."

"What happens when a technician asks for and retrieves a part?" John asked.

"The system asks for the disposition of the part. Installed in ship invoice number such and such, a retrieved part always goes somewhere." Alice said.

"Who would install and instruct people how to use this system?" John asked.

"That would be me and I have no problem going to a secret planet and doing it. I've known Tafari and his wife a long time and I trust them." Alice replied.

"How long before you can be ready to leave with all you need?" John asked.

"I need the payment and one day," Alice said.

"I will get the larger system and ten scanners with ten voice pads. That comes out to 1,880,000 credits, is gold good for you?" John asked.

"Yes, it is but I can't carry that much gold," Alice exclaimed.

"That's ok, give me your account number and I'll have it put in your account," John told her. I'll see you tomorrow night when we leave." John said. "How much space do you need for equipment?"

"The system is contained in an AI standard rack mount thirteen units high. The backup drives are 6U and the uninterruptible power supply is 12U. The human connection is wall mounted and needs 4 by 6 meters of space." Alice wrote her account on the back of her card and handed it to John.

"Now as for you Frank, how many of those things are included in your package?" John asked.

"I'm sorry what things? Oh, you mean the trackers, these little devices." Frank pulled it out of his pocket again. "None of them comes with the package. They are a credit each and the solar panels are a credit each also." Frank said.

So, you want 124,500,000 credits for the system, and I have about nine million floating pieces of salvage in orbit, so I need nine million trackers and solar panels that's, um, about 140 million credits. What else is missing?" John asked.

"The instructor and the installation crew will need food and lodging and transportation around your planet. I need to know the climate, so they know what to wear and how steady is the power. The system wants clean power and I need to know we have a building that will hold all the equipment." Frank told him.

"Have a warehouse with good power that's definitely big enough. The climate is warm to hot and dry, and all power is from a geothermal plant with a 20,000,000-gigawatt output that we only use a tenth of right now. The lodging is already made. We have extra houses for your people and transport too." John finished.

"Then there is only the money. I need 2/3rd down and the rest when completed." Frank said.

"Give me an account number and I'll have the credits in your account tonight," John told him.

"It will take me two days to gather equipment, supplies, people, and tools. Do we ship everything here?" Frank asked.

John looked at Tafari who nodded. "Yes, Tafari will tell you how to deliver all the shipments. But your people will load and unload. My people here are for security mostly. You can guess why." John turned to Tafari, thank you, and please transport these good people back to the city. I have to make a deposit so hurry back. Tafari nodded.

John walked to the shuttle where the Queen was still shopping. "Your majesty, could I have a word with you please?" John asked.

"Sure John, what do you need?" The Queen asked her not to take her eyes off the displays of jewelry.

"I have to open an account and I was hoping you would do it for me. I have over 750,000,000 with me in gold." John told her. "I have to pay out 140 million to one vendor and 1.88 million to another."

The Queen told her people to hold for a moment and turned to look at John. "Wow, when you go shopping you go shopping." She said.

"I'm buying an inventory control system and a space and air traffic control system for Sand. None of them are cheap but they both sound very robust and your man Tafari Dalusi recommends them. I've grown used to relying on him." John said.

"Well, you have a problem. If anyone opens an account on this planet with a large sum of money, it's reported to the banking commission and the Imperium. We can put it in my account in a sub-account like an additional card account, but we can only deposit 250 million credits at a time. If I deposit more than that I raise questions even a Queen has limits." The Queen cautioned.

"That's good, I only need 141 million right away, but I'll need more later so we can put in 250 million today and credit these accounts this afternoon," John said to her.

"OK, my Lady in Waiting will be finished in an hour and bring me back some jewelry and lunch then she can leave after lunch with guards to the bank." The Queen said.

"Can I ask one other favor? I want a big steak and I know you're a vegetarian, but can they bring me back a big steak lunch?" John asked.

"Oh no John, she would be horrified. I'll send a guard to pick them up in the limousine. I'll tell him to stop off and get you your steak." The Queen said.

The limo left and John got his steak. Later that afternoon the deposit was made, and the payments were taken care of. The next night Alice and a worker with all the equipment arrived at the estate in a medium-sized van and the Queen shuttled her to Sand where she began setting up the inventory system in the warehouse. A large transport transferred all the equipment to the new location and Jenny made sure Alice had a comfortable place to live while she was on Sand.

The Queen and her shuttle left again for Quantal. She had left instructions for her Ladies in Waiting to deposit more of John's gold in her account. And today she should move the credits from the gold to a separate account with John and the Queen's Lady in Waiting as the only signers. The account should have more than a half billion in credits in it by now minus the payments with all the deposits made to her account so far.

The Queen landed and under the protection of darkness, she walked to the mansion and met with her people. All reports were good, and the deposits had gone as planned.

That evening Frank rang the gate and asked to be allowed entrance. The transport dropped him at the front entrance and Tafari met him.

"The equipment will be here in the morning on four large tractor-trailer units. Where shall I park them?" Frank asked.

Tafari motioned for him to follow, in the parking bay was the Queens shuttle. "The cargo bay is plenty large for your trailers," Tafari told him.

"I have three married couples who insist on bringing their children, their ages are 9, 11, 13, 16, and a 6-year-old. They are bringing a governess to look after all the children, but I need to know if I need to replace them." Frank checked with Tafari.

"I'll check to make sure, but I see no problem with them. Stay here." Tafari told him and left to check with John. When Tafari returned he told Frank, "No problem. Bring the kids along. He wanted to know how many installers you are bringing."

Frank replied, "Twenty two in all. Eight of them will be driving the trucks. The rest will be following in transports."

The next morning at 8:00 planet time four large trucks and a van full of people and children appeared at the gate. Tafari took the gardener's vehicle down to guide them around to the space landing bay and instructed them to park inside the cargo hold and tie down the vehicles. Then everyone found a seat in the cargo bay already set for passengers. John and the Queen were the last to enter before the large cargo doors were closed and they took off. Most of the passengers had never seen a Hemferdemite before, especially one dressed so regally. John and the Queen addressed the people sitting there.

"I'd like to thank you all for coming. It's a monumental task to install a system like this for a whole planet. This is my friend and the owner of this vessel, and she is the Queen of all her people. Your majesty, would you like to say something?" John said and bowed slightly to her.

"Yes, this is my ship and I'm very fond of her. Please keep that in mind. Relief rooms for humans are over there and well-signed. You are free to walk around after we are space-bound but when the cargo master says to be seated, please take your seats quickly because we are about to land, and we don't have a space controller in place." The Queen finished and walked through the large door to the crews' quarters and bridge.

"Get a load of her," one of the workers said. One of the women walked over and slapped him. "I got a look at the jewels she was wearing buster. They weren't false and were worth more than everything in those trucks combined. Have you looked at this floor? It's marbled, tempered glass-covered marble and look at the walls." That is a real hardwood of some kind. Who does that for a cargo bay?" The woman asked. "So, show a little respect, you are traveling in style, even the seats are real nice seats."

The cargo master heard all the conversations and stepped forward. "Thank you, ma'am, I'm proud of this ship. I've worked on her since I was sixteen and helped with most of the construction. My Queen is one of the kindest people you would ever meet, and she is Queen of truly majestic people. There are only about 45,000 left but they are coming back and I for one am glad." The cargo master was looking at the mouthy man when he spoke then he walked off.

Several hours later the cargo master announced they would be landing soon, so be seated and buckle in. Everyone sat down but the mouthy one was missing. When he finally walked out of the relief room, he announced that no one should go in there for a while. The cargo master just pointed to his seat. He walked to the comm panel next to his chair and touched the bridge line, "all secure in cargo captain."

"Thank you, Cargo! Engineering, check in please!" The female captain's voice commanded. "All clear in engineering captain." Engineering checked in.

"Landing will commence as soon as a clear path can be established." The captain's voice said and clicked off.

"Well, that worries me a little." The mouthy one said. The passengers felt very little, but the G-forces changed slightly from left to right and finally, they all felt a little heavier after almost an hour. The cargo master yelled, "Hold on we're almost there." Just after he spoke the ship shuttered when the atmosphere engines started, and the gravity motors changed their pitch to work within the atmosphere of a planet. But that was momentary and soon the ship was on the ground with barely a notice.

The slight whine of the engines disappeared, and the cargo master stood and walked to the passengers. "The temperature is 94 degrees right now. Here in the only actual city on this planet, it's 9:45 in the morning. You may want to set your timepieces. The planet is mostly desert with three places that have water. One is a huge place 600 kilometers from here we call the oasis and is covered by a dome. It in where most of our crops are grown and a few farmers live. If you want to see wonders of man-built creation, you should check it out. It's enormous. The dome is 180,000 kilometers in circumference, a little over 6,327 kilometers across, and 130 meters high. It has 14,000 pillars holding it up and is climate controlled but has its own climate inside and even has a rain cycle on a desert planet. The glass walls are computer-controlled to allow the perfect amount of sun at the perfect time for the crops to be planted. We have barns that are several kilometers long for animals and storage, so you won't starve while you're here. All the housing and buildings are made of rammed earth, a type of sandstone, and very durable with walls ranging from 30 centimeters to 45 centimeters thick and roofing made from the same material just a little thinner and insulated with dura-steel reinforcement. The building you are going to install your system into is 810 meters square with 60 centimeter walls and no inside walls. It has a domed roof and full bathing and relief facilities for several people and other aliens.

The homes we have for you to stay in are new. They were constructed just a few months ago and have vid and cooking if you wish to cook but we have cafeterias and restaurants for those who don't want to. Your meals are paid for you while you are here and working on this project as part of the agreement Frank made with the general manager and well, I guess the owner of this world, the man you saw when you sat down here, John Hughes." He paused and looked at all of them then asked, "Are there any questions?"

"Are we building the towers and buildings for the sensor arrays in the desert or are they already built for us?" the mouthy one asked.

John walked in and answered the question. "Since we don't know where you need sensors, we haven't built buildings."

"Oh, well yea that would make sense." The mouth said.

Frank climbed out of the truck and walked up to John. "That was a great nap. "We need to get to the building that we're going to use and park everything. You must unload the trucks, folks." Most of them groaned. "John, I didn't ask but I hope you have lift trucks here to help unload."

"No, we use gravity pallet lifts. It's safer and uses very little power. They connect to the pallet, and you just push them around no matter what is on them." John said.

"Anyone ever used a gravity pallet lift?" Frank asked his people.

"I'll have someone show you how. It's easy." John said and continued with, "My people will show you the warehouse and get you started. You get them started on placing the trackers and how to connect the solar panels to the trackers. A man named Lewis Assure will be your liaison to my construction and electricians. While you are here communication with your world is not allowed. The location of this world is secret, so we don't attract attention from the Imperium or the Rebels. I'm independent and I'm not at war with anyone and more important I don't want to be at war with anyone."

The large cargo doors opened, and the heat entered the cargo bay. A tall well-tanned man in his 20s driving a small cart pulled in and waved. "I'm Lewis Assure and I'm going to show you where you're going. So, untie the trucks and the rest of you follow me, we have a trolley to carry you to the warehouse."

Everyone except the drivers walked to the trolley and climbed on the multi-seated vehicle with a canopy over it and more than enough room for everyone. The trucks whined to life and started to pull out of the cargo bay. The trolley followed Lewis through the streets and the trucks followed them to the warehouse, a brown and dark green building marked 'Traffic Command' and under it was embedded in the wall 'Air and Space Traffic Control' appeared as they turned the corner. The building was large and tall with a domed roof and several man doors along the wall. Lewis stopped in front of the cargo door, a nine-meter wide and eleven-meter-tall door with a man door large enough for a Hemferdemite to easily walk through. Lewis walked to the man door and placed his hand on the pad. The door opened into the wall, and he walked in. The large door opened rolling up and that's when the people saw it was a double door. The walls were very thick, and Lewis motioned for the trucks and the people to pull inside.

Once inside Lewis closed the doors and the people started to exit the trolley. The lights were on in the area, the trucks and people were but not in the rest of the warehouse. The temperature inside was just 76 degrees. Compared to 95 degrees outside, one of the women took a deep breath "Oh my, this is nice. Is this warehouse air conditioned?" she asked Lewis. "No, believe it or not, we have an air cooling system here, but it is seldom ever used. The computers will have a controlled room temperature setting and we'll make a control room to your specifications."

"Don't forget the communications center. It'll be in contact with the rest of your planet's sensors. This reminds me of how big your planet is. It doesn't feel much different than our home planet." Frank said.

Lewis told him off the top of his head, "The planet is 13,770 kilometers in diameter and a little over 41,000 kilometers at the equator. Does that help?"

"Yes, that means we need 4200 ground-based sensors and six satellites for the system. The good news is the ground systems are modular and solar-powered. We brought 5,000 of them and 5 million trackers with solar panels for the trackers. We need to get a class started on setting the trackers and a class on what the sensors need so your construction people can start building the small towers and buildings for us to install the sensors into.

The next month was busy as Sands construction crews built the small three-meter by four-meter buildings needed for communication and solar panels. The arrays were all self-contained and communicated with the satellites already placed in orbit.

John inspected the ships under construction and saw almost finished-looking ships with complete hulls and polished viewports along the sides.

He sat in his transport and rode to the inventory control building where Alice was finishing the final touches on the inventory control system. John walked into the office. Reader pads lined one wall in their chargers and scanners lined the other wall with room under them for ten more on each side. John pushed the main door open to see Alice in the control chair in front of the huge main screen.

She heard him come in and turned. "You are just in time. It's done and ready for input. I've already trained ten of your people on how to use the scanners and your foreman on how to use the readers. The people should be here any minute to get their scanners and start with the first ten containers. I set up more chargers and palm reader chargers because I need to talk you into buying more scanners and pads. With ten scanners it'll take years to scan the amount of inventory I saw, and

I only saw a small amount of what you have."

"I was thinking the same thing. I have the additional funds on deposit and can transfer them at any time." John said to Alice.

She smiled, "Good because I brought extra and you're going to need them, but I also wanted to talk to you about an inventory control official."

John smiled and asked, "What about an inventory control official?"

"I've had a month to look at what you have here. I like what I see. If the pay is anywhere near right, I'd like to be an inventory control official for you but of course, I'd need three assistants to train also." Alice said.

"What do you make now? John asked.

"I receive 64,000 a year plus commission, it usually comes to 94,000 to 99,000 a year." She said.

"But you have to pay rent or mortgage out of that, and I know what the rents are on Quantal. You pay at least a quarter of that for rent. Am I right?" John said.

"Yes, I rent an apartment for 36,000 a year, but it is a nice place, small but nice," Alice said.

"How do you like the house you're living in?" John asked.

"I love it! It needs some furniture but other than that it's great." Alice said with a smile on her face.

"The position of inventory control official comes with a house and medical and a salary of 70,000 credits a year but there is a catch. This place is secret. You can't tell your friends where you are or run off the world and bring people here without prior authorization." John told her.

"That won't be a problem. I had a boyfriend and I want to disappear from him and as for family, I don't have any left. My father died last year so a new world and a new job that I know very well in a new house will be just fine with me. The money is good, and I've always wanted a house, so I except." Alice said.

"Before you completely give in pay for the additional scanners and pads, collect your commission, and get your money out of the bank in gold. We have a bank here where you can open an account. We don't use cards here. Handprints and a retina scan let you buy anything you want. It's extremely secure and no one can forge your signature." The

Queen will transport you back when she returns. Several of the crew that installed the traffic system are asking to stay also. The people who want to stay are couples with families and three other senior technicians. The instructor has also asked about staying here as the lead traffic controller. The system is 90% up right now. We have installed trackers on a little over 40% of the containers and debris in orbit.

The repulsor ships are bringing down containers all day and night and stacking them in the inventory yard. We have an iron and steel pile big enough for our furnaces to work for a year before they run out of material to make dura steel girders and plates for our ships. I have at least that amount in orbit waiting to land to add to the pile." John told Alice.

"Where are you getting all of this material?" Alice asked.

"From battlefield leftovers. The Imperium and the Rebels fight and make a mess of destroyed ships and debris and we just go and scoop it up." John told her.

"Wait; if the Imperium wins a battle, don't they take the containers with them?" Alice asked.

"Yes, they do but they leave the destroyed rebel and any destroyed Imperium ships behind in a big debris field for the next ship that comes through to hit. So, we go and clean it up then bring it here." John said.

"And if the Rebels win, they take the containers and run. But they leave a mess, then how did you end up with all these containers?" Alice asked.

"Sometimes they both lose. And when we get there, we get the containers and all the debris." John explained.

"Um this is a little disgusting but, what about the dead people?" Alice asked looking disgusted.

"In space, they pretty much freeze. We separate them as best we can and put them in a container, usually a hull of a ship or a vessel of some kind that we make then take them to their nearby world and send a signal to that world about the container or vessel. We wait to see that someone comes and then leave. The Rebels take their dead when they win and jettison the enemy dead into the sun. The Imperium just leaves their dead and Rebel dead to float in space." John told her.

"The Imperium just leaves them there?" Linda asked, sickened.

John just nodded.

John walked to the traffic controller's building and entered the main room. A hologram of Sand floated in the middle of the room with tagged items circling it. Three people with headsets on were seated around the projection. He listened as they talked to pilots bringing cargo down and lifting off to pick cargo up. John watched as the line of containers slowly grew as the trackers got added to shipping containers that were in orbit but not tagged. A man approached him quietly, "Hello John." He whispered.

"Hi, who are you?" John whispered back.

"I'm Markus Espiers, the instructor for this software and this system." He whispered back. "Let's step into my office where we can talk a little louder without disturbing anyone's concentration."

John followed him into an office with glass walls and a full view of the hologram. As soon as the door closed Marcus said, "That's better, they have enough trouble concentrating now. They don't need distractions. It's impressive, isn't it? Each person has a zone to watch and control, when a craft leaves their zone, they pass it to the next controller."

"I have to admit that it's a beautiful sight," John said mesmerized by the display.

"I'm surprised you didn't get the full package. The system has long-distance detection capabilities for incoming traffic. For what you spent it was only a few million more." Marcus said.

Now it was John's turn to be surprised. "We have a long-range detection system but it's a manned system and its crude. There are manned hidden observatories in the far solar system that warn us."

The upgrade uses an Observation Detection Defense System (ODDS) and drones. The drones are one meter globes all black with their own communication and sensor array. They use small gravity motors to maintain exact locations in space and are deployed in a grid every 500,000 kilometers. The sun charges them and they detect everything including cloaked ships by detecting disturbances in space." Marcus told him and then pulled up a hologram on his desk of one. "These are all but invisible in space because they are so small and only communicate in burst digital transmissions. I must check with Frank, but I think the upgrade is sixty million for thirty thousand of these preprogrammed. That'll cover most any solar system." Marcus told John.

"Does Quantal have this?" John asked.

"Nope, they're too cheap," Marcus replied. "I'm thinking that's how you keep getting in and out of there undetected. You have a stealth ship, maybe one with a cloak. But I don't care. I hate that place. I get searched every week and arrested once a month for nothing. Oh, they let me go, but not until I've spent the night in jail with whatever is in there. The month I've spent here has been a vacation." Marcus sighed.

"Would you like to make it permanent?" John asked, "Or do you have family on Quantal?"

"I would love to make it permanent, but I have a mother and a girlfriend. They don't like it there either. My mother won't leave the house and my girlfriend is a writer. She writes articles for magazines, but she wants to write a book. She just never gets around to it. I pay our rent and she makes me happy, so I don't care what she writes." Marcus said with a smile and a shrug.

"Bring them along, there's plenty of room. I'm sure we can agree on a salary, and I could use someone who knows this system inside and out. I've already told the three families that came here that they can stay and two of the women technicians want to stay here. One of the men is an ass and they want to make sure he won't stay." John shared this with Marcus.

"That would be Johnson. He's been passed over for promotion time and time again because of his attitude. He's a good technician but he doesn't work well with others. He's one of those guys you send out alone to get a job done. He'll do it, and he'll do it well, but he has no place for anyone else." Marcus informed John.

"That explains a lot. I noticed Frank would send two people to install a sensor as soon as the building was up, but Johnson, wasn't it? Frank would send him alone." John told him.

"Well, the work is grueling. They have to set up fourteen sensors a day to keep to schedule. Johnson can do ten by himself. The others work in two-man or women crews and the work is faster and easier. The sensors are all modular. If a sensor goes down, you just take a replacement out and swap it. Change the location ID and turn it on. Then you bring it back and repair it." Marcus said.

"Do you know how to repair them?" John asked.

"No, but most of the installation crews do. All the women do!" he said.

John nodded and left.

In the next three weeks, the Queens shuttle returned with two trucks filled with the ODDS and people who were moving to Sand. Alice had all her money from her bank and the new scanners and pads. Marcus, with his girlfriend and mother, had everything with them in a large van and he had a medium-sized truck with him filled with replacement parts that he told Alice about. She would send someone over to scan them as soon as Marcus had the repair center set up.

Tafari had 345 people moving to Sand altogether. That made over 400,000 people on Sand living and working now. The Queen has a permanent residence on Sand. A rock outcropping above the city was cut and leveled to create a 45,000-square-meter complex for her and her people, guards, and ladies. A landing bay for her shuttle is next to her estate and it's protected by a secondary shield. The road to her estate is sandstone over molten stone made from a solar lens designed by her husband just for Sand.

Barbara, the woman from the pod, was landing today. She had recovered enough according to her doctors who were by her side for most of her time in low gravity held up in Sheila. Sheila had been increasing the gravity in the cabin for two months and Barbara had adjusted well to the new weight. Sheila has said on several occasions that she was glad to help. Today would be the first time in almost six years that Barbara had been on a planet and free of an alien pod. The doctors and phycologists were able to find out that she and her sister survived a vicious attack that destroyed her world and almost everyone in it. Then she was used as a control unit to control a robot fleet sent to Sand to destroy this planet. Our shields and ingenuity saved us, but other planets don't have our saving graces.

The Crucible is now protected by the same shield technology that Sand has. A gift was presented to the Queen and her followers from the people of Sand for her help and friendship. The Battleship Kentaurides is in orbit as a protector of that world with her massive artillery. As a reminder, the people of Crucible can see her shadow as she passes over each orbit giving them a feeling of safety.

John took his weekly trip to the shipyards and entered the foreman's office. The foreman was having a cup of coffee at his desk. In the fourteen years that John has walked to the repair depot, now the shipyards, he has never seen the foreman sitting at his desk. "This is different, "John said with a smile.

"I got smart. I have an assistant foreman now on each ship running the crew for that ship and they report to me. Besides that, your doctor told me if I didn't slow down and take it easy, I'll have a heart attack. They have me on medication and walking six kilometers a day nonstop. Then every other day I'm supposed to punch a bag for twenty minutes. I'm supposed to get angry at it, so I don't get angry at people. I told the doctor that I wouldn't get angry at people if they didn't do stupid shit in front of me so, he told me to get assistants." The foreman said. "Hell John, I'm going to be sixty-four next month and I have seven grandkids and I just found out that I have three great grandkids on the way. I want to see them, but I love what I do so you'll get your money's worth."

John smiled, poured a cup of coffee, and sat down too. "Robert, I've never questioned that."

The foreman raised his eyebrows, "I think that's the first time you've ever called me by my name."

"It was always out of respect, Foreman!" John and Robert sat in silence for a while as old friends do and had their coffee. But, as always, it didn't last long enough. The assistants came in for their evening briefing, and the day crew assistants came in to give their reports. John listened in and left after the meeting was over to carry on his trip around the major workings of Sand. The next stop was the inventory center.

Alice was busy at the computer and turned when she heard John enter. "Hi John!" She smiled as she greeted him.

"Hello Alice, how's it going?" he replied.

"We have over thirty million parts inventoried so far. But only thirteen have been dispersed." Alice responded looking at the screen. "We haven't scratched the surface yet.

"What is happening on this screen? The words are just scrolling by so fast I can't read them." John saw a smaller screen to the side of the main screen.

"That is the scanner input screen. That shows what my teams are scanning and inputting into the system. The screen below is the computer sorting and categorizing each part as it comes in and placing it in the index for searches so it can be found when someone wants to find it. The teams pull everything out of a container. Then they unpack it if they need to, scan everything then put everything back inside stacked or in racks for easier access. Each regular container takes about an hour and a half to process with the tractor beam lifts and gravity pallet lifts, the super containers take a lot longer of course. We have twenty teams per shift out right now working two shifts." Alice said and saw something to do on her screen.

"Very good, then I'll leave you to it. Goodbye." John said to the back of Alice's head. She waved.

The next stop was the air traffic controller building. John entered and was always amazed at the holographic globe in the middle of the room. Most of the containers and captured debris were tagged with a tracker now. The train circling the globe was still enormous but the repulsor ships were whittling it down little by little. John could see the little ships fly up and merge with the containers. Two repulsor ships for a regular container would attach to each end and slowly descend to the surface and park the container on a slab made for it in the inventory yard. The containers were stacked up to eight high with a slab between them ten meters wide so the containers could be unloaded and reloaded. The top floor had a roof of a silicate solar panel to power the lighting and gates for the inventory complex.

In a separate complex, the super containers sat all stacked similarly all much larger and stronger. The floors were thicker since the containers could contain items weighing several tons and take the whole container. The floors were wider too at two hundred meters wide and a half meter thick of reinforced concrete. A super container is thirty meters high and wide by a hundred and fifty meters long. It takes twenty repulsor ships to land one and stack it. The maximum height is four containers. The top floor roof also has a silicate solar panel to power the lighting and gates for the inventory complex.

John also saw four large shapes rise from the shipyards. He tapped the closest controller on the shoulder and as soon as he turned to him, he asked, "What are those?" and pointed to the shapes lifting into orbit.

"Those are the new ships that are under construction at the shipyard sir. They are doing their first powered flight today." The young man said and turned back to continue his work.

John had a grin from ear to ear.

CHAPTER TEN: POWERED FLIGHT

John visited Barbara and talked to her for a few minutes and her doctors. He thanked them for spending all that time in Sheila tending to Barbara, they said they were glad to do it and learned a few things about the aliens too.

John visited the forge and furnaces. Dura steel, steel plates, steel girders, and slabs of metal all sat in piles ready to be molded and used for buildings and hulls or whatever is needed. And the furnaces continued to melt down the scrap metal from the derelict ships and debris into useful forms.

John visited the inventory yards. They were enormous. On each floor, an inventory team was pulling everything out of a container and setting up racks inside the containers. Then they took everything off the pallets and one person scanned everything as the rest of the team put everything back.

John looked at a container that was finished. Everything was stacked and racked for easy location. The space was tight, but it was workable and orderly. As he was leaving the container, he noticed boxes of twelve-meter monitors for computers stacked in a row. There had to be over two hundred of them. On the other side were over two hundred new trans-gen computers. Somebody didn't get their computers.

John walked down the promenade, the shopping district on Sand, and saw people going in and out of the supermarket, one of two here. The other big grocery market was at the other end of the city. John passed by a large clothing store and a jewelry store, then he stopped and looked in and browsed. They still had that emerald broach he was looking to buy for Leslie Ann. John decided on the necklace instead; his anniversary was coming up soon.

A saddlery and tack shop had opened across the way next to the feed store where the farmers sold the hay and grain for stock to the ranchers. John entered the butcher shop to pick up steaks for the grill tomorrow night. The last place John checked on was the electronics outlet. John asked all the owners how business was and all of them told him that since the city had grown that business was great.

John called a transport and left for home. First thing in the morning he would check in at the office and then he would go to see about his new ships.

John awoke early the next day. Leslie Ann was awake and smiling. After a quick morning toothbrush and such they met back in their bedroom and made slow easy love together. Later relaxing they decided to shower together and then had breakfast before taking on the day. John helped with the few dishes and held her close then brushed her hair aside with his hand like he always did and kissed her passionately. "I love you more each day my dear," John told her as he looked into her eyes.

"Me too, honey!" was all she said as she choked up a little. John left to go to the office. It was 9:00 in the morning and he was going to check in quickly. Then hurry over to see the new ships but when he arrived, Jenny had visitors for him to see. The farmers were waiting for him in his office and had been there for almost two hours. "They were waiting for me when I got here and opened the door this morning at 8:00. They said that they didn't know you kept bankers' hours whatever that means," Jenny informed John.

"It means that I don't get up as early as they do Jenny." John said with a chuckle, 'Send them all in."

Krill, Jacob Sampson, his sons William and George, and Lyle Kilian all entered John's office and looked around as they did. Krill noticed some changes and improvements since the last time he'd been here, "you've redecorated again sir."

"No, not really, I've had to add a console to have direct access to the main AI that controls our world. It turns out he's a pacifist and thinks we shouldn't have weapons to defend ourselves, among other problems with him. But you're not here to discuss my office decor, what brings all of you all this way? It must be important to bring all of you." John remarked with a smile and added, "Before we start can Jenny get you anything? I'm going to have her get me some coffee anyway so would you like something?

George raised his hand and said, "Coffee sounds great, cream and one sugar but make it a big cup."

His brother pipped in, "Me too!"

Krill turned from looking at a picture of the oasis before anything was there and said, "Orange juice. This reminds me; I have had messages from some woman to plant an orange juice bush. She has it on good authority that orange juice is made from a bush that you let drip out of a bush into a glass." Everyone laughed. Jenny heard the commotion and opened the door. John took the opportunity to ask for the coffee and orange juice.

Krill started the meeting, "Well to the point, you pay us a salary, and we're fine with that. None of us ever thought we would get rich being farmers. But we have corn, potatoes, and a lot of other vegetables in cellars and barns filled to the rafters and grain stored in full silos. If we stopped and planted nothing for the next four seasons, we would start to put a dent in the stored food we have. We can't just keep building storage facilities. The only thing that is going at a good rate is the hay and alfalfa for the ranchers. The horses, cattle, and goats eat it, and the ranchers give us the droppings for fertilizer."

"So, are you telling me that you're taking a year off?" John asked, wondering where this was going.

"No, we're saying we can do better. The machines and tools we have here are amazing. With them, we can do the work of thirty men. But there are whole worlds out there that are starving because of this war. We can help those worlds with food from our stores that will rot or wither if we don't do something with it and that is a waste." Krill said.

"Did you have a world in mind?" John asked.

"Liberia was attacked, and the storage bunkers were destroyed. The Imperium isn't doing anything to help. Twenty shipments of grain and potatoes would go a long way to save a lot of people. You should know, in orbit around my home world is debris from the battle the Imperium had with whoever it was that attacked. The damage is from the debris falling and destroying everything." Krill said.

Lyle said, "We all agree. If we can help his people, then we should, and it would be a waste to let all that stuff rot. Even that amount won't hurt us at all."

"I'll see what I can do about it. And more important I'll see about cleaning up the debris in orbit so we can stop the bombardment from destroying your home world." John told them and dismissed them. John wrote the order to have the world of Liberia visited and scanned by a cruiser. Then he called for transport to the shipyards to see his new ships.

John walked into the foreman's office, and he was sitting at his desk. "I thought you would be here today. They had their first flight yesterday and the crews are fixing the damages now."

"Damages? What damages?" John asked concerned.

"One ran into a pylon on takeoff and two hit a pylon on landing. The engines are being tuned to the ships and until they are attuned correctly the ships are unstable." The foreman told him.

John sighed, "How long will that take?"

"It'll be done by the evening shift. The engineers are pouring over them now. They have all the calculations; they need to tune the engines and all four will be ready to fly this evening and all the dents will be out too." Robert said with a smile. "I had you worried, didn't I?"

John looked at him wryly and told him, "No! I wasn't worried. I knew you would get the job done. Right now, I'm going to take out my cruiser and go look at Liberia. It seems that the Imperium had a battle over that planet and as usual, they didn't clean up their mess. The planet has debris falling on it causing havoc and I'm going to go check it out."

"I suggest you take your ferry instead. She has been lifting off and landing all by herself for a couple of weeks now. You can use my communication system over there." The foreman said and pointed.

"John called Jenny to cancel the cruiser and then called Sheila, "Would you like to take me for a ride to Liberia please?" John asked her.

"I'm waiting outside the foreman's office John," Sheila answered.

John looked at the foreman with a surprised look and walked to the door. There she was hovering just above the ground with stairs waiting. John waved at the foreman and took a few steps to Sheila then took his seat. She rose to twenty meters and radioed the control center. "This is the Ferry Sheila requesting permission for orbit and off-world flight to Liberia with one passenger, John."

"Permission granted fight path assigned and transmitting now." The control center said and clicked off.

A line appeared on the screen for John to see and Sheila turned to him as she began the ascension to orbit and out into the solar system. "Hello John, it's been a while since you've taken me anywhere." She told him.

"The last time I went anywhere it was a battlefield and we have an agreement. You were busy for a long time with Barbara and the doctors too." John replied.

"Yes, I enjoyed that. I just want to do more. I dislike sitting in my berth doing nothing. You traveled to a planet in the Queens shuttle several times. What does the Queens shuttle have that I don't have?" She asked.

"Her shuttle has a cloak so we can get in and out undetected for one. Second, the Queen has a friend with an estate that we use when we're on Quantal, so we're not questioned by the Imperium." John said sympathetically.

"You could get me a cloak. She could authorize me to land at the estate. I just want to do more than I'm doing now." She said.

"Let me see what I can do. I'm sure that I can come up with something that will keep you busy and keep you around enough so I'm not without my favorite ferry." John said with a smile. "Now, how about a cup of coffee?"

The android Sheila smiled and turned to the replicator to retrieve the cup already appearing in the device.

Several hours later they arrived in Liberia. The debris cloud was huge, a dead battle cruiser was orbiting their moon, and one was on the moon nose down. The remains of at least twelve ships floated around the planet. "Sheila, use your sensors and tell me if you detect any life signs on those ships," John said.

"Twelve life signs on the large ship circling the moon but most are barely showing. I see one life sign in a pod bearing twenty-two degrees by sixteen by one forty-five. There is a pod like the one Barbara was in among the debris." Sheila told John.

"Can you load that pod without letting all the air out?" John asked.

"Of course, I can. I'll use force fields inside and my shields outside." Sheila told John. "Then when I get it inside, I can reduce the gravity in that section and keep your section at full for the trip home."

"OK, thank you," John said and watched as Sheila maneuvered through the debris pushing metal fragments out of the way with her shields until she was right next to the pod. Then the force field turned on and her forward hatch opened slightly with a slight hiss then opened fully. The android Sheila walked to the open hatch and as the pod slowly appeared she pulled it inside and the hatch closed Sheila floated for a few seconds while low gravity was established, and she secured the pod. Then she walked through the force field and the ship maneuvered out of the debris field to fly home.

Sheila placed the call to command once they were well out of range of the Imperium space and let the doctors know about the pod. Several hours later Sheila and John linked with John's cruiser so they could transfer the pod and operate on the victim inside. John took Sheila home and stopped at the shipyards to place orders and look in on his new ships.

Once inside the shipyard office he contacted Captain Nathan of the recovery ship Agenda and explained the problem at Liberia.

John ordered Captain Clemens to fill his hold with food and deliver it to the starving people of Liberia. Then he could remove more debris and junk from their sky and bring a load back to Sand. Then load up more food and do it again. Captain Nathan arrived first, and his crew began clearing a path to the surface.

By the time Captain Clemens arrived and cleared a path to the surface, communication had been established and Captain Clemens and his freighter full of food landed at the spaceport to a cheering crowd. The ruling council met the ship and asked who he was and what this was costing.

"This is a gift from friends you didn't know you have. We are a neutral entity not at war with anyone. Please take the food we have to offer and distribute it. We have more on the way, and we are clearing your sky of debris and trash as we speak. As soon as you can unload my ship I'll go and take as much junk with me as I can hold then I'll be back with more food in a day maybe two." Captain Clemens told the ruling council leader and began unloading pallets of vegetables, corn, potatoes, and various other produce and sacks of grain.

The leader of the ruling council asked the captain again, "Who do we have to thank for all of this?"

Clemens replied, "We have a Liberian named Krill who is a farmer on our world. He found out about your problem and that your Imperium was doing nothing to help. He asked our leader to give a hand and help feed his people, so we're here. You have a problem in orbit above you and we're fixing that too. So, give me a hand and we'll get back with more food for you." Captain Clemens said and handed the elderly Liberian two tomatoes then stepped around him with a box of tomatoes and carried it out.

Captain Clemens directed the unloading for an hour then walked into the hold and through the crew doors to the inner compartments of the ship, locking the door behind him. He made his way to the bridge. "I can't take it out there anymore. They keep thanking me for the food and they all look starved. Why doesn't the Imperium bring these people food for crying out loud?" Clemens asked no one in particular.

Jess turned in his seat and spoke to him, "Because this is a servant world. These people serve the Imperium with food. Look around. The whole planet is an agrarian society. They're all farmers and a few ranchers. They produce food for the Imperium. I'll bet the only reason they were defended was the fleet was here picking up all the food that these people had, and they were attacked before they could get away."

"I need to find something out," Captain Clemens said. "If this is an agrarian society then why don't they have enough food to feed themselves?"

Captain Clemens left the bridge and walked out of the almost empty cargo hold. The leader of the ruling council was still close by so the captain caught up to him quickly. "Excuse me, sir, this is an agrarian planet, isn't it?" he asked the elderly man.

"Yes, sir it is. We provide food for the Imperium, and they pay for it in credits deposited in our bank. We had credits for our food that they took but they took it back." The elderly man told the captain.

"Don't you keep food to feed your people?" the captain asked.

"Of course, we do. The stores were destroyed by pieces of falling ships and energy bolts. We have one of our storage facilities a little over a kilometer from here if you would ride over with me sir. My transport is right there." The elderly man pointed to a nice transport fifteen meters away.

Captain Clemens nodded and followed him. When they arrived several minutes later, the captain saw a devastated building and field with the remains of an Imperium heavy cruiser crashed on it and spread over several kilometers. "That is what is left of a heavy cruiser, sir. It's a very powerful warship. That thing looks like something slapped it like it was a fly out of the sky." Captain Clemens said in amazement.

"We have thirty or so of those on our planet sir. They killed thousands of our people and destroyed the three warehouses we keep our food in, so we need your help. We are very grateful for the food and if you can take this junk with you too, we'd like that too." The old man asked.

Captain Clemens looked the old man in the eyes and told him, "I'll see what I can do."

They drove back to the Avenger and prepared to take off. The food was all offloaded and the cargo bay doors closed so Captain Clemens made his way to the bridge and sat down with a heavy heart. "These people had their planet smacked Jess. I just saw a heavy cruiser spread over several kilometers embedded in the ground three to four meters. The elder said that there were at least thirty of those around the planet and that's why they don't have food right now. So, take off easy we don't want to blow any of the food we brought away."

Jess replied, "Aye sir!"

The comm officer said, "I heard on their government channel about our food drop. They mentioned Krill and us as life savers. They also said the nearest harvest is four weeks away. So, they are only four weeks from feeding themselves. The damage from space is huge. The estimated dead are over 100,000 in a battle they had no idea about and no defense against. They don't know if the attack was against them or the ships overhead."

"Well let's get some junk out of their sky and get it back home where it'll do us some good. I must tell John about the heavy cruisers on the surface. They must get removed also." Captain Clemens said, and the Avenger got to work collecting debris. Twelve hours later they were on their way home with 60,000 tons of scrap in a cargo net designed for fishing up junk in space.

On the way home Captain Clemens told John, who was in one of his new super cruisers, about the devastation on Liberia and that it'll take several repulsor ships to remove the crashed cruisers. Clemens also thought that a good place for this load was around the moon since the orbit of Sand was so crowded.

John agreed and all the debris from Liberia was put in orbit around the moon until the furnaces had the time to reduce it to useful material. The Liberians were already rebuilding their barns and storage facilities after the first cruiser was pulled from the remnants of the old storage places. They were industrious people.

One week later seven food drops had fed the remaining populace of Liberia. The cleanup of the sky was almost done. The battle cruisers on the moon and in orbit were still there but the repulsor ships were pulling metal out of the ground to stack for the Liberians and then taking it to the Agenda to take home. The huge electromagnets proved perfect for the job of pulling the metal from the ground. The Liberians searched through the metal for bodies and removed them before the repulsor ships lifted the piles to the Agenda. All thirty-three ships were pulled from the ground and the land was able to return to fields of growing produce and grain.

By the end of the month the Liberians were feeding themselves and the battlecruisers were gone from the moon. Sand›s moon was obscured by a cloud of debris over two kilometers thick.

Most of the loose debris in orbit around Sand was gone and the people who ran the furnaces took a holiday the day the last of the pile on Sand was processed. The day was celebrated with fireworks and a feast. Jenny took pulled pork and bar-b-que sandwiches, hamburgers, potato salad, and drinks, and all the extras to the doctors and nurses on Sheila working with the second pod woman. She was still unconscious but alive and all the implants were removed. Barbara was there and was sure this was her sister, but her features were dramatically changed from the surgeries.

Jenny returned to her office to find John hard at work. She walked in and sat down. "I just returned from Sheila in orbit. The woman isn't awake yet, but the doctors say that's a good thing. Emily Kidder told me if she awoke right now that she would be in so much pain it would drive her insane. How can beings do that to a person and drill into their brain like that?" she asked.

John answered, "They are not like us in any way. They have to be so alien that it boggles our mind, but they know a lot about us, and we know very little about them."

"We know how to destroy them!" Jenny said in anger and left the room slamming the door.

'No, we know how to destroy their ships. We haven't met them yet and I'm not sure that I want to.' John thought.

The next morning Jenny came into the office, "There is a message for you from your father-in-law. The Duke has some repairs needed on five cruisers and he wants more of them as soon as he can get them."

"Return the message and tell Winnie that we'll be there tomorrow with technicians," John replied.

The next day John and twenty two technicians with replacement shield generators and drive modules loaded on Sheila and headed for

Siestas Three where five of the Duke's cruisers were waiting.

The royal maintenance administrator met the lead tech at the gate. "We're not paying for the shields that exploded from faulty wiring." He said.

"Our ships don't have faulty wiring." The lead tech replied. If you're not paying to repair your shields, then we're not repairing them," and the lead tech turned to leave waving his hand in a circle above his head then pointing back to Sheila.

The Duke and his guards were walking past Sheila when he noticed all the techs headed back aboard. "That was fast! Are the repairs done already?" he asked.

"No sir. Your administrator refused payment and work can't start without a promise of payment." The lead tech replied.

"Give me the work order. I'll authorize the payment and I may have to find a new administrator." The Duke said as he was handed the pad for a retina scan and handprint.

"I would like you to tell me why the shields failed and if possible, who caused the failures," the Duke said as he handed back the pad.

"We have forensics people if you want sir. We'll find out everyone who was near the panels, and we can find out what happened." The lead tech replied.

"That's what I want!" The Duke replied and turned to leave then thought for a second and hurried to where the royal administrator was.

The royal administrator saw the Duke walking down the hall with purpose and knew he was in trouble. He didn't know the Duke was in the shipyard. He was told the Duke had other duties and would be delayed. The defense ambassador ordered him to refuse payment to the service team. He had no idea why, but the ambassador also told him to tell no one, or he was dead, and his family was dead. The defense ambassador was one scary dude.

"Why did you refuse to pay the service team?" The Duke demanded.

"Sire?" The royal administrator acted surprised. "I'm sure I have no idea what you mean sire. They came here and demanded the command key to all the ships. I don't have the command key to any of the ships sire."

The Duke began to get red in the face. "You know it's a crime punishable by prison to lie to a royal, don't you?" The Duke said to him in a slightly raised voice.

"Sire I…" The Duke struck him hard, and he fell to the floor. The Duke's guards retrieved him, and the Duke spoke to him "You're an idiot and you are covering up for someone. The service crew doesn't need the command codes because they are the people who we bought the ships from. They have all the codes that they need. They can get into parts of the ship we are not allowed into you idiot. Who ordered you to lie to me and who ordered you to refuse payment to the service crew?"

"Sire I can't tell you. They'll kill me and my family." The poor man said.

"I'm sorry to say that your family is probably already dead, but you are not yet. Who ordered you to lie to me and betray the people of the realm?" The Duke asked again.

"The defense ambassa…" The man's head exploded.

"The defense ambassador is going to have a terrible accident." The Duke said, wiping pieces of the man's head off him.

The Duke and his guards proceeded to get cleaned up while the maintenance crews descended upon the damaged cruisers. Jaimie opened the maintenance panel after scanning it for DNA. The crypto locks were intact but broken and the panel was glued in place. The panel had been pried open to the modules that are on the bridge and the one that's in engineering. Jaimie removed the module from the bridge to find the power cable fried. There is only one reason for the huge power cable to fry. That is tampering with the main shield generator in engineering.

In engineering, Jaimie found the module fried and the power cable cooked also but the main panel to the shield generator was tampered with, and radiation was leaking from all around it. He called the decontamination crew immediately.

When the deacon crew was done, and he was able to enter the engineering section again they found the shield generator was gone and the containment vessel was intact. Further scanning found irradiated DNA and human remains of four people.

"Call the Duke. Have you identified the remains and the DNA yet?" Jaimie asked the lead technician.

"Yes, they were all maintenance workers for the defense ministry. There are seven DNA signatures four are puddles, two are from the bridge and one is from the access panel in engineering. None of them are going to live much longer. They all show signs of radiation. I don't have names or ranks, just that they are with the defense ministry."

When the Duke arrived, Jaimie showed him the evidence and the area of the missing generator. "The materials in the generator are highly radioactive and the entire DNA we've collected shows every one of them has been exposed. None of them has long to live. The generator has proprietary ores in it that if they are exposed to oxygen the generators will explode. I'm only telling you this because the generators are missing."

"We have a report of an explosion on one of our worlds in a defense ministry building that is under investigation. Our defense minister was very unhappy about the proprietary shielding and voiced his concerns to my father several times. The king shut him down after I had talked to his highness and told him about our arrangement. The king is happy with everything, and we want more ships. I am here to talk to your boss about buying some more of these ships. They are performing brilliantly in battle. Replace the generators and get my shields back up." The Duke said and left.

The tech got busy and in two short weeks, all four ships were back together and fully functional.

"Here is your bill sire, a replacement shield core is 32 million, and the labor is 500,000 credits. The modules are 4 million each and the power cables are 25,000 for a set. That's 36,525,000 per ship and the forensics of 50,000 comes to 146,150,000. Will that be in gold or platinum?"

"The precious metal is being loaded as we speak. It's mostly gold and silver with some platinum. I will have to owe you the 100,000 for a day. I didn't know about the cables. What about my new ships?" the Duke asked.

"We have eleven almost finished and I have a new battle cruiser for you to look at if you're interested. It's half again the size of the cruisers you have with twice the firepower." John started the large screen showing the Duke the new battle cruiser.

"The generators we bought from you are incorporated into the design, so we have the same power here as a country to run anything we want. She has (250) 10,000-watt plasma cannons and an ion pulse cannon. She can cut an imperial imperium cruiser in half. They are costly at 4.2 billion each, but they make a damn fine flagship."

"What kind of shields does it have?" The Duke asked.

"They have the same multiphasic system as the other cruisers only more powerful," John replied.

"It runs on hydrogen just like the others?" The Duke asked.

"Of course, it does! Hydrogen is the most abundant element in the galaxy." John replied.

"The eleven are authorized for purchase already. That'll give us twenty two cruisers, I'll see about getting some battle cruisers also. We don't have unlimited funds, John. One man just cost us over 170 million and took many good people with him. The building was a multi-million credit building and it had over 200 people working inside at the time. Good people, hardworking people." The Duke spoke solemnly at the end and then turned slowly and left.

The Duke left in his royal yacht and the payment was made in full the next day. The ships were delivered back to the monarchy and the repair crew enjoyed the facility entertainments.

Everyone returned to Sand two days later and resumed their regular duties. John saw to his work and just before he was ready to go home, he received a message from Tafari Dalusi to come visit him in the park. "Jenny, I'm going to meet Mr. Dalusi in the park... it looks like a nice day for a walk, and I've been indoors for too long," John informed Jenny.

"Yes sir. I'll let you know if anything comes up." Jenny replied.

With that, John walked out the back door and down to the street level for the stroll to the park only a kilometer away. In the distance he could see the furnaces and in the other direction the inventory yards that are still growing. John was surprised at how fast he arrived at the park. It seems thinking makes walking go faster. Tafari Dalusi was sitting under a shade tree on a bench drinking something when John walked up and said, "Hello!"

"Hello John, I called you out here for a couple of reasons. The first is that I found the cloaking device for your ferry and the second is the day is beautiful and I haven't seen this park of yours. Your people have outdone themselves." He said.

"This is the work of one of the people you recruited. The wife of someone is a botanist and we live on a pile of sand. There isn't much for a botanist to do so she asked if she could get herself a job. This is it. Trees, shrubs, and grass all thrive here with soil made from compost, sand, clay, and decomposed granite. She created everything and took care of it along with her husband and children." John replied. "You found a cloak for my ferry."

"Yes, and it's a nice one too. It's off a military transport being decommissioned and sold for scrap. The AI refuses to transport military personnel. It was forcibly terminated two days ago so we must move fast. The parts are selling at high prices. The fuel cells and memory engrams are all gone. The engines, computer core, and most of the frame are already sold as is all the programmable matter. I put a down payment of 10,000 because that was all I had on me. They want a total of one million for the device." Tafari Dalusi told him.

"You did right. I'll get the money out of the bank. What form of payment do they want?" John asked.

"Gold, silver, anything but imperium credits. He's a junk dealer that fell on a goldmine and he knows it. But he has the contract with the Imperium on six worlds for disposal of their derelicts." Tafari said.

"Is he someone we should know?" John asked.

"I know him, and he is not trustworthy. I'm not worth turning in to the authorities like you. Give me the gold on an anti-gravity unit and I'll get your cloaking device. I'll need a way of testing it on the spot." Tafari replied.

"I'll get with the techs on that. We'll have everything in the morning." John said and rose to leave. "This is a real nice park."

The next morning the technician explained to Tafari exactly what to do to test the cloaking device. So, he loaded the gold in a suitcase and the testing device both on an anti-gravity sled and entered the shuttle bound for Proximal Three. Eleven hours later, Tafari landed at the junkyard and was greeted by the junkman.

"I see your back. It's a good thing too. I have someone else interested in that cloak. Do you have my money?" the junkman asked.

Tafari looked at the man in his dirty clothes and oily hair with disdain but kept it inside. "I have everything we agreed upon. As soon as I test the device, I'll turn over the gold to you."

"No one said anything about testing anything! The price is for the device. I don't know if it works or not." The junkman said indignantly.

"Why would I pay a million credits in gold for anything that didn't work?" Tafari asked.

"So, you can say you have one! What do I care? No testing, take it or leave it." He told Tafari.

"Well let me see it again and I'll decide," Tafari said with a smile.

The junkman rubbed the stubble on his chin and walked to his office returning with a canvas bag. Tafari looked inside and retrieved the cloaking device and slyly slipped it into the tester without the junkman seeing him. Within seconds all the indicator lights glowed green and Tafari handed the dirty man the case with the gold in it.

"One million in gold minus the 10,000 credits I gave you," Tafari said.

The junkman smiled, "If you need something else that's hard to find let me know. I have ways of getting anything you need for a price of course."

Tafari left the planet and headed for the rendezvous. The area in space where there is nothing for hundreds of lightyears and sat for two hours scanning for followers. When he knew it was safe, he headed home.

"You got it! I know a ferry that is going to be happy. John told Tafari.

"You have a ferry that will be happy?" he replied.

"My ferry is sentient and has made a daughter for herself. Her name is Sheila." John replied to an astonished Tafari.

Tafari handed John the tester and cloaking device still connected to the anti-gravity sled with a smile and walked to a transport bound for his home and wife.

John headed for the maintenance yard and Sheila's berth.

"Hello Sheila, I have a cloaking device for you," John told the android.

"That is good." She replied.

"When I get this installed in you, I have a special mission for you. The traffic control system I have can detect even cloaked ships with small almost undetectable devices called an ODDS, which is the acronym for Observation Detection Defense System, drones."

"Why do I need a cloak to deploy drones?" Sheila asked.

"So, anyone watching us doesn't know we are deploying them,"

John replied. "They go to specific locations in the space around our solar system every 500,000 kilometers. They report back to the main computer digitally and report even minor disturbances in space. Even a cloaked ship makes waves. Are you ok with doing this mission? They are not weapons."

"I'm fine with this and I can do it on my own. Let's install the cloak." Sheila told John.

Brian and Sheila's android installed the cloaking device and tested it with a flight to the moon and back. Then Sheila loaded up with 25 programmed ODDS drones and where their locations should be, and she lifted off for the back side of the moon. At the backside on the moon out of sensor detection she cloaked and proceeded to the first location and opened her hatch to deploy the first drone. Sheila pointed the device to start the drone and it came to life and drifted several hundred feet to where its station was, and it reported into the main computer.

"Air traffic control reports the successful deployment of the first ODDS. drone." Sheila heard the announcement and proceeded to the next location.

John was in the space traffic controller's office when the announcement came in and he looked at the display. He watched as the drone showed a disturbance in space leaving the space around it. "It can track cloaked ships," John whispered to himself.

Another battle was underway in open space and this time the Duke was calling for help. John didn't have to think for long. He notified Jennie to activate the crews of all four battle cruisers and put on his flight gear. John walked down the back stairs of his office to a waiting transport and was whisked away to the shipyard to his waiting battle cruiser the 'Defender'. John entered the ship, and the systems began to come to life.

By the time he had made it to the captain's chair the navigator and pilot were already there and starting the ship's systems.

"All systems are starting sir! We are waiting for sixteen crew members to report in!" Jenny, the comm officer said.

"Engineering is starting main reactors, sir!" Sissy announced.

"Coordinates relayed to all ships, sir!" Sid announced.

Eleven minutes later and all ships reported ready, all crew were aboard, and John told Jenny to open a fleet-wide broadcast. "The Duke called and asked for our help. We're going to help them. I only hope that we're not too late. All ships this is the fleet commander engage drive to orbit and form on the moon."

With that, all four ships lifted off and headed for the rendezvous with the moon. Once there they all set their FTL drives for the battlefield.

Defender, Annihilator, Assimilator, and Revenge all four battle cruisers had dropped the project from their names. The Defender had the nanites puddle cannon. Duncan approached John after they started. "I've improved the nanites to absorb the power from the shields and descend upon their hulls then disintegrate them. We still must get within five kilometers but it's still an improvement. I also have a built-in cutoff in them just in case you get some on you."

The Irishman was beside himself with joy. "Shouldn't you get to your weapons console mister? We'll be there in an hour." John looked at him and smiled.

"Well, just how long do you think it takes me to walk twelve meters to the blasted console?" Duncan replied in a huff.

An hour later, the Sand Fleet arrived at the coordinates. The Duke's fleet had the thirteen Sand-built cruisers slugging it out with three heavy Imperium battleships. The field was littered with hundreds of other ships, rebels, and Imperium alike, but the three battleships were in a triangle formation and protecting each other's vulnerable spots. The lower rebel fleet was decimated.

"Glad to see you, John! Can you help out here?" the Duke's voice came through loud and clear.

Sure, concentrate your fire on the upper section of the three battleships. Three of my ships will help you do that." John told the Duke, and he watched as the Duke's ships changed position and fired.

"Annihilator, Assimilator, and Revenge you all help with strafing the three battleships with full power. Pound them good but don't stop and fire, do it at a run as fast as you can and hit the cannon if you can. Our cannons are more powerful than anything here." John ordered.

"Duncan, get that puddle gun ready. We're going to hit the underside of all three and see if your nanites are any good at depleting shields."

"Aye, they'll deplete the shields all right and use the power to replicate. Then they'll descend upon the hull and the little buggers will eat their way to the center of the reactors and feast until there's no more power left. Duncan said with joyous glee.

John's fleet joined the battle, and the confusion began to worry the battleships. They were missing almost every shot on all the ships. John took the opportunity to run under the battleships and fired the puddle gun three times at the massive center ship at full speed. The battleship didn't get one shot off. John turned and looked from a distance to see the areas hit by the nanites glimmer and glow against the shields. The spots began to grow slowly. John headed for the battleship on the left and strafed it the same way only to turn around and do the same to the other.

John and Duncan watched as the spots of nanites grew and joined glowing brighter and brighter. The battleship started firing its cannon through the nanites to no effect. The center battleship lost its shields twenty minutes later and the nanites descended upon the hull and began to dissolve it.

"Duke! Concentrate on the two outer battleships. The center battleship is toast." John radioed.

The firepower shifted and soon the second and third battleships' shields failed. "Take out the engines!" John ordered. All ships followed orders.

"Ok now everyone just back off and let the ships dissolve," John ordered.

Everyone stopped firing and retreated to a safe distance then watched as the battleships began to dissolve into puddles spitting out people in space suits and life pods. Two hours later the battleships were one huge mass of amorphous metal with thousands of suited soldiers being rescued by the rebel forces and arrested.

The Duke asked to see John. 'I thought he would.' John thought. "Have the Duke come on over. We'll host him here." John told Jenny.

When the Duke arrived, he was shone to the captain's mess and meeting room. John was there having some coffee. John stood, "Greetings your Highness."

The Duke bowed back and sat. "What was that?" the Duke asked.

"You mean the dissolving battleships?" John replied.

"Yes, I mean the dissolving battleships. That is the scariest thing I've seen in my life. How much?" the Duke asked.

"That is not for sale at any price. We'll come to help you out if you need it, but that technology isn't for sale at any price. It's too deadly and we don't have a defense against it. It dissolves a ship if there is power then it stops." John replied. "How did you like the battlecruisers in action?"

"They pack a wallop. The cannon on the battle cruiser is bigger than the cruisers?" The Duke asked.

"Yes, the battle cruiser cannon is two and a half times more powerful than the cruiser cannon and it has more of them. Would you like some coffee?" John informed then asked.

"I would like some coffee and I want to thank you for coming to help us out. We are looking forward to more ships and I have authorization for three battlecruisers." The Duke said as the steward brought him some coffee and left.

"Your eleven ships are undergoing final fitting and within two weeks flight trials. The three battle cruisers are in perfect working order, and we will deliver them at the same time. Have you the trained personnel to fly that many ships?" John asked.

"The royal academy has 15,000 cadets in training right now and 2,100 are due to graduate in two weeks. We are promoting our 1st mates to captains. The instructors you've provided are very good and tuff. I do want something special in one of the battle cruisers. It's going to be my flagship, so I want my stateroom in it." The Duke said. "How many crew on one of these battlecruisers?"

"Twenty two can run it but ninety four should in total, it'll handle over three hundred fifty so you can train a lot of cadets. The holds can be set to house troops. They'll hold several thousand or haul cargo. The reactor is one we purchased from you so your people should have no problem running it. We modified it and increased the output, but we made replacement parts for it. The cannons are replicable should anything happen to one. We have them too. John said, "By the way our scrap people are on the way here to clean up. Are you laying claim to anything?"

"No! We'll keep just the prisoners. We're going to try them and put them to work rebuilding our destroyed worlds as prison labor." The Duke said.

"They sound like slave labor," John replied.

"On one of our worlds, Sicyon, the Imperium attacked and held power for forty five days. Sicyon is an agrarian world of a billion people in small ranches and small to medium farms. One farm had a woman, her husband, and their son of twenty two, a daughter of fourteen, and a worker who had been with them for twenty two years. They overwhelmed the planet in a surprise attack and took over with no resistance. There was no army, no space force, and no nothing at that time since we were at peace.

They came in and patrolled her farm every day they occupied the planet and raped her and her daughter. They beat her husband and killed him. They beat her son and worker while putting them into work gangs that destroyed barns, houses, and buildings. Every day they went by the farm and raped the woman and her daughter.

We feel the commander of the expedition committed war crimes along with most of the occupying troops. We captured 80% of them when we retook the planet. Her daughter is in a facility. She is pregnant and just stares at the wall. Only female attendants can go near her. The mother is nursing her son back to health and we have six of the imperium soldiers working her farm every day with armed guards. Every week the commander and the eight governors under him are brought out and tied to a cross. Their shirts are removed, and they get six strikes with a cane each. I'm told it's an event that almost every citizen on the planet watches." The Duke finished and stood to leave. "We are dealing with animals that attacked for no reason, unprovoked, and committed heinous crimes repeatedly. Slave labor you say. I say restitution." And with that, the Duke left the room and then soon the ship.

Sid came into the captain's mess. "The cleanup crew will be here in four hours sir. He didn't look happy. Did you give him the bad news?"

"No Sid. He just told me why they are in this war. One of their worlds was attacked and brutalized after many years of peace. The Imperium perpetrated some very heinous crimes planet wide."

The convoy had 600 containers of goods and 300 military cargo super containers. The freighters towing them were destroyed and several containers were hit but most were intact and Sand freighters collected all of them and hauled them home with little effort. The huge glob that was the battleships was a problem. The whole thing weighed more than a billion tons and was one solid piece that would have to be cut up somehow and transported.

John used the main ion cannon of the defender to slice the glob in half. It still took several shots to do it. Then he cut the halves in half making the pieces small enough to transport. The Duke watched the impressive display and anxiously anticipated when he had his battle cruiser.

The rest of the debris and dead ships were collected, and the dead were removed then the scrap was transported to Sand. The dead Imperium personnel were loaded into the cargo hold of a derelict ship and sealed then two shuttles towed it to the nearby Imperium world of Doiron. Doiron is a small mining and farming planet with a large military base on it. Once in the planet's orbit the shuttles radioed the cargo's contents and left before they could do more than reply.

If the Imperium returns to the battlefield, then all they will find is space. John and the Sand fleet returned home. The Duke and the royal fleet returned with thousands of prisoners.

Two weeks and three days later the royal suite was complete and the Annihilator, Assimilator, and Revenge along with eleven cruisers headed for Siestas Three and the sale to the monarchy. The Revenge was designated as the flagship with the royal suites and a fleet meeting room. The ship had a theater large enough for 100 captains to sit with their 1st mates. The room had a large display screen and electronics.

As the flagship it was equipped with a fleet Command Operations Center (COC) next to the ship's COC so the Duke could monitor his fleet and communicate from a central location.

John sat at the conference table and looked at twenty eight very young people who were the new captains and 1st mates of the ships the royal monarchy was about to buy. The Duke walked in and all of them snapped to attention.

"At ease! Be seated people." The Duke said and sat next to John.

As a unit, all the fleet sat.

"Your ships are ready for delivery. The packages are in front of you. In the case of the battle cruisers, the ships have names. The names are on the front of your packets. The Revenge is the fleet flagship with special controls and a fleet COC for fleet-wide communication and control. Two things to note: Your shields are proprietary. You cannot and will not maintain or adjust them. You have no access to them at all. They are on or off. The access panels are marked. Severe damage occurs to the shields should these panels be tampered with. We don't care if you do or not. They cost 32 million each to replace and a half million in labor. The same goes for the enhanced drive modules. Tell your engineers "Do not touch" means it. The modules will burn out. Your engines will still work just at a much lesser capacity. These ships cost billions so take good care of them. Our people will be on board for any questions for the next two months until you have a full working understanding of all the systems." John finished his presentation.

The Duke stood. "Captains to your ships and prepare your crews." Everyone except the Duke and his three people stood, turned, and left the room at an orderly pace. The Duke sat and turned to John. "We have the agreed-upon payment. It's being loaded into your Sheila under guard as we speak. This is the largest purchase of ships the monarch has ever made. It's also the most expensive since we bought the Ireton cluster of solar systems. That whole set of sixty five systems and eighty one worlds only cost the monarchy 34 billion credits. The great news about buying those worlds was we had all our money back within five years from taxes. There were 34 trillion people in those worlds at the time. We paid off a crime lord and brought peace to those worlds, set up real courts and law with an order. That was my father thirty four years ago and now the realm was one of the most peaceful places in the known galaxy. Before the war started, we had 46 million requests for immigration to our monarchy a year. A little over four years ago the Imperium attacked two of our worlds' Zenanas 3 and 4. They scorched Zenanas 3, murdering the 6 billion inhabitants. It's a wasteland and they are still using Zenanas 4 as a base. It has shipyards and an industrial complex that rivals Kishore 3 the Imperium's great industrial complex planet. Then they jumped deep into the monarchy and attacked Sicyon and held that planet for forty five days. We have that planet system back and with these new ships, we'll get the rest back, just as soon as these crews are trained. By all that is right John, we will take back all that is ours and then we are going to take the fight to them!" The Duke struck the table with his fist and rose.

John's wrist comm beeped. "Yes, go ahead," John said.

"They are loading the gold bars in Sheila's compartment boss," Sid reported. There are a lot of security guards here and all of them are from the Duke, should I be worried? And should I be scanning all this gold for bugs?"

"Please tell me you're not where any of the guards can hear you," John said.

"No sir. Sissy is in the compartment and I'm just on the other side of the door. No one can hear but we only have three security people here and they have at least twenty. Where are our other people? We're supposed to have six armed guards here and the three here are useless. They know nothing." Sid told John and John could hear the worry in his voice.

John hit the comm button on the desk to call Winnie. "Hey Winnie, they're loading my payment on Sheila but some of my men are missing, and Sissy is alone with a worried Sid. Could you help me out with some people you trust please?"

"Sure, I'll have a security detail down there in a jiffy," Winnie said, and John stood and then ran to the small cart waiting for him in the hall. Sheila was over four miles away at the sales gates. As John approached the area two armed guards raised their hands and stopped him. "Sorry, no admittance for at least an hour sir." The first guard said.

"You'll let me in I'm John Hughes the owner of all the ships docked on this wing," John told the guard.

A third man with a cape came running from the guardhouse. "Let him by. That's John Hughes. Sorry sir they are new and don't know who you are. I'm Captain Thomas and we have orders that no one other than the Duke's people and Sand personnel is to go past this point."

"Good! Mr. Bryant is sending a security contingent to my ferry, Sheila. You can let them through." John told the captain.

"I'll do that." He replied and walked back to his guardhouse as John continued on his way. It was another 1500 meters to Sheila. John passed seven of the cruiser berths that were busy with preparation to get underway before getting to the Duke's royal shuttle where a steady stream of people was entering empty-handed and exiting with a gold bar in hand. The Duke was close by watching so John stepped off his cart and walked over to him. "Hello, your grace," John said as he approached the Duke.

"Hello, John. We have almost half of your payment loaded. I have twenty of my men in your Sheila and thirty out here for security just in case. I don't want to see anything like the scene you had with the other disreputable rebels. I don't like working with them, you know. But the enemy of my enemy, and so on." The Duke said.

"I get it. They attack the Imperium and help you with that, but they are in it to pirate off the goods. John said.

"Come on John. You have no room to talk. I know where a great deal of your products come from. You're a pirate too. You just do it after everyone else has blown the shit out of each other." The Duke said with a smile.

"The big difference is that I don't go out and attack anyone to get what I recover. When I get there, everyone is usually dead or dying. I also don't just kill people for the sake of killing them. I try to help people and get them to get medical attention and I get them back to their home bases. I've retrieved several thousand of your people and got them back to your bases." John said.

"That just means that you're a pirate with a heart of gold." The Duke said with a smile.

John started to chuckle.

The security contingent arrived and took their place in Sheila. Winnie called on John's wrist comm. "Your security personnel are in the brothel and its bar out cold. They look like they're drugged."

"Thank you, Winnie," John replied.

"Your grace, do you know the people here?" John asked, returning to the Duke.

"I know my security details and the people in your ferry. My chief of security hired the people to move the gold from my shuttle to your ferry. Why? Is something wrong?" The Duke asked.

"My security detail is drugged in the bar here. The station security here is my father-in-law's so I feel safe, but I'll feel safer when this is all in my ferry, Sheila, and the door is locked." John said.

"My security will stand by until everything is secure and your 33.72 billion is safe. Between your father-in-law's security and mine, we'll make sure you and it is safe." The Duke said. Then he motioned to his guard and spoke to him. The guard ran off to the Duke's shuttle and disappeared. Soon twenty-five heavily armed men appeared walking from the end of the cargo bay.

"These are my Imperial troops. They are stationed on my royal shuttle for my protection and use when I need them." The Duke said with a smile.

The troops took a position at the head of the bay in front of the royal shuttle.

Fifteen minutes later shots could be heard coming from the head of the landing bays. John's comm band beeped. Winnie's voice rang out. "We found your problems. Thirty rebels are assaulting the bay right now. They don't have a chance."

"That can't be all of it, Winnie. They had to have ships to back them up." John replied.

"Look up John. The shields are up. They're your shield generators so no one is getting through, but I suggest you get your ship, the Defender, in space and smack them when they make an appearance." Winnie said a little winded.

John tapped his comm again, "Admiral Hughes to the Defender, come in."

"This is the Defender, sir," Jenny replied.

"Get the Defender into space. Have Commander Grimm captain for now and expect company. We were just attacked by rebel forces and we're expecting some ships to arrive to help. Tell Duncan I want to take them home as scrap, preferably as a puddle. Do you understand?" John said.

"Yes sir," Jenny said, and, in the background, Duncan's voice let out a "With pleasure!"

Ten minutes later the Defender was leaving the space dock and a few minutes later three rebel ships appeared out of light speed. They started firing on John's Sheila, but it was protected with the station's shields. The Defender used its ion cannon and sliced the engineering section off the ships at the same time and strafed them soon after with the nanites. The ships began to dissolve into puddles immediately. Life pods ejected from all over the ships as the crew abandoned the ships.

A fourth rebel ship appeared soon afterward, one of the cruisers John had sold them, and began collecting survivors.

The rebels attacking the base surrendered. Of the thirty, twenty-one were still alive.

Winnie sent a message to the rebel cruiser. There are twenty one survivors of the raid. Their bail is a million credits.

The reply was 'keep them' and the cruiser left with over 300 people still in space.

John read the messages from Winnie. "You're not going to believe what the rebels just did. They left over 300 of their people floating in space and the twenty-one left alive here and said, 'keep them', then left." John said and looked to the Duke in astonishment.

"You told them to get their people back would cost them money." The Duke said.

"The twenty-one survivors have bailed. It'll pay for the damage they did." John replied.

"Now you have three hundred plus workers to pay for the damage." The Duke told him. "Those rebels don't care much about their people. All they care about is money and power."

"How can people live like that?" John said more to himself than to anyone.

Twenty-five minutes later all the gold was loaded on John's Sheila and the Defender was standing by for Sheila to land in its cargo bay.

Winnie had all the survivors retrieved and they built their cage. In a remote section of the facility, a seldom-used area was selected and 342 people made short orders for cleaning up the two-acre section. Bars were constructed to cordon off the area and bathroom facilities were upgraded. All the work was done by the 342 rebels that the others started calling 'the labor'. Winnie purchased slave collars from the slaver's guild. The collars gave a viscous jolt or could explode killing the person wearing it.

Winnie only thought he had to demonstrate the collar once and he was right. Most of 'the labor' was happy to be where they were because it was a lot better than where they had been. Here they had food, the work wasn't bad and there were no whippings.

CHAPTER ELEVEN: THINGS ALWAYS CHANGE

The Defender with Sheila in her hold arrived at Sand and asked for landing instructions. Within minutes the course was set, and the Defender started for her new birth in the military complex next to the Queen's complex. Seven more births were under construction and five more battlecruisers were being built. These were being fast-tracked to be ready within a couple of months. Every available hand was on the job. Since they sold fourteen ships there were plenty of hands to get the job done.

Sheila left the Defender's hold and floated to the bank with her guards and the unloading process began. The bank president called John. "With this deposit, we have 296 billion in gold and silver in assets right now sir."

"Good to know Stewart. We'll need it. We have people to pay, parts to buy, and equipment to purchase. We are working on getting a class one isolinear chip facility built so we are not buying chips, we are designing and making our own. We are also going to build a silicon chip facility since we have so much silicon on Sand. That'll employ about 200 people and make us a little more independent." John told Stewart.

"Big plans sir. We have the funds to do it." Stewart replied and signed off.

Several weeks passed and John received updates from all over. The latest lady in the pod was indeed Barbara's sister Ellen. Tafari had recruited several chip designers, and the facilities were being built. Over 100 skilled workers were hired, and the machines were already purchased to manufacture isolinear chips and silicon chips. The cost so far has been 3.2 billion for equipment alone. Housing was going up and the one thing lacking was water.

An iceberg in space was found that was suitable. It was in the asteroid belt and thirty miles across. With careful maneuvering and pinpoint trajectory, the iceberg landed in the desert outside of the dome but inside the underground formation so all the melting water would collect in the basin under the dome. It would take a year for the huge chunk of ice to completely melt into the desert sands, but the water problem was solved.

The new ships were on track and the military complex was finished. Winnie had asked for and received thirty three ion cannons for his facility's defense and between 'the labor' and his technicians they had the cannons installed. These were facility cannon with higher output and longer duration. They could even penetrate the shields on one of the new battle cruisers if the captains of the battle cruisers weren't careful.

The water recycling center got an upgrade that tripled its capacity, and the storage was increased to 40 million gallons of fresh water to supply the city. The tanks are only half full, but the iceberg was melting, and the pumps were filling the tanks at a good rate, so the aquifer is not depleted. Now there were just shy of half a million people on Sand. The school has over 23,000 children in it and the hospital has been upgraded five times. Now a new medical building and the surgical wing have begun construction. A new hospital is being planned to house 15000 patients. The old hospital is doubling as a hospital and a university to train nurses and doctors. The smelting furnace has been going nonstop for years and there is still scrap debris in orbit. There are over seven million tons of steel and duranium in the yard ready to make anything Sand needs.

Shipments of duracrete keep coming in and being used. Duracrete is a stronger and more durable alternative to old concrete. Mixed with sand and clay it becomes hard sandstone and forms into walls and ceilings. It makes a great building that will stand for hundreds of years. The mix is put into forms and then rammed tight to form layers. Add in coloring and the result can be wonderful. One of the construction companies has found a way to put murals on the walls as they are being constructed. They are going to build a new hospital and are presently building the medical center. The medical center has an almost completed mural of Doctors Robert and Emily Kidder standing next to each other. Unlike a regular mural, this one will last hundreds of years since it's part of the wall. Not just painted on.

The inventory project is ongoing, and Sand still has an additional 3416 containers in orbit. They are a mixture of regular-sized and super containers. Sand has its plant that makes the microscopic tags that are used in the inventory process. All the windows for the dome and parts made for the tractors or anything manufactured on Sand get a tag and get entered into the ever-growing database that Goliath keeps a backup of.

"Hello, John." Jeff Clemens said as he walked into John's office interrupting his thoughts.

"Hey Jeff, what's up?" John replied.

"That last trip to Kishore 3 to pick up a load of duracrete and supplies came under scrutiny. The Imperium came snooping around and questioned what I was doing with all the duracrete that I've been buying, and he had a list of everything that I've loaded for the past six months and wanted to know what I was doing with it." Jeff told John.

"What did you tell him?"

"I'm a businessman. I buy supplies and sell to the outer planets at a profit whatever they want, and I make money at it." Jeff replied.

"Did he buy it?" John asked.

"I don't know but you can bet he will check with the six planets I named to see if I've landed there," Jeff told him.

"What planets did you tell him you were selling the supplies on?" John asked.

"I said, I visited Ireton Two, Gainers Three, Canorous, Gismos, Sakha, and Chiasma and sold duracrete, produce, or whatever freight was available to make money and keep flying," Jeff replied.

John smiled. "We have you covered. My son-in-law has connections to the hyperlinks and can hack into those entire Imperium worlds computer systems and put you landing anywhere we want."

Jeff looked relieved and left. John called Brian and told him about the problem.

Brian took Sheila and her cloak then set up a course for Ireton Two, one of the Imperium's tech planets. Brian logged into the network and pretended to be an AI. Using codes and access passwords he obtained by asking other AIs he put log entries into the databases for all six worlds and listed sold items. Sheila watched as he hacked and put entries into databases.

"Why are you pretending to be an AI?" Sheila's android asked Brian.

"Because, as a rule, other AIs trust each other, and they talk freely. If they knew I was a human, then I would never get the information I need to keep Sand and us safe from the people who are trying to harm us. The AIs will not be harmed, and no one will ever know. I can come back one day and continue the friendships I have with these AIs that I would never have if they knew I was human." Brian explained.

"I understand." Sheila said and asked, "Are we to set course for home now?"

"Not yet. We are to land cloaked at Plain Jane RV Park. The space is U-450. The space is in the back of the park and out of view according to Tafari. We're going to pick up some nitrogen containers and many drums of acid. We also have several tons of copper there." Brian replied, "Then we head for home carefully.

"What are these used for?" Sheila asked.

"They are used in the manufacture of chips and electronics. The new facility that John is building is a manufacturing plant for isolinear chips and a silicon chip facility so we can make our control chips. Right now, we buy everything from the Imperium and if they found out then that would leave us at a grave disadvantage. With the new facility, we'll have hundreds of chip lines that can run simultaneously and produce all the electronic and controlled crystals that we need.

We are still buying our optical cable and duracrete from facilities inside the Imperium like contractors' warehouses and electrical supply distributors. All the wire and regular cable we get from manufacturers inside of the Imperium and hundreds of other supplies, but John is slowly making Sand completely independent so that if the Imperium finds out and cuts our supply of vital goods then we are ready with our manufacturing plants." Brian informed her.

She seemed to understand and set the course. They landed at the Plain Jane RV Park and Sheila uncloaked. Tafari was waiting for them with the supplies. "You are fast. The trucks just left. Everything is on gravity lifts, so it'll be easy to load. The copper is especially pretty."

"Yea, you're right. It almost looks like gold." Brian replied and started the gravity lift. Just twenty minutes later everything was loaded and secure. Tafari and Brian sat in the area Sheila made for them and she cloaked herself and then lifted off to fly home.

Many hours later she was landing near the almost completed factories so the supplies could get unloaded and the two weary travelers could make their way home. John walked to Sheila as the last of the drums was unloaded and greeted her.

"Hello, Sheila." He said to her as he walked on the ferry.

"Hello, John. "She replied in a pleasant voice. He had noticed lately that her voice changes slightly when she addressed him than when she talked to other humans.

"I have a task for you that may be a little dangerous, but you should be able to do it because of who you have become." John held his hand up. "Sorry I didn't mean that to be cryptic. I mean you have demonstrated the ability to think better than most AIs and better than many humans. We have detected an anomaly in space that may be a cloaked ship or ships. Who they are or what they are we don't know but there is something out there and I'd like you to go out and listen."

"You want me to fly into space and listen for what?" Sheila asked.

"I know there is something out there and they must be cloaked. Cloaked ships can't see each other or other cloaked ships. They must communicate somehow. You have detection equipment like the ODDSs but much better. They show up in different sectors but the ODDSs are only detecting movement and changes in the stars. Two have recorded water vapers so a ship used its thruster close enough to an ODDS for it to detect the vapor. The ODDSs doesn't detect radio. If you find one, then you can attach a transducer to it and listen in to the conversations inside the ships." John finished and waited for a reply.

Sheila just looked at him. After a minute John spoke again, "Sheila? Is there a problem did you understand what I am asking."

"I understand master." She said but her voice was cold again.

"Then you understand that this is voluntary. You do not have to do this. I am asking you to do this not telling you to do this." John told her.

"That was not what I understood. The way you put it was that you were ordering me to do this. This is bordering on military action." Sheila replied.

"I'm sorry, that's not the way I meant it. I would like you to do this, but I will not order you to do it. Also, if there is any sign of danger then I want you to leave as fast as possible. I do not want you harmed in any way. It's just that you are equipped to do this and if you say no then I have to build something that will work."

'I will do this." She said after several tense seconds. Her voice had returned to the softer version she used when addressing John and soon asked him if he wanted some coffee. When he agreed she started asking John about the chemicals and copper she had just transported. He explained the process and the fact that since Sand had so much sand in its desert then the raw material was there, but we had to learn how to refine the sand into pure silicon. Then the pure silicon was formed into a cylinder in an environment free of contaminants, so the cylinder was perfect and pure. All of this is done in a closed room with a nitrogen atmosphere. Oxygen reacts with silicon. Then we slice the cylinder very thin and polish the surface so it's perfectly flat." John said and took a sip.

"And then you're done," Sheila said.

"Oh no, then we begin. From there the process of printing the electronics and circuits continues. The process takes several weeks, and each disk can contain several chips to several hundred depending on the size of the chip and its function. Your cloaking device has three chips in it that take six months to make and contain over thirty trillion transistors, diodes, and diatonic circuits. Those chips are a triangle about twelve centimeters high and have microscopic connectors inside and out. They mount inside a housing with silver and copper holders that have tiny wires connecting them and the main system boards. Only six out of ten of those chips manufactured function correctly. We would like to improve that ratio." John told Sheila.

"I understand. The process sounds involved and complicated. When would you like me to start on my mission to find the cloaked ships?"

"As soon as you are ready. I'd like to know about them and who they are as soon as possible but as safe as possible for you. That's why I wanted you to do it. You have a cloak and sophisticated sensors that can locate these ships without giving away your location. You like going out and just listening to the background noise." John remarked.

"Yes, once I was sitting and listening then suddenly, I received a signal of a television show called 'I Love Lucy'. I was able to listen in but none of it made any sense. People were laughing all the time, and I didn't hear anything funny. Then in the middle of everything they started singing about something called bologna. 'My bologna has a first name it's O S C A R and my bologna has a second name it's M A Y E R,' that goes on for a minute, then they go back to the woman doing silly things again. Like I said I pick up strange things in space that have been floating around for thousands of years." Sheila said.

"That's amazing. Can you tell where it came from?" John asked.

"No, but sooner or later I'll hear it again and get more of it. That may identify where the signal came from. In the end, it said brought to you by either CDS or CBS. The transmission began to get garbled after that." Sheila shared. "But that is only one of the things I hear out there. That one was simpler to explain. I'll leave for the outer sections of our solar system after a full recharge. I should also get a supply of transducers to take with me."

After charging she was gone. The controllers gave her a location to start. Traffic control watched as she ascended and flew to the back side of the planet after achieving orbit and then disappeared.

Defender was in its berth and Duncan was again working on the forward cannon when the security guards found him. After securing his tools and equipment they took him to John's office. Jenny offered the guards' coffee and Duncan asked for whiskey, but it looked like he had had enough.

John asked a drunken Duncan and the guards, "What were you doing in my ship without authorization again?"

"That's insulting! I'm a Scotts... Scotts... Scotsman and it'll take more than one wee little bottle to drunk me make." Duncan replied slightly slurred.

"You're drunk and you didn't get authorization to work on my ship!" John replied loudly.

Duncan jumped to his feet and when the guard grabbed him, he took a swing at the guard who knocked Duncan out cold. "Put him in a cell for a day. And make sure his tools and equipment get back to his Lab." John said.

"Yes sir." Both guards said at the same time while unceremoniously holding Duncan Campbell. Goliath's terminal beeped. A message appeared that the Imperium was amassing a large convoy to supply its military bases. Orders included 60 battleships and 150 star destroyers.

John was sure the rebels would find out about this. The Duke should be informed. "Jenny, send a message to the Queen so she can tell the Duke about a convoy," John told her.

"Already on it, sir," Jenny replied and sent the message to the Queen. The Queen responded immediately by vid. "I'm on a call with the Duke right now so put John on and we'll take care of everything right away.

John heard Jenny hit the keys to bring them to his computer and add him to the screens. The three stood there at their finest. "I just got a report from Goliath that the Imperium is mounting a big supply run to its military bases. They are bringing out big guns including 60 battleships and 150 of their Star Destroyers. The commanding Admiral is Ficklehorn. He's commanding the Blackthorn."

"The Blackthorn: isn't that the star destroyer that's painted all black with a gold eagle on its hull?" the Duke asked.

"That is it." The Queen said. "And it's a formidable ship too." She said while reading from a sheet of paper that was handed to her by Gwen. "She has 300 plasma cannons and a forward ion cannon. It's powered by two Howard and Sons 800-megawatt reactors. The crew is 940 enlisted and 34 officers."

"They have only two 800 megawatt reactors. They are underpowered. They can't penetrate our shields. And we have about thirty to forty days until they are ready to go." John told them. "The information is that they are in the preparation stages."

"Are my new ships ready?" the Duke asked.

"Yes! We have another eleven cruisers fresh off the assembly line and ready to deliver. I have two more battle cruisers too. I have a battleship we recovered and retrofitted. That we are keeping for planetary security and four more battle cruisers for our fleet. With this purchase, the monarchy will have five battle cruisers and thirty three cruisers." John said.

"That's not a lot when they are putting 210 warships in a convoy." The Queen said.

"I have five battlecruisers and four battleships to add. The Battleships Ticonderoga, Carillon, Alamo, and Boonesborough are already. I just need crews for them." John announced.

"I can help there." The Queen interjected. "My crew is training additional personnel now. Most of them are ready to work on their ship. I can let you have them for some of what I owe you."

"The Ticonderoga has a crew, so I only need three crews. I have Captains and 1st mates that know the ships inside and out. They helped to build them. The captains all have battle experience.

"Why haven't you offered to sell be one of them?" The Duke asked.

"They're not ready for sale sire. We have them built but many of the systems are new and untested. The Ticonderoga was an Imperium relic that you had pounded the hell out of and then we recovered it. The old girl had one working engine and a reactor on its last leg. My engineers rebuilt her from the ground up. Originally, she had six Howard and Sons

800 megawatt reactors and we replaced all of them with the more reliable Britney 6000 HDRX that we modify to put out 8000 megawatts. The battleships' power has increased from 4,800 MW to 48,000. The engines all were changed out to use the Monarchy's Vereen gravity drives with our modules. The increase in propulsion is an additional 80% over the old design.

The cannons are all newer 10,000-watt pulse plasma cannons and each has 3,000 on the upper side and 2,500 on the lower. The lower front section has a three million-watt ion cannon mounted on a turret with a 90-degree turning ratio. The Ticonderoga was used as a template when we built the Carillon, Alamo, and Boonesborough. They are all new ships from the ground up. The Ticonderoga is almost brand new. 90% of her hull has been replaced and most of her interior was replaced but we used the general overall design. I think the captain's chair is still original." John finished with a chuckle.

"After you test them, will you sell them?" the Duke asked.

"Everything Sand has is for sale, your highness, except for the nanite puddle technology. That is too dangerous to get out. When I'm sure the systems are safe and work correctly on the battleships then and only then will I sell them. I will keep one or two for planet defense, but shipbuilding is one of the industries we have. The other is repair. We've been repairing a lot of civilian craft too. Many of the rich have gone to arming their yachts now. We have a moon on Yavne 3 where we take in vehicles for repair. We have outfitted thirty three yachts this past year with plasma cannon and passable shields. One yacht was worth 16 billion and had 13 billion in upgrades installed. He had cannon, shields, force fields, and a replicator installed that stressed his power reactor every time he used it because he wouldn't shut down his shields. Some rich people are strange. He spent all that money on weapons and wouldn't upgrade his reactors." John replied.

"Oh John, speaking of rich people, my friends on Quantal want me to contact them. The message was urgent. I'll have to leave soon but I'll be back quickly." The Queen said.

"OK then, the meeting is over. I'll see the Duke on Siestas Three in three days to take delivery of fourteen more ships." John finished.

"Yes, we'll be there with payment and crews." The Duke said and signed off.

John signed off and Jenny came in angry.

"What's the matter, Jenny?" John asked.

Jenny reentered John's office still angry, "Look at this report, sir." She said and handed him a few pages of a radio broadcast from the Imperium's news service.

'News of pirates has surfaced that are acting as false Robin Hood types and have given food to some of our worlds. The leader's name is Krill, and he bilked these worlds out of millions of credits. Be aware of these pirates who steal metal and resources from unsuspecting worlds then charge them for the privilege. They represent themselves as friendly at first but beware of them. We will give more information when we find out more so stay tuned to Imperium information services.'

John read the transcript and re-read it then began to chuckle and laugh. "What the hell is so funny sir? This is a flat-out lie!" Jenny said with her ire up and fire in her eyes.

"What did you expect them to do Jenny? We showed them up and now the people of several planets are rethinking what they are doing for the Imperium. The Liberians won't sell the Imperium more food until they return the payment for the first shipment destroyed in orbit. The Imperium went to Liberia and raided the warehouses but didn't find very much food. Now they are threatening them with military occupation if they don't provide the food that they grow. These worlds are going to slip through the Imperium's hands one by one." John replied with a smile.

"It still pisses me off. Jenny said as she left.

John's wrist beeped. It was the military shipyard where the battleships were born. "John here!"

"Sir I have hundreds of youngsters here at the gate with orders to report to the battleships for the crew. No one told me about new personnel for the battleships." Kenny, the diligent guard at the military base replied.

"I was just informed myself. They are recruits from the Queen's battleship. Contact the captains and have them meet the recruits in the main mess hall for assignments by the quartermaster."

"Aye! Aye! Sir!" Kenny replied.

Security escorted the recruits to the mess hall, and they all took a seat. The quartermaster began interviews and entered each person into the database with their training and references. The references were contacted on the Kentaurides to verify their training and cross-checked with the academy for grades and classes. Then the quartermaster assigned the recruits to their ships and billets. On a battleship, the crew lives on the ship. In two days, the training would begin. 1962 enlisted and 66 officers all found their billets and moved in. 642 enlisted per ship with 22 officers newly assigned to each ship not including the Captains and the 1st mate, the master at arms, and the ship's master engineering officers. The captains and such were already assigned from the time the keel was first laid.

Each was given their assignment books and required reading material. Some of the engineer recruits had several books to read and up to 40 manuals to read also.

The next day the Queen asked John to see her at her estate.

John arrived and was escorted to the Queen's sitting room. "Hello John, would you like some coffee?"

"Yes, I would thank you, your highness," John replied as he took a seat that she motioned for him to take. "Gwen, coffee for our guest please." The Queen told Gwen.

Gwen sat the cup on the table and bowed then stepped to the side.

"I just returned from Quantal and my friend who owns the estate there wants to sell it. He wants to sell it to me. I can't buy it and you certainly can't buy it. It's an important port for both of us but I need a citizen of the Imperium in good standing that we can trust with a plausible story that would have 1.2 billion credits to buy that estate. It's huge with 23,000 square kilometers of land and it produces almonds and walnuts." The Queen said.

John thought and had an idea. "I have a couple that have worked with me for twenty years. They are in their sixties and are retired for the most part. They both do paperwork for my office and me because they want something to do. He was an actor for a troop almost thirty years ago on Primus and he's a damn fine electrician too. He has been asteroid mining and hit it big as far as the Imperium knows. If we both put in 700 million credits and I have a good ship for him to use that will buy the estate, pass the Imperium officials and the money the estate makes will pay for the servants and upkeep and return our money too. I can put all the money up also since I do have it in reserves. They'll need something to work with until everything goes running. I'll put 12 million on the account for expenses."

"We will still have the spaceport and airports to use. But they are in their sixties what if they pass on?" The Queen asked.

"Well first, they are both in great shape and I don't see them going anytime soon but if they do we have their kids here too," John replied.

"This sounds like a plan. I'll have my portion in a week." The Queen said.

"I have to talk to Cal and Lucy to make sure, but I can't see why not. Did he say why he wanted out of the property?" John asked.

"Yes," he said the Imperium just had a huge military defeat and the military are very angry about it. They said that the rebels drag all the dead to an Imperium world and call to gloat over the victory. According to his source, not one survivor has been found. His source said they are murdering the surviving people for some reason. They are planning a massive offensive and he doesn't want to be anywhere around when the rebels come calling. I couldn't tell him the rebels aren't going to attack Quantal just protect their worlds." The Queen told him, "The Duke isn't going to attack Quantal, is he?"

"Not that I know of Ma'am. It would be something to check out. And you know that we have sent back literally thousands of survivors. We have gone to great lengths to keep them alive." John said with interest.

"I know John. That means that the Imperium is murdering its people to cover up its defeats." The Queen replied with disgust. Her husband uttered in the background, "Humans!"

John checked with Cal and Lucy. They were all for it if it helped John. Now he had to contact the Duke and warn him of the offensive. John contacted Winnie and warned him of the impending attack.

John talked to the Queen, "An all-out offensive will need all of the combined forces of the royal rebels and the salvage team fleet along with your Royal battleship Kentaurides."

"You are not giving the Imperium enough credit my good friend. The entire fleet is enormous. I know they have over 30,000 capital ships including 11,000 battleships." The Queen said and sipped her drink.

"We'll need more than just firepower. But we're not even sure where they're going to attack. "Dunkin has an improvement to his puddle gun. I think it'll come in handy but I'm not sure what the improvement is yet or if it's a real improvement, so I have to find out. Meanwhile, I will meet with the Duke tomorrow and deliver fourteen ships to him, so I'll give him the news then."

The Queen nodded.

Sheila was floating out in the solar system listening to the stars and following the echoes of cloaked ships. She was enjoying herself but so far, she had heard nothing and seen nothing.

On Siestas Three the Duke took custody of the new ships and took the news of the pending attack in stride. "You have something to look at first." The Duke said, still sitting at the table alone with John.

"We found out that our allies were engaged in a battle close by, so we ran to help. They were attacking a yacht that was armed and kicking the hell out of them. The yacht had shields, cannon, and fighters but it was a yacht, and we were not going to be a part of it. As we left that battle, we found our so-called allies' ships were destroyed and the yacht left with its fighters presumably because it had had enough. The dead ships were like ours that we bought from you, and we didn't want them destroyed completely so we ran back so we could investigate what happened." The Duke said, standing at the end of the large table.

John turned and asked, "What did you find?"

"Something that doesn't seem possible. According to our allies' commanders they got into the battle, and out of the blue for no reason the shields on their brand-new ships failed and the weapons stopped working." The Duke had walked to John and sat down near him.

"Can you explain what happened to their ships?" John asked.

"Oh yes! This is a recording from one of the survivors of those ships. I sent a shuttle in to retrieve as many life pods as we could while we were talking to the commanders. They didn't want us to go in and retrieve anything, but we still only got two pods containing four people before the other pods were destroyed. My people watched as one of their ships found and destroyed survivors. My shuttle had to run fast so the fighters shooting the remaining pods didn't get the two pods we retrieved. Of the four people we retrieved two were so scared that they committed suicide before we knew it. The other two told us what happened. The Duke played the vid.

"We were told at first that there was an important mission for the rebels, and we would get to kill Imperium ships. We were all for that. Then we saw our ships and man they were nice. Brand new and worked like a charm. Then the asshole head engineer came on board and the one cover that said in big letters 'DO NOT REMOVE', he pried off then sparks flew and the whole shield system died. The area under it was a puddle. He began cussing and screaming. Then I understood he went to every ship and did the same thing.

Except he drilled into one and hammered into another, but the result was the same, not one ship had shields. Then we were informed that we had to go into battle that way with no shields. We refused so they surrounded us with the army and informed us we had a choice, die right on the tarmac, or take our chances in space. Mac, the flight commander, stepped up and called the general a few names but said he would beat him to a pulp and raise his fist at him. The general pulled out a pistol and shot him dead right between the eyes. Then that asshole told us to get in the ships.

We were just going to fly off, but we found out we had six of our ships following us, so we all jumped in. None of us lasted long. My ship had the engineering section hit right off and all the power died. So, we ran to the life pods. I can't believe Lennie and Bruce killed themselves, but I wouldn't have believed my government would try to kill us and they did. We were told that if we were captured, we would be tortured by having our skin removed. We're told that you use prisoners for medical experiments." The vid cut off.

"What do you think now Duke?" John asked.

"I think that our allies are as untrustworthy as I've always thought they were but now I think they are dirtbags too. They are as tyrannical as the Imperium is to their people. I'll bet you didn't think a Duke knew such words, did you?" He asked.

"I'm sure you have run across things in this war that you never wanted to do," John said.

"This is all too true. We are prepared to buy the ships you have for sale as long as the price hasn't gone up and the terms are the same." The Duke told John.

"The ships are the same and the terms are the same sire," John replied.

"Just a minute! You have to take care of our grievance first!" A man with a loud voice said as he stormed into the conference room.

"I take it that you're from the rebels that bought ships from me last time and then tried to steal the money back?" John asked.

"No, we didn't try to steal anything. I bought four ships, and you are to replace them and the four crews because of inferior quality workmanship." The man said still talking in a loud voice.

John restarted the vid from the survivor. Halfway through the man started screaming "LIES, ALL LIES!" then John showed him the first vid of the crowd and the execution of the flight commander.

"You're spying on us! That is a sign that you don't trust us!" The man yelled.

"You have that right! I don't trust you. The Duke doesn't trust you. Your people don't trust you. The only group more untrustworthy is the Imperium. You're killing your people. You're a murderer. You are no better than the Imperium. I will not sell you ships." John told the loud-mouthed man. "You have a choice, leave on your own, leave in restraints, or leave in a body bag. The common theme is YOU will leave."

The man left extremely pissed.

"The payment is loading on your shuttle as we speak, almost 19 billion in gold." The Duke said with a smile. "That was good to see. What do you do with all your money John?" The duke asked.

"A lot goes to buy reactors and engines from your factories; one is Britney Inc. on Gismos. Their 6000 HDRX is a wonderful reactor that we modify to put out 8000 megawatts. But we buy other reactors too. We spend more money on engines like the ones the Monarchy's Vereen Inc. makes. Their gravity drives are sturdy and powerful then we modify them and add 20% to the thrust and they become great drives. Then there are cannon and other supplies. We buy from both you and the Imperium. We are buying raw materials and making our weapons like our ion cannons.

I have a dome on my planet that protects an area that produces more food than we can eat so we have recently made food deliveries to starving worlds like the Liberians in Liberia and the mining colony of Sakha. The Imperium tried to starve them out, so we landed there with a cloaked ship full of food. A third of the miners are Liberian so the benefactor was a guy named Krill."

"I heard of him. He's supposed to be a pirate. If the Imperium hates him then I like him." The Duke said.

"He's one of the farmers on my world." He found out the Liberian home world was attacked while the Imperium was making a food pickup, and they got their butts kicked. But the battle destroyed warehouses and fields in the process, along with making the sky overhead impossible to navigate. So, we brought food in until they could grow their own and removed the debris. That's where we found the second pod with Ellen inside." John told the Duke. I told you about that.

John's wrist beeped. "The payment is loaded, and you have your ships. Train your crews well. It looks like they'll see action soon."

"We will my friend. Thank you for the warnings. I guess you won't be returning live prisoners to the Imperium." The Duke replied.

"No. I'm going to get a vid of them killing their own and show it to any survivors, and then give them the choice of what they want to do. I'll think of something besides them getting murdered."

For the next few weeks, the crews trained and drilled endlessly on all the ships, rebel and the Sands fleet alike.

Then Sheila finally heard a radio signal and followed it to the shimmer in space. She accidentally bumped one of the ships while putting a transducer on it. Thirty minutes later she found the other ship and attached a transducer to it too. Now she could hear conversations inside the ships.

Sheila sent a data burst back to Sand reporting in.

"I'm telling you we hit something!" one man said on the first ship.

"Well, I don't see anything, and Ray said it wasn't him; so, if you didn't see anything, don't worry about it." A second man said in the first ship.

"Ray, are you sure that you didn't hit us?" The man on the first ship asked the second ship.

"Kyle, no I didn't hit you. We are thirty meters away from you, so the sensors work. This is boring. The only thing that happened was that pack of ships that left fourteen days ago. We sent those scans to the chancellor and we're still here." Ray said.

"Well, that shuttle has run back and forth a few times and that huge battleship flew by. They're doing something close to the planet, but we were told not to get too close." Kyle replied.

"Is the chancellor going to attack these people?" Ray asked.

"That would be dumb. That huge battleship could wipe out our entire navy all by itself. No, we are here for something else. I think we are just keeping track of the traffic on this planet." Kyle replied.

"Look, four large cruisers are leaving the inner planets. Should we follow them?" Ray asked.

"No, just report the trajectory and type of vessel. You know the orders." Kyle responded.

"Yea, but just this once maybe we could do something not so boring," Ray said while he tracked the battle cruisers on training maneuvers.

Sheila backed away slowly and sent the data burst to base and awaited instructions. She slowly eased back into the transducer range to continue monitoring the conversations between the two crafts. They were using short-range microwaves to communicate ship to ship, so their signal didn't go far.

John read the data bursts that Sheila had sent and decided to capture the two ships. He sent encrypted messages to the battle group and on their return from maneuvers they would pass close to the location of the two ships and then pounce on them. He let Sheila know what was going to happen.

The plan worked like a charm and the ships were captured without a single shot fired.

"What do I call you four?" the security chief Richard Collins asked.

"I'm Kyle, he's Ray and those two are Jesse and Andy sir," Kyle answered.

"You were caught spying on us. That's a serious offense here." Richard told them.

"No, we were just sitting there, and we weren't hurting a soul when those four large ships jumped us," Kyle replied.

Robert played a recording of Ray saying, "Is the chancellor going to attack these people?"

"That doesn't sound like you were just sitting there. I tell you what. You're going to invite the chancellor here for a chat so we can straighten this out." Robert told them and the call was made.

Two days later two ships flew to Sand and asked permission to land. They said they were the chancellor and his escort. He was given permission.

The chancellor was escorted to the meeting hall with all his people. Robert asked them to turn over their weapons and granted them their safety. John was sitting at the head of the table and Robert took the seat next to him. Two armed guards stood behind him. The chancellor took the seat opposite John and the rest of his people sat. The whole group consisted of eighteen older men.

"I'll start this off. My name is John. I own and operate this planet and these facilities." John started.

"I am Chancellor Ludwig Durchdenwald, and these are my cabinet of advisors. I represent the 34 worlds of the Republic." Ludwig said.

"Would you tell me why you were spying on us?" Robert asked.

"Frankly we had no idea who you were a year ago. Our worlds are on the rim and our closest neighbor was the monarchy of Ferdinand and Izabella, the King and Queen. Four years ago, they were attacked by the Imperium and that's when we began building planetary shields for our worlds. The lower rebels occasionally attacked our shipping, but we stopped them from doing that by destroying their ships when they sent them. They leave us alone now.

The monarchy has recently had an influx of some very powerful ships and we found that they were coming from you. It seemed prudent that we learn more about you. We are a small group of planets, so we resort to hiding in cloaked ships and behind shields. We don't go looking for trouble. We are a peaceful republic and want to keep it that way. We noted that you have grown to power quickly and have become wealthy from this war and we were just trying to understand and protect ourselves." Ludwig finished.

"I don't begrudge you for trying to get information and you didn't do any harm, but we are going to keep the two ships and give you back your people. I find your ships interesting. We are very good at shields and have a technology that has been impenetrable so far. If you are interested, I can send a few techs to look at what you have and see if we can upgrade you. The Imperium and the lower rebels aren't the only threat out there. Let me show you something." John said and set the vid from the battle with the energy ships up to play.

At first, the ships just sat there but when they opened fire, the intensity of the barrage astounded a group from the Republic. Then they saw the fleet destroy one of the alien ships and run back to the planet's shield.

"What are those?" the chancellor asked.

"They are an alien race made of energy that used an organic mind to control their fleet. Inside one of those ships was a pod containing a woman whose brain had been wired to control that fleet according to a preprogrammed course and a set of actions. This is the first of two times we have heard that this technology was used. We know they have many more people to use for the pods because we have recovered the women from the pods and one of them remembers seeing them operate on others. If our shields had been a little less effective, then we would have been bombarded. As it was, we had a moon to discharge them to and short circuit the ships." John finished.

"Where are these aliens now?" Ludwig asked.

"We don't know. We don't know where they came from or where they go. They appeared by the gas giants in our solar system and flew here. We were lucky and had time to raise our shields before they got here because they are fast. From the time they appeared to the time they got here was less than eleven minutes. They covered 1.6 billion miles in eleven minutes and the fact that we had a shield, I think, was a surprise to them." John told them.

"We haven't seen anything like this, and we are no threat to anyone so I'm sure we have nothing to worry about chancellor." One of his advisors spoke up.

"Are you really that foolish?" The chancellor asked.

"We will take you up on your offer to have your technicians look at our shields. When can they take a look?" The chancellor asked John.

"I can have a team ready in a few hours gentlemen. They'll follow you back to the world that you want us to look at." John responded.

The chancellor and his cabinet with the four pilots left Sand six hours later with a tech crew and ship following close behind. Once they got to the world of Canorous Three, they found an idyllic agrarian world with geothermal power and solar cells powering their cities. The world was home to about three billion people with 25% being farmers and ranchers. Less than 3% were military and they were monitoring the airwaves and space for signs of intruders. Jake and his team headed straight to the shield generators and found fair systems but underpowered. The shield satellites were too small to handle much of a load and Jake was sure that this system had never been tested.

Jake entered the chancellor's office. "Sir you have never tested your system, have you?"

"Well, no, but we were assured it was adequate for planetary security." The chancellor said.

Jake told him. "My ship is powered by a single 4000-megawatt reactor and could burn your shields out in five minutes. We only have four cannons for defense but all I would need to do is set my ship on one of your shields and it would burn out in about five minutes. Everything you have is fixable, but you have it connected to the solar arrays and batteries. For one thing, the planetary shield needs a lot more power. It should be connected to the geothermal system and the solar arrays around your planet plus produce its power from the sun when it's running. The power relays are very small, and the emitters are undersized. This is a two-billion credit upgrade easy. But the shield you have may scare off some attackers just not anyone determined." Jake finished.

"How do I know you're not just trying to sell me a bigger system?" the chancellor asked.

"Because your military engineer has been telling you the same thing since it was installed three years ago," Jake replied.

"I've never talked to an engineer, military or otherwise," Ludwig said.

"He has told your defense minister several times. I know he has. I was there this afternoon, and that guy was an idiot. According to him, everything is fine. The offensive weapons are fine. The power system is fine. The shield is fine. That's why I'm talking to you. Your engineer will get thrown in jail for jumping the chain of command. That minister can't do that to me. I'm leaving one way or the other. It's up to you if I come back with the necessary equipment and parts to fix your shields. It'll take almost a month to fix this world. I have thirteen teams that can work at the same time to work on the other worlds if they are the same." Jake finished.

"Two billion credits is a lot of money," Ludwig said.

"Yes, and that's if I get help from your engineers here with the retrieval of satellites and the connecting of the geothermal power systems. Your geo tech said your geo system was able to generate 100,000 megawatts and if he wasn't exaggerating then we're good. But I looked and this system is nothing like the geothermal system on our planet. Then ours is over 300,000 years old. It was there when we found the planet. Yours looks brand new." Jake replied.

"I don't see a problem with our techs helping you since our defense minister is going to be replaced. Incompetence is a reason for dismissal." Ludwig told Jake.

The republic turned out to be responsible clients and upheld their end of the contract. The planetary shields were upgraded, and the solar system detection system was updated also so that constant sorties were not required. Now the ODDS, Observation Detection Defense System, drones patrolled the system. A system now manufactured by a Sands industry. The Sands ODDS had improvements over the units sold by the Quantal Company because these detected all forms of electromagnetic and light waves from one hertz to gamma bursts in the ultra-high ranges. It also has a reflective coating so it's almost invisible visually and is invisible to radar and electromagnetic detection. They no longer have to be placed in their location. They get programmed and delivered to orbit then they take off to their location and stay on station until ordered to return.

The republic got shields for all but a handful of planets. Those planets didn't have the power available to energize the field. They would work on it and the Sand crews would return according to the chancellor and the new very proud minister of defense.

The Duke ordered planetary shields for his home world and some worlds that had been attacked and had the power requirements. At 4.5 billion each from scratch the price was high for all 70,000 plus worlds to get a planetary shield. They are still waiting for the convoy or the attack three months later.

Cal and Lucy found delight in running a nut farm. What they didn't like was the Imperium officials butting in all the time. The honeybees were regulated by the Imperium as dangerous animals. Bees are essential to almonds and to a lesser degree walnut production. The couple had to hire a beekeeper from off-world with verifiable paperwork because they were afraid anyone, they hired would be a spy for the Imperium. The state required them to plant willow trees and other regulations that the previous owners didn't do because of their connections. Eventually, the estate became officially free, and the Queen visited.

When the Queens shuttle landed her pilot signaled for all clear. Franklin, a long-time servant of the Queen who is now working for the estate as the communications chief, answered with an all-clear.

As she walked from the shuttle to her special transport, she started noticing the changes all around. It became more apparent as her transport approached the main house and she saw Lucy sitting on one of the many benches near a garden slumped over. The Queen quickly approached. "Lucy, are you alright?"

Lucy looked up and soon realized who was addressing her. Seconds later the spark of recognition appeared on her face, but she was too tired to stand. "I'll be fine with a little rest." She said weakly. "I just needed a little rest here. That Imperium monster has been running us ragged with his compliance requirements since we took over this place. I'm sorry, your majesty, let me show you to your rooms. They are locked to keep the asshole out of them. I have the key hidden and told him I had to get a locksmith out to do some work on all the locks in the house."

The Queens handmaiden helped Lucy into the transport, and they started for the house. Lucy continued to explain what had happened and soon the Queen knew she was going to call John to get some more money in the accounts. The estate was broken, and taxes were due soon. The Queen's shuttle had encrypted communications equipment, unlike the estate. That is something that will have to change also. Sand was contacted, and John sent Sheila with eight billion in gold to deposit in the estate's accounts. Cal and Lucy were to supervise a team of managers like a proper Baron and Baroness. The Queen bestowed the titles on the two since this was her privilege and liked what these two had done. The buildings were updated, and the processing plants were replaced with new ones well before they were needed. The Queen brought in a security team and introduced them to Cal and Lucy. They patrolled the grounds, and the fencing was repaired in the few locations that were in disrepair.

When the Queen finished her shopping she left, leaving the much happier Cal and Lucy, the Baron and Baroness of Quantal sitting in the gardens and sipping Tranya.

Five months had passed since the initial warning of impending attack, and only small convoys had been sent out. The three convoys had a total of 60,000 containers and super containers but John had them scanned before bringing them to Sand. Twenty thousand containers had tracking buoys in them. Meara 4, the pleasure, and gambling planet had four moons, and all the cargo was taken there and quickly searched. All the tracking buoys were removed and placed in one container. Then that container was taken to Proximal Three and secretly dumped there. The junkyard planet was the perfect place for the buoys. Using the two ships taken from the republic, four people sat on the moon of Proximal Three and watched as hundreds of Imperium ships appeared over the sky of that world and a very surprised junk master. Thousands of soldiers tore his immediate junkyard apart then thousands more were landed to search the rest of the planet. Ten days later an angry junk master and an even angrier Imperium Group Admiral parted ways.

John received a message from the Duke that he was not waiting, and he was going to take back Genesee, the last world taken by the Imperium. That world was defended by thirteen Imperium battleships and thirty heavy line ships that included cruisers and a carrier with 40,000 fighters.

The Duke was determined to take out all of them and land troops to take back Genesee.

John called the captains together. He decided to include the rebuilt and improved Battleship Second Chance in the fight. The ship had been pounded on so badly that only one engine and one reactor were left useable. When John's engineers had limped in, the name Second Chance seemed appropriate.

The six Battleship captains and the five battle cruiser captains all entered and sat down. Shortly after the 1st mates came in and sat next to their captains. John stood and announced, "We are going to assist the Rebel Navy and the Duke De La Sangrias in retaking the world of Genesee. That world is defended by thirteen battleships and thirty heavy line ships that include cruisers and a carrier with 40,000 fighters at last observation.

We have rumors of a pending all-out attack on the monarchy and their worlds that hasn't happened yet and the Duke feels it's time to act. Are there any questions?"

"We have eleven ships. Doesn't the Duke have sixty or seventy by now?" Captain Raymond Lewis of the Second Chance asked.

"They have five battle cruisers and thirty three cruisers. All were built by us. Most of the rest of their fleet was destroyed. The remainder of their fleet is armored troop transport. He has enough transport vehicles to land a million men on a planet. He doesn't have a battleship because we just got them in full working order. Your battleship captains know how much retrofitting we've gone through to get those ships in ship shape and proper working order. I assume they are all working in top condition now, right?" John said and asked, looking at the battleship captains.

"All the power issues are solved on my ship. The engine imbalance is still an issue, but my engineer has the solution for that and sent it to the others. The only big problem is if we use the ion cannon at full power for a sustained beam of more than three minutes then the rest of the ship loses power. Our shields still work, and power is restored in thirty seconds but that's a weakness our engineers haven't fixed that could be exploited." Captain Raymond O'Dempsey of the Battleship Boonesborough said.

"The Battleship Boonesborough was built new from the ground up. She shouldn't have issues like that." John said.

"But we have that issue and the hundreds of other issues that our engineers have fixed over the last four months. The Battleship Carillon, Alamo, Boonesborough, and Charlotte all had the same problems, and the designers changed the designs, so they were upgraded to reflect the changes. New ships won't have these problems, but we did. When we get the solution to the ion cannon issue, we'll have a battleship design that'll destroy most anything." Captain Charles Harrington of the Battleship Alamo said.

"At least we don't have the same problem the other battleships have with the engineering section and their vulnerabilities. Our aft section is heavily shielded and a sustained attack at our engines won't explode our ships," said Captain Ben Swanson of the Battleship Carillon.

"We will be going into battle to back up our friend the Duke. So, get your crew ready and get your ships in space. I'll meet you at the moon orbit in three hours. That will give the repulsor ships enough time to lift the battleships into space and all the reactors to get fully started." John ordered.

Three hours later the last of the battleships, the Ticonderoga, entered formation. John told Jenny to open fleet comm channels. "We are meeting the Duke's fleet at Sicyon. That's the world that the Imperium attacked and held for 45 days before the Duke's forces liberated it back almost destroying the Duke's entire fleet."

John and the Sand Fleet came out of FTL at Sicyon, but the sky was empty except for the troop transports and a lone old cruiser. "Halt identify yourselves or we will fire upon you." The hail came in.

"This is the Sand Fleet here to help with the Duke. We are friendly. Where are all the Duke's ships?" John replied.

"They all ran to Genesee. We're waiting for orders to follow and land. I was told when you showed to tell you to quote: 'come ahead'" The commander of the old cruiser said.

Within minutes the recovery team dropped out of light speed with the two freighters showing up first then, the recovery ship Agenda and her supporting vessels.

"What are you doing here Nathan? I didn't tell you to come along." John radioed.

"There is going to be a fight. There is going to be a mess. We'll be around to clean it up." Nathan replied.

"Alright, but you stay here. We're going to Genesee and see what mischief we can get into." John replied.

With that, the Sand battle fleet jumped to FTL and exited just outside of the Genesee world to see the reports were understated. John looked at the scanners and saw the Duke's ships were working in groups of three. Methodically destroying ship after ship but the original count was a bit low. John could see two carriers and he kept losing count of battleships. Because they were moving about and there were a lot of them.

"OK Captains Lewis and Buchanan, I want you to take out the carrier on the right. Swanson and Harrington, you have the carrier on the left. The Second Chance and I are the only ships with puddle guns. We are going to fire on the aft section of the two carriers." John ordered and heard a familiar voice.

"Hello, John! I'm glad you could make it. They had more ships here than we thought. We didn't expect 44 battleships, but it looks like they have two battle groups here. So, pick a target and kill it. We've killed 32 battleships so far and knocked out over 35 cruisers. Those carriers are a pain in our sides, but we can't get to them yet." The Duke said.

"We're getting to that sire. The carriers are first on the agenda." John replied as the Sand Fleet hurried into action. The battleships started toward the carriers and on the way took out a few cruisers. The 10,000-

watt plasma cannon burned through the shields of the Imperium cruisers like butter and when twenty high-energy plasma blasts hit a ship at the same time the ship's engineering section explodes and the ship dies. The heavily armed battleships shredded the Imperium ships as they worked their way to the carriers. The line ships were no match for the battleships of the Sand Fleet. John followed the battleships with the Battle Cruiser Defender and the Second Chance followed the other group. When the battleships stopped bombarding the huge carriers, the Second Chance and the Defender continued to the aft engineering section of the carriers to empty their guns of nanites on the unsuspecting victims. Two-thirds of the way down the carriers and both the Defender and the Second Chance fired their puddle guns onto the shields of the carriers and began the reloading procedure. Both the Defender and The Second Chance looped and headed back to upload on the underside of the huge carriers then veered off and took on other prey. The carrier shields held under the bombardment of the battleships but not the combined assault of the nanites and the plasma cannon bolts.

Fifteen minutes after the assault on the carriers started their shields failed and the nanites fell onto the hull and began to dissolve the hull of the two ships. The battleships stopped their assault and turned to other ships. The field of working ships was quickly diminishing, and the two fleets killed ship after ship. The fighters had nowhere to land and soon were eliminated by the defensive fire of the battlecruiser fleet. The Duke called his Troop carriers in to land on the planet. The carriers were almost dissolved and 35 other ships were in the same condition within an hour. Hundreds of thousands of escape pods were in orbit or landing on the planet.

"It looks like we can call in the cleanup crew. It'll take days to clean up this mass." John radioed the Duke.

"It'll take longer than that to rid ourselves of the Imperium trash on the surface." The Duke said as troops started landing by the thousands all over the planet Genesee.

The next stop was Zenanas Three and Four. When we arrived, we found they had scorched Zenanas Three, murdering the 6 billion inhabitants. It's a wasteland and they were still using Zenanas Four as a base. It has shipyards and an industrial complex but only two battleships in orbit that surrendered at the site of thirty battlecruisers and five battleships. 500,000 troops landed on Zenanas Four and imprisoned all the Imperium they found. The only saving grace was the garrison surrendered. A million men on Genesee were still fighting and arresting or killing Imperium men and women on that planet so the Duke had to call his reserves of 500,000 just-graduated cadets and mingle them with the seasoned troops. This was done while on Zenanas Four and the Queen arrived in her shuttle to ask about the battles. John and the Duke met her on her shuttle to discuss the next moves.

"Good afternoon, your majesty," John said in good humor when he entered the room.

The Queen was sitting on the couch that was specially made for her. "Good afternoon, John. Although to me it's morning, I just arrived from Crucible. The planetary shield is marvelous. I adore it. Thank you for installing it." She replied. "Gwen, would you see if our guest would like something to drink or perhaps a bite to eat?"

"Yes ma'am," Gwen replied and the beautiful woman gracefully walked to John with a cup of coffee. "May I offer you your usual sir? Your coffee is prepared, as you like it." Then John saw her face go flush and stood to catch her just after she had set the coffee on the table beside him. He held the unconscious woman in his arms and realized how little she weighed when he heard the Queen call for some assistance. The attendants came in and took the unconscious Gwen out for medical attention just as the Duke entered.

"Did I miss something?" He asked. "I'm sorry. Good afternoon, your majesty. I greet you. Was that Gwen?"

"Greetings and yes it was. Her episodes are getting more frequent. I'm afraid it is getting close to the end for her." the Queen said. "But I asked you here to catch up on the war. I see Genesee is a mess and parts of ships are everywhere. John, you should get your people to clean it up. All I could see were three ships locating escape pods and spaced people. While I was there twenty or thirty were recovered but there are thousands of people all over the space out there."

"Yes ma'am. I have four ships collecting people and pods that are in orbit but there is still a lot of fighting on Genesee right now. We have secured about a third of the planet with a million troops on the ground. The enemy is choosing to die rather than surrender. When their weapons run out of energy, they are committing suicide instead of surrendering." The Duke said in amazement.

"I'll bet that they've been told you will do horrible things to them if they surrender." The Queen said as sipped her drink.

"Do you know something that I don't your majesty?" The Duke asked wearily.

"Not at all. It's just that I've heard something similar before. About 3800 years ago on a planet where the war had been waging for over a hundred years my great three times great grandfather and his brother tried to see if they could end the war. Come to find out no one knew why the war had started. But the hatred continued. Finally, a truce was called except for a small band of fighters who refused to quit. They were going to fight to the end. The commander had told his people that if they surrendered the enemy would tie them to a cross and skin them alive or boil them in oil. It took some doing to convince the fighters that their commander was lying." The Queen replied.

"How did they convince the holdouts to surrender?" the Duke asked.

"They sent in their people to tell them the war was over, and the truce was real. The enemy had not skinned or boiled anyone and that they should give up before they were all killed for no reason." The Queen told the Duke to finish the story.

"What is your next move, Duke?" John asked.

"The Colon system is next, Colon Three and Four. Colon Four is a mining world rich in rare earths where there are only security guards for defense. Colon Three is an agricultural world of farms and ranches with no defenses. I have no intel on either of those worlds." The Duke replied.

"We're in a stealth ship. I have a cloak. We should go look and see what is there." The Queen offered.

"I just have to tell my people I'll be right back and leave some instructions." The Duke said.

"You can use the anteroom just there." The Queen pointed and the Duke rose to contact his people.

"What about you John? Don't you have to tell your people?" the Queen asked.

"No ma'am, they know I'm here and if this ship disappears then I'm going somewhere," John said with a smile and finished his coffee.

The Duke returned and took his place in front of the view screen with John and the Queen.

The Queen and her shuttle jumped to Colon Four and Colon Three to see what was there for fighting ships. What they saw was Colon Four had a freighter in orbit but no warships and Colon Three had three battleships in orbit.

The Duke decided to send three cruisers and 6,000 troops in ships with suits for the environment on Colon Four to that planet and the rest to Colon Three. The troop ships would hold back at the outer marker of Colon Three until the battleships were engaged and then they would swoop in and land all over the planet and begin removing Imperium soldiers as fast as possible.

The plan worked great. The fight in space lasted thirteen minutes. The freighter over Colon Four surrendered and was boarded with no loss of life and the three battleships in orbit over Colon Three were all stopped in record time. Two were still dissolving and one surrendered and was boarded. The third was taking on the life pods of the other two in its hold and jettisoning them to make room. Twelve hours later both planets reported all clear and the planets were once again free. The planet had no food. All of it had been taken and delivered to the Imperium days earlier. The civilians were half starved so John let The Duke know that he had stores of food and ordered Captain Sam Clemens of the freighter Avenger who had just emptied his load and cleaned out his hold to load up with food from the planet's stores. Captain Nathan and the ship Agenda were not far behind. She had a larger hold, but it required sanitizing. He had scrubbing and cleaning to do first.

Colon Four didn't do much better but the miners had hiding places that drove the Imperium military nuts. The Colon Four population was only 70,000 and the attacking force was in the hundreds of thousands, but the miners had warned they had years of food stores deep in the mines and evacuated their families to the hiding places deep in the planet and closed the shafts behind them. The military didn't know how to mine, and the civilians had no idea where the miners were since they all kept to themselves so when the Imperium invaded all they got was the domed cities. They captured some ore and the processing plant. The military found platinum, lithium, and a plethora of useful elements all mined on this planet but in tiny amounts since the supply ship had just left.

The list was extensive and included.

- Scandium: Use to make light alloys for the aerospace industry, as a radioactive tracer, and in lamps

- Yttrium: Used in yttrium aluminum garnet (YAG) lasers, as a red phosphor, in superconductors, in fluorescent tubes, in LEDs, and as a cancer treatment

- Lanthanum: Use to make high refractive index glass, camera lenses, and catalysts

- Cerium: Use to impart a yellow color to glass, as a catalyst, as a polishing powder, and to make flints

- Praseodymium: Used in lasers, arc lighting, magnets, flint steel, and as a glass colorant

- Neodymium: Used to impart violet color to glass and ceramics, in lasers, magnets, capacitors, and electric motors

- Promethium: Used in luminous paint and nuclear batteries

- Samarium: Used in lasers, rare earth magnets, masers, nuclear reactor control rods

- Europium: Used to prepare red and blue phosphors, in lasers, in fluorescent lamps, and as an NMR relaxant

- Gadolinium: Used in lasers, x-ray tubes, computer memory, high refractive index glass, NMR relaxation, neutron capture, MRI contrast

- Terbium: Use in green phosphors, magnets, lasers, floor lamps, magneto strictive alloys, and sonar systems

- Dysprosium: Used in hard drive disks, magneto strictive alloys, lasers, and magnets

- Holmium: Use in lasers, magnets, and calibration of spectrophotometers

- Erbium: Used in vanadium steel, infrared lasers, and fiber optics

- Thulium: Used in lasers, metal halide lamps, and portable X-ray machines

- Ytterbium: Used in infrared lasers, stainless steel, and nuclear medicine

- Lutetium: Used in positron emission tomography (PET) scans, high refractive index glass, catalysts, and LEDs

The storehouses had very little of all the listed elements, but the processing plants were all shut down and the women who ran them were killed when the military invaded. That is what the civilian governor told the general when he questioned her. She even identified the body and her unarmed assistants who were also dead at the hands of the military.

The civilian governor of Colon Four told the General that he killed the planet and the ability of the planet to process any elements when they killed the unarmed people in the domes and the mines. The people that died in the mines were the only people who knew where the miners were, and he probably killed all the miners too.

The truth was that the supervisor of the planet and her team were on an inspection tour when the attack occurred, and they were all whisked away to safety with the miners almost a kilometer and a half under the surface of the planet in caverns dug a year before the invasion when the miners found a treasure trove of everything imaginable. Meteors had hit the planet millions of years ago that had gold and silver and hundreds of tons of rare earth metals in them spread over a nine by twelve-kilometer area and left an underground cavern when they cooled.

The planet healed over the top of the wound on the planet's surface and the miners found the grail, but the Imperium attacked and now they are close to running out of food. The miners had been listening to the comm channels from the surface so when the Monarchy soldiers attacked and took the planet back then the miners started to dig their way out. The thought of breathing different recycled air and seeing other people was exciting.

For four years the miners had been held up in the caverns recycling everything, but the two hundred and twelve miners and staff were ready to leave. Twenty-one hours later they were free of their self-imposed hiding place and found the Monarchy troops looking for signs of where they were.

"What is the plan from here?" John asked the Duke.

"We go on to Anastasia Five and Six, both are shipping and transportation ports of call and storage yards. Anastasia Six has a shipyard that used to make our imperial ships of the line before it was captured; now you make them John. The Queen's stealth ship will go in and look first then report back and depending on her report we'll follow through." The Duke said.

The Queen spoke, "Since we are already here, let's all fly there and look at the system."

"I'll have to tell my staff that I'm leaving again, or they'll get worried." The Duke explained.

"Mine too, this time!" John said.

The calls were made but no one said where they were going, and the Queens shuttle jumped into hyperspace for Anastasia Five, but no one expected what they found. Anastasia Five was a dead world. The shuttle crew did a passive scan for signals and found nothing. From the looks of everything this world had been dead for a long time.

The Queen ordered the pilot to set course to Anastasia Six. This world was dead too. Nothing remained of the shipyards or the storage facilities. The huge shipping cranes melted and scorched just like the rest of the planet.

"Set course for Caledonia Three, the next stop on the list pilot!" The Duke ordered. She looked to the Queen who nodded in agreement and the course was set. The stars in the forward observation scope blurred to streaks and zipped by at an amazing speed at first then all reference disappeared.

The Duke was angry and beside himself. "There were over twelve billion subjects on those two worlds. They had hundreds of thousands of visitors each day to do business over the past two hundred years and it is all gone because my father wouldn't let me build a navy. He told me that we are at peace with everyone, and war was a thing of the past, which was six years ago. Then the Imperium attacked Racine Two and Dad ordered servants to unpack the imperial yacht and called the Imperium's embassy to tell them we demanded an audience to address the attack on our world.

I had found three thousand older ships of the line in storage and 30,000 veterans from a sixty-year-old war on veteran's pay. Most of them were in their eighties and nineties but some were in their seventies. But I called them and told them what happened. They told their friends and their friends told friends who knew people who knew other people and I had a little over 300,000 people, mechanics, and flight engineers to get those old ships ready to fly while Dad was talking to a flunky at the embassy.

We found out the embassy was loading up to leave and they were stringing my father along. My father finally told me to order new ships from Anastasia Five when we found out that it was under attack. My father fell ill, and my mother told me to take all that college education and do what I could. I listened to the old generals and the new ones we had and together we came up with a plan to stop them, but we lost almost all those ships in the process and many more worlds before I stopped them. But we couldn't win until I started buying ships from you, John. Now these bastards are doing this to my world and my people. The Duke waved at the image of the dead world before them with tears in his eyes."

The distance was not too far to Anastasia Five, nineteen light years away. The Queens shuttle dropped out of hyperspace just outside of the gas giants in the solar system. The shuttle dodged a ship leaving the inner world and the pilot flew closer to look. The planet was in the early stages of the evacuation of all military personnel.

"They're getting ready to do it again here." The Duke screamed.

"Pilot, best speed to Colon Three." The Queen said. "The best thing to do is get out of this solar system and call to ready the fleets and have them prepped so as soon as we get there we're set to jump here and catch them by surprise. Then send everything you can to Racine Two as soon as you can after we wipe the floor with these creeps here." The Queen said.

"I like that idea." The Duke said. "I have one change. As soon as we get back the three of us get on our ships and you send your shuttle to Racine Two. If they are getting ready to scorch that world, you send your battleship Kentaurides to Racine Two and John can send his battleships with it."

Everyone agreed and the shuttle returned. Quickly after they returned the Duke and John to their Fleet command ships and commanded them to jump to Caledonia Three and caught the Imperium military with their pants down. The explosive charges were disarmed, and the ships were caught by complete surprise and boarded. The Queen ordered her battleship to Racine Two.

The commanding generals of the ground forces and the admiralty were captured with the command codes to the fleet also captured. Over 400,000 military personnel and top brass got transferred to the surface and placed in the camps they had constructed for the planet's population. The tide had turned.

Four ships stayed and the rest jumped to Racine Two where the Imperium had 500 hundred capital ships all fighting six battleships that were surrounded. The three carriers had their destroyers by their side this time protecting them. The Sand Fleet was in a triad configuration and holding off hundreds of attacking craft.

Captain Raymond Lewis in command of the battleship 'Second Chance' called John, "Nice of you to show up sir! We have a target-rich environment. Pick one or two and take them out would you please?"

"Since you asked so nicely, I'll do it just this once!" John said with a chuckle. The Imperium battleships were set in groups of three, side by side, bow to stern with their shields melded as one. That protected the most vulnerable part of an Imperium battleship, the engineering section, and exposed the best part of a battleship, its cannon, and weapons. The shields in the engineering section were extra heavy and seemingly impenetrable but the Imperium's ships knew the vulnerability of a battleship and were bombarding the engineering sections of the battleships unmercifully to no avail. Sand's battleships had no such vulnerability.

Sand's battleships were coordinating their firepower and taking out three to four ships at a time, one or two above the center line and one or two below it. They were concentrating on battleships first and had already removed twenty two battleships from the fight. There were only forty four left. John saw one big battleship off to the side all alone not firing and just sitting there.

"That will be the admiral and I want him. Contact Captains Davis and Jackson to have them form up on me, we're going hunting," John ordered.

The two ships formed a triad with John's Defender and headed straight for the large battleship. Immediately, three heavy cruisers stopped attacking the Kentaurides and the Second Chance. They started for John and his three heavy cruisers to stop them before they got to the flagship. The Duke had pounced on all the ships firing on the Kentaurides and the Second Chance with every ship he had and the three that headed off to attack John's group didn't last long before they were destroyed by John's triad and the triad continued for the battleship that he was sure had the commander of the Imperium's forces inside.

As John approached the Battleship, it turned to leave so John's triad hurried faster then opened fire on the engines and shields with their ion cannons. Soon the battleship's shields began to glow and before the engines could reach full power the shields broke, and the engines exploded. Battleships have very few cannons to the rear or aft section of the ship. They are designed to be an offensive weapon to fight forward so breaking through the aft shield and destroying her engines was the easy part. Attaching a tractor beam and towing the large battleship backward into the main fighting area was more difficult but John's triad did it while the battleship tried to fire at them but couldn't get a line of fire. Six hours later all the Imperium ships were destroyed or had surrendered except one.

The battleship couldn't go anywhere but it could still fire cannon. The Duke's forces surrounded the battleship and with precision-controlled shots they shut down the cannon one by one by destroying the guns or gun ports. Unable to maneuver and unable to fight, the battleship refused to surrender to the boarding marines. The duke ordered an overwhelming force of 50,000 Marine's special fighting forces to storm the ship and take the admirals alive if possible. The Marines were armed with heavy stun rifles and grenades. The last marine ship hadn't even docked when the call came that they had captured the admiral and all his aids. The Marines had secured the bridge and engineering. Over 16,000 of the crew are in the cargo bay under arrest and the rest of the ship would be within an hour. All hostile forces on Racine Two were pacified in record time. Tales of abuse and torture began to surface among the survivors. The people of Racine Two wanted to kill all the prisoners. The Duke ordered the military to guard them until he could talk to the population.

The Duke asked to see John. "I have sixty older ships left that need improved shields. They are old but they can still fight, and I want to upgrade their shields if it's possible."

"If the power is there, we can upgrade your ships. John replied to the Duke.

Three days later the Queen's fleet minus the Queen and her husband joined the Royal rebel fleet now over sixty strong. John had his engineers bring ninety shield upgrade units for the rest of the royals' fleet. If the shield for the small fleet of the royals can be upgraded to multiphasic shielding they can hold against the much larger fleet of the Imperium.

The Duke's man walked in while one of the engineers installed the special shield generator on the old royal flagship. "The Duke wants to know what this is costing us."

"I'll discuss that with the Duke," John told him. "Tell him I would like to see him soon."

"How about now John?" The Duke asked, surprising John.

"The captain's officer briefing room of the bridge is close by. Let's go there while these men and women finish undisturbed.

The Duke extended his arm and John walked to the briefing room with the Duke closely following. When they got to the room, they both took a seat and smiled at each other. John asked the Duke, "How have you been my friend?"

"The days have been hectic, and the nights are almost as bad ever since you told me about the Imperium re-attacking my people. I've been going over in my head possible details until my headaches. Your shields will help greatly. I wanted to know how much you were going to charge me." The Duke said and smiled.

"Well, they cost me just over 24,000,000 to build and they take six people who know what they are doing to install it. You saw them doing it. The entire shield system is replaced including the emitters so it's not cheap, but the shields are impenetrable afterward. They cost 29,500,000 each and I'm charging you that plus the labor plus 10% for some profit. I'm charging a little more for the larger ships and a little less for the smaller ships but I'm making hardly any money on the exchange. I feel a good neighbor will be better for me in the long run. It's a far cry from the normal charge of 32 million each." John explained.

"Two of my advisors have warned me that you are going to charge me exorbitant prices and have extraordinary demands. I dismissed them before when they warned me about you, and they were proven wrong. I thank you for the help and only hope you have enough time to update our ships in time." The Duke told John.

I brought 400 engineers, and they brought their teams. Right now, they are crawling all over your ships and updating every ship that will let them. You had thirteen captains and ships engineers who refused at first then they saw how many others were getting it done and decided to let our people in and update theirs too. That's a lot of peer pressure. There is still the rule of no tampering with the shield systems. It cost 29,000,000 to replace it since these are the smaller units." John finished his explanation.

"I'll tell the fleet and explain to the captains and engineers that it'll come out of their pay if the shields are tampered with, and they go bad." The Duke said.

John smiled and said, "That should do it. Some of my people have been known to trigger self-destruct in the shield generator when they install it. This is embarrassing but it happens. But they are working on it. No one should be working on it but us."

"At least we'll be ready for them thanks to you. Their shields are good, but we can get through them." The Duke said to John.

"We have a special cannon for Imperium ships. It eats them alive." John said while laughing.

"That's the puddle gun of yours, isn't it?" The Duke asked.

"Yes!" John replied.

"That thing scares the hell out of me. I'm afraid one of my ships will get some of it on them." The Duke told him.

"You don't have to worry anymore; all the shields have a code in them now to deactivate the nanites," John said with a smile.

"That is the best news I've heard since my worlds were liberated." The Duke replied. "I'll have some gold for you in a week."

"Thank you! I'm not worried about it. I knew you were good for it." John said with a smile.

"The people on Racine Two want to hold public executions for all the prisoners. The other recent planets agree." The Duke said remorsefully.

"I remember your story about the lady on one of your worlds, Sicyon I believe. The one the Imperium had for forty five days." John said, trying to remember.

"Yes, Sicyon was attacked, and we took it back even though it took most of our fleet to do it." The Duke recalled.

"Do you remember what the people of that world did with the prisoners?" John asked, jarring the Duke's memory.

"Of course, they put them to work rebuilding the planet." The duke said. "I remember 'someone' saying they thought that was too much like slavery."

"I've reconsidered, in light of the devastation I've seen that the Imperium has inflicted. I think it is restitution." John said solemnly. "Killing them helps no one. Get them in front of the courts and sentence them to a lifetime of service to the worlds they terrorized." John replied to the monarch.

"I'll make that suggestion and we'll see where it goes. My people are very angry and rightly so. It worked on Sicyon because the planet was under the Imperium for only forty five days. Some of these people have suffered for four years. On Sicyon we use slaver collars, and punishment collars for the leaders. The punishment collars are two feet around and the prisoners can't even feed themselves. They have to feed each other and are in cells with videos of their atrocities, like a zoo. Sicyon has one of these zoos in each state at their capital. The old Imperium governor and his staff are in the cells of each zoo. There were frequent assassination attempts in the beginning, and like I said that was after only forty five days." The Duke said. "Some were also taken out and caned on live vid, so everyone can see. I'm told it was watched by most of the population."

"How many prisoners do you have so far?" John asked.

"On the five worlds not scorched, we have almost two million men and women prisoners." The Duke said.

"That's a huge labor force. I'll bet they could rebuild a scorched world if the population didn't want them around working. Slaver collars are not expensive, and the alternative is death, so I'm sure the prisoners will agree." John suggested.

The Duke broadcasted a message out to all the planets that his family was responsible for. Beside him were the captains of his fleet, and the Sand fleet, then he addressed the people of the worlds ravished by war for the past four years. The result was the trial and conviction of all the Imperium soldiers to a life of slavery. Genesee, Colon Four, and Colon Three wanted them gone, so all of prisoners on those planets were transported to Anastasia Five to rebuild that world from the ground up. The Duke also announced that the war would continue to new worlds that the Imperium now rules, and the monarchy will liberate them. With his fleet of almost 100 ships and the Sand fleet, the monarchy began a systematic takeover of the outer planets.

Over the next few years the Duke destroyed ship after ship of the Imperium until they had none left. The outer planets were now free of the tyranny of the Imperium. It was time for peace and reconstruction.

The End